SEARCHING LOVE

SAINTS PROTECTION & INVESTIGATIONS

MARYANN JORDAN

Cover design: Cosmic Letterz

ISBN: print version 978-1-947214-17-0

ISBN: ebook version 978-1-947214-16-3

Author's Note

I have lived in numerous states as well as overseas, but for the last twenty years have called Virginia my home. Many of my stories take place in this wonderful commonwealth, but I choose to use fictional city names with some geographical accuracies.

These fictionally named cities allow me to use my creativity and not feel constricted by attempting to accurately portray the areas.

It is my hope that my readers will allow me this creative license and understand my fictional world.

I also do extensive research on my books and try to write on subjects with accuracy. There will always be points where creative license will be used to create scenes or plots.

This book marks the last of the Saints Protection &
Investigation Series. It was a spin-off from my Alvarez
Security Series and next will be the spin-off, Lighthouse
Security & Investigations Series.
Like all my books, my readers are the life-blood of my
writing. They fell in love with Gabe and demanded more
books like that...and I was happy to accommodate because
they are my favorite genre of books as well.
So, to my faithful readers...the ones who one-click when they
see a pre-order. To my re-readers...the ones who tell me that
when they cannot find a book to read, they go back and re-
read my series again and again.
Thank you, from the bottom of my heart!

Though the evening sun was still high in the sky it had dipped behind the tree line, creating shadows and making visibility more difficult. Nathan Washington did not mind for himself since intuition always took over, but he hated the thought of someone not familiar with their surroundings to stumble.

"Come on, girl," he said, "let's get going."

The beautiful, red-haired female with him looked up and grinned before taking off, running ahead. The twists and turns in the path did not appear to cause her any delay but, then, she rarely stayed on the path anyway, instead heading wherever her instincts told her to go.

Nathan jogged along behind her, admiring her form. Long legs. A svelte 110 pounds. Silky hair. Deep, soulful, brown eyes. A nose that constantly worked. Long ears, a wrinkly face, and, right now, a tongue lolling to the side.

Scarlett, his four-year-old bloodhound, was on the scent and he hustled to keep up with her.

When the call had come in from his good friend, Jack Bryant, telling him his services were needed, he and Scarlett had immediately hurried to the scene. Jack's wife, Bethany, owned Mountville Cabin Rentals, situated at the base of the Blue Ridge Mountains, next to their property. Arriving at the main house at Mountville, he saw Jack standing with his arm around her.

Bethany started to move toward him, her face pinched with fear, but Jack's arm kept her in place. He towered over his wife, his stance protective. Looking at his friend, Nathan took in the hard set of his jaw and the small shirt held in his other hand.

"This is from the little boy," Jack said, his words clipped. "The parents said that they were walking back to the cabin from a hike and didn't notice Jimmy wasn't with them all the way. They have four kids and he got separated somehow."

"Got it," he said, taking the shirt and holding it down to Scarlett, allowing her to sniff. A moment later, he and Scarlett had taken off, moving swiftly past the crying mother and father holding their other three children. With shouts of, "Please find him", ringing in his ears, he blocked out all other thoughts and focused on the hunt.

"You got it, girl," he encouraged, as she left the trail and leaped over a small tree in the woods. Through the thickets and down a slight ravine, Scarlett loped along, her nose down, tail wagging. Tall pines, aspens, maples, and oaks filled the forest, their rough, dark trunks easily providing a hiding place for a small child. The surroundings were beautiful but, to a lost child, the forest could seem ominous.

He hated that the frightened child had left the trail, but where the undergrowth parted and leaves coated the ground, it was easy to get confused, thinking you were still on a path. Nonetheless, he had every confidence that his well-trained bloodhound would be able to keep up with Jimmy's trail.

As each additional minute stretched on he was afraid of what he would find at the end of the trail. His years as a member of an Army search and rescue team had left him with that. Shaking the negative thought from his mind, he crawled under a downed branch, keeping pace with her.

Ten minutes later, Scarlett's pace picked up and he sucked in a quick breath. He could tell they were close, so he began calling out, "Jimmy! Jimmy!"

Suddenly, Scarlett came to a stop, her haunches lowering to a sit, her sides heaving and her tongue hanging out. Just in front of her was a little boy, his bare arms and legs scratched from the low growing brambles. The child turned his tear-stained face up toward him, his eyes wide.

Squatting down, Nathan said, "Hey, Jimmy. I'm Nathan. Glad to see you, buddy. My dog's been looking for you…I think she'd like to say hello."

Jimmy wiped his nose and stared at Scarlett before saying, "I want to find my mommy."

"Well, she said she misses her little man, so let's go find her, bud. But, first, here's some water and a granola bar." He pulled the water bottle and treat from his backpack. As Jimmy drank thirstily, he also poured more water in a bowl for Scarlett. "See, she's thirsty, too."

A slight smile crept across Jimmy's face as he watched Scarlett drink.

While Jimmy was distracted, Nathan turned away slightly and called on his radio, "Jack. Got him. He's okay. Coming back now." Reaching his arms down, he said, "Can I carry you? You must be tired."

With only a second's hesitation, Jimmy's arms shot upward, allowing Nathan to pick him up. Looking down to Scarlett, Nathan said, "Okay, girl, take us back."

Scarlett looked up and her intelligent eyes sought his before she loped back along the path in the direction they had come from.

Soon, they were leaving the trail and heading back down the main road toward the cabins when he saw a group of people rushing toward him with Jimmy's parents in the lead.

"Jimmy, it looks like we have a welcome party coming our way."

"Mommy!" he screamed, and Nathan set his feet on the ground.

Scarlett stayed back with him as they watched Jimmy engulfed by his family. Jack and Bethany hurried past them, heading straight to Nathan. Before he had a chance to brace, Bethany rushed to him, throwing her arms around him.

"Thank you, oh God, thank you," she gushed, tears in her eyes.

He looked over her head, observing Jack's expression, now relaxed in relief. As Bethany let him go, Jack moved in to shake his hand, pulling him in for a back slap as well.

"Words can't express, man," Jack started.

"No need. That's what me and Scarlett do," he smiled in return.

Before he had a chance to walk away, Jimmy's parents hustled over, both pulling him in for hugs of their own as Jimmy proudly introduced them to Scarlett. He knelt down, one hand rubbing behind her ears as he said, "You stick with your parents from now on, yeah?"

Jimmy nodded as he mimicked his actions, rubbing her ears as well. "She found me good, didn't she?"

"Yeah...she found you good," he chuckled, his heart lighter.

It took a few more minutes before the family completed their effusive expressions of gratitude before heading back to their cabin, but Nathan was ready to leave. He loved his job but the accolades that often accompanied made him self-conscious.

"Son, we do good because it's what we should do, not because someone'll thank us for it."

He could hear his father's words, so often spoken as he grew up, ringing in his ears. Patting his leg, he looked down, grinning as Scarlett's eyes peered up at him. "Come on, girl."

He offered a chin lift to Jack, knowing his friend would understand his desire to leave. Grinning, he observed Jack pulling Bethany back to his side to keep her from running over again, waving as he and Scarlett climbed back into his old truck.

As the truck rumbled down the road, he thought of Jack's previous business offer. Saints Protection & Investigations. Jack, while still in the Army Special Forces, had worked with a team of highly trained members making up a multi-task force consisting of SEALs, SF, CIA, explosive experts, and others. Finding the diversity worked well, Jack recreated the idea of an exclusive multi-task force once he was a civilian. He recruited from SEALs, FBI, SF, Police, ATF, DEA, and CIA for his new team. Top of the line equipment, weapons, security systems, vehicles, and computers— everything the Saints Protection & Investigations could need—was at their disposal. And, as Jack liked to say, they took on the jobs nobody else wanted or could solve.

Private and government contracts provided lucrative rewards, but every one of the ten men who were Jack's elites would have done their jobs for a lot less money. The chance to investigate crimes and protect, without the bureaucratic bullshit that hampered each of them in the past, was the perfect enticement.

Nathan had worked several cases for Jack on a contractual basis, but had never taken him up on his offer of full-time work. Sighing heavily, he wondered what held him back. Snorting, he knew the answer...*I'm a loner.* Since getting out of the Army, where he had worked beside, and then lost, some of the best men he had ever met, he preferred the solitude of his work now.

Twenty minutes later, his truck turned onto the

gravel drive and he carefully avoided the potholes and ruts. Looking over at his favorite girl he grinned widely. *Hell, my only girl, right now.* "You likin' this, Scarlett?"

She turned her head to offer him a baleful stare and he could have sworn she was talking. Laughing, he reached across and rubbed her head before she returned to her outside perusal as they drove toward home.

Pulling to the side of his cabin, her baying joined the cacophony of his other hounds, penned in their runs in the back. Getting out, he walked toward them, the sight of his small kennels warming his heart. He raised bloodhounds, training them for wilderness tracking before selling them to the police, military, or investigators. He also fostered rescue bloodhounds when one of the local agencies needed him. He was often called to work independently by the sheriff or police across a four-county area, as well as by the Blue Ridge Mountain Forest Service. His operation was small, but it gave him enough money to care for his dogs and keep his cabin.

"Hey, Beau. Red. Persi," he called out the names of the dogs he currently had in residence. Beau and Persi were his, and Red was a rescue that was almost ready for adoption. Persi was pregnant and he grinned, thinking of the litter of more red bloodhounds he would soon have. Walking into the large shed, he flipped on the light switch. The insulated building held shelves of food and medicines on one side, with the inside portion of the dogs' runs on the other.

Blaise Hanssen, a friend of his who also happened to be one of Jack's Saints, was a veterinarian and had helped him design and build the kennel. Blaise's wife,

Grace, was also a dog trainer. Formerly working with drug dogs, she now trained companion animals.

As he moved to get the food ready, the three dogs loped through their doggie doors and into the building, still baying for attention. Dishing out their food, he watched as they ate, Scarlett joining in with her dish. After they finished, he let them out and they bounded along as he headed to the cabin.

Situated in thick woods, he owned twenty acres around his cabin and loved the solitude. It gave him a great place to train the dogs to track, as well as giving him the privacy he craved.

Walking through the back door, the dogs trotted down the hall to their pillows in the living room as he stopped in the utility room to kick off his boots and wash his hands. Moving into the kitchen, he opened the refrigerator, pulling out the leftover stew from the previous night. Once it was heating on the stove, he sliced a few thick pieces of bread and slathered them with butter before placing them in the oven to toast.

Resting his hip against the counter, he casually looked around, satisfied with the projects he had completed on the house. The cabin had been a steal when the owner was ready to unload the property, so the price had been right. He had spent his first year out of the Army living in the ramshackle place, renovating it one step at a time. The electricity, the well, pump, and septic system worked fine but, while the cabin was well built and solid, it needed a complete overhaul on the inside. He opened up some of the inner walls to offer more space, new insulation, new windows, and refinished the floors and gutted the kitchen and bathrooms before adding the utility room. Though it might not be a showplace, even now, it was home.

And, most importantly, it was off the beaten path.

The bubbling of the stew captured his attention and he refocused on dinner. Pouring it into a bowl, he took the crispy, buttery bread from the oven and moved over to the table to sit. The cabin did not have a dining room, but the kitchen extended toward the living room and held a small table. It did not matter if it was just him eating, his mother's words on dining etiquette had been drilled into him. *"No matter how great the feast or poor the fare...you should always eat at the table with the television turned off. Mealtime is for conversation."*

As he sat, he looked over at the dogs lounging on their floor cushions. Noticing his attention, Scarlett raised her eyes to stare at him. "I know, girl, it's just me sitting here, but I'm a creature of habit, I guess." He finished eating and rinsed out the dishes before placing them in the dishwasher. With a final wipe of the kitchen counter, he moved into the living room and settled onto the sofa.

The walls were thick, hewn logs and the fireplace was formed out of stone from the mountains. The sofa was tan and the deep-cushioned chair was brown, so the red braided rug on the floor brought a bit of color into the dark room.

Scarlett moved to climb onto the sofa with him, her head in his lap. He did not bother to turn on the TV knowing, after a rescue, his mind needed to process the events. And he needed to focus on the fact it was a search and rescue…not recovery. *I did enough of those in Afghanistan. Thank God I haven't had to see another one since then.* It felt worthy to find the body of a fallen soldier that had been lost, but to find them alive would have been so much better.

He sipped his whiskey, his gaze on the unlit fireplace. He forced his thoughts to Jimmy. His tear-stained face, with hope flaring in his eyes as he looked at Scarlett. The emotion pouring from his parents when their arms encircled their child again.

Other rescues slid thought his mind as well. Children who had wandered away. Hikers who had become dehydrated and disoriented in the woods. A teenage runaway. Going with Blaise to find Grace's car when she had wrecked in the mountains.

Then his mind, as it often did, moved to a search from two years ago. Called by Jack for a special task, he first had to track several women who had been drugged and had wandered into the woods. Then, the Saints needed him to find Blaise's sister, Bayley, and another woman, who were running for their lives, lost in the woods at night.

Nathan and Scarlett had found Bayley easily, but as she was reunited with her brother and her boyfriend, Nick, another Saint, she begged him to find the woman she had been running with. As they left, he and Scarlett continued their search deeper into the woods. He had no idea that what he would find would stay with him for so long.

2

TWO YEARS EARLIER

After seeing Bayley safely reunited with Blaise and Nick, Nathan tromped through the woods, following Scarlett, noting when she stopped suddenly. He approached cautiously, observing his dog's stance, alert and still. Looking through the trees, he saw a figure in the moonlight.

"Agnes?"

The woman, whose face was hidden in shadows, replied, "Yes. Please stay where you are. I was supposed to meet the FBI agent, Harlan, but he was shot."

"I know. What can I do to help?"

"I need protection and...he's the only one I trust."

Her voice was melodic, even with the shakiness of fear. He rubbed the back of his neck with one hand while the other stroked Scarlett's head, wondering what to do.

"I was going into witness protection. I don't trust anyone other than the man who I had contact with."

Pulling out his phone, he called Blaise. "I need you to do something, but no questions."

"You got it," Blaise assured.

"Get to Harlan, the agent, and tell him to call my number. That's all."

"I'll take care of it," he promised.

Nathan and Agnes passed the time barely speaking as he knelt next to his dog, his hand caressing her. He introduced Agnes to Scarlett and a small smile slipped over her lips.

"Is she named after the heroine in Gone with the Wind?" she asked, softly, her voice barely above a whisper.

He looked toward her and smiled, finding the feminine, yet husky, voice reaching through the dark woods and encircling him. "I loved that movie. My grandmother used to watch it when it would come on TV and, one Christmas, when my parents bought her a video player, I got her that as her first movie. We'd watch it over and over." Ducking his head, he chuckled in embarrassment, wondering why he offered that tidbit to a stranger...*I've never told anyone that.* "I guess that sounds kind of wimpy for a teenage boy, doesn't it?"

The wind blew gently, rustling the leaves overhead. Agnes swallowed audibly, as though fighting tears. "I think it sounds beautiful."

He stared at what he could see of her face, still in the shadows, his heart warm at her show of acceptance. They continued to sit, talking quietly, while waiting on the phone call. She kept looking up and he finally looked upward as well, asking, "What are you looking at?"

"Oh...I, well...I've just never noticed so many stars before."

Nodding, he explained, "It's the mountains. We're far away from the city lights, so it makes the night that much darker and the stars appear that much brighter."

"Oh..." she replied, her voice full of wonder as she continued to look skyward. "I think that there's probably a lot of things I've never really noticed before."

"Maybe now you can," he said.

She sighed, replying, "Maybe...maybe someday."

A few minutes later, his phone rang. Answering it, he said, "Here she is," and he handed his phone to Agnes. She stepped forward, still in the forest shadows, and took it from his outstretched hand. She said very little, agreeing to whatever Harlan was laying out. Disconnecting, she handed the phone back.

"What now?" he asked.

Agnes fiddled with the bottom of her jacket for a second, saying, "I need to get back to the road where we were run off. Harlan will have someone there to meet me."

"You sure you can you trust him?"

"Yeah. He told me who to look for and, well, I've got no other options."

"So, you're going into witness protection?"

Nodding slowly, Agnes replied, "I have no choice. I have to make things right." Shaking her head, a groan slipped out. "Bayley quoted Agatha Christie just before she left. It fit so perfectly."

He looked at her quizzical gaze, and she quoted, " 'I've had a long life of experience in noticing evil, fancying evil, suspecting evil and going forth to do battle with evil.' " Sighing heavily, she added, "I've got to see this through. Or else evil wins."

His heart pounded roughly as her words hit him, and he was struck with the realization that the woman in front of him was the bravest person he had ever met. Unable to think of anything to say that would come close to touching her strength, he stood silent, cursing his inadequacy.

Her gaze dropped to Scarlett, still sitting next to him, with her tongue lolling to the side. "I'd like for you and Scarlett to lead the way back and I'll walk behind."

Brows drawn down, he asked, "Why? Why can't I see you?"

"I'd rather stay a bit of a mystery to you…it feels safer that way."

With a short nod, he turned, deciding that to give her what she needed was the best way for him to honor her strength. Looking down, he patted Scarlett's head. "Come on, girl. Let's go back."

With his dog happily jogging along in the woods, Nathan followed at a pace slow enough for Agnes to follow. As they approached the road, he saw a dark SUV parked with two men standing next to it, their dress and demeanor screaming FBI. They approached Agnes and hustled her into the back seat. As the SUV made a three-point turn on the narrow road, it offered him a glimpse of a dark-haired, young woman, her eyes piercing his as a slight smile played about her lips before she lifted her hand in a small wave goodbye. He felt the strangest sense of sadness seeing the enigmatic woman taken away.

When the rescue was over and he had made his way back to the Saints, he learned that, while Agnes had been born into a crime family involved in human trafficking, she had risked everything to work with the FBI to put a stop to it.

Tossing back the rest of the whiskey, Nathan stood, his morose memories still as fresh as if it had all taken place yesterday. It made no sense to spend so much time thinking of a woman he would never see again. Rinsing his glass, he looked over at the dogs and called, "Come on...let's go."

They rose from the rugs and dutifully followed him outside. The light from the porch illuminated their path as he let them run to take care of their business while he walked to the kennel. The woods were still, the little creatures having already burrowed in for the night. The crickets chirped and, in the distance, he could hear the frogs croaking from the creek.

He grinned, thinking of his father's words to him when he was younger and they were walking over the farmland toward the woods at the back of the property.

"Your mama knew what she was doing when she named you. Francis Nathan Washington. 'Course, I always wanted to call you Nathan, after my grandpa Nathaniel, who was a good and kind man...probably one of the best men I ever met

in my life. But, your mama was raised Catholic, and since we were living on a farm with all these animals, she said she wanted to name you after a saint that loved nature. So, son, that's where you got the Francis from. You've gotta love of nature inside you, boy, and know that nature comes from God. Just always appreciate it, treat it right, and respect it."

Looking up, he was able to see the stars bright in the sky, as the moon rose over the tree line. He grinned, thinking it had been a couple of weeks since he called his parents. Deciding to do that the next day, he patted his thigh and whistled, calling the dogs over to him. Placing Red, Beau, and Persi back into their runs, with goodnight rubs and hugs, he shut the door.

His hand resting on Scarlett's head as she stood next to him, he filled his lungs with clean, mountain air before walking back to the house. Once inside, he locked the doors and turned out the lights. Climbing the stairs to the loft bedroom, he moved into the bathroom as Scarlett jumped up on the bed.

After a quick shower, he trimmed his thick beard. His light brown eyes dropped over his body's reflection in the mirror. He had packed on a few more pounds since his time in the Army, but daily workouts with the dogs had managed to keep it mostly muscle. A few minutes later, he climbed into bed, grinning when Scarlett groaned as she shifted to the side. Rolling over, he stared at the stars through the window, still wondering about the sense of disquiet he felt, unable to discern the reason.

Sighing deeply, Agatha Christel lay in bed, staring at the stars through her window, for once taking little comfort from them. The night was cloudless, giving her a perfect view, but in the city, they were not as bright as they could be. And she knew firsthand how bright they could really shine, in the right environment.

She was the only employee of the women's shelter that lived on the premises and was given the bedroom rent free. The attic room she called her own was small, but cozy. The brass bedframe was an antique that someone had donated to the center when getting rid of some furniture. The sheets were clean, although worn soft with time. The handmade quilt, in blues, yellows, and greens, had been made by one of the women who had stayed for a while in the shelter. A dresser painted white was next to the bed, a small lamp on top. The only other piece of furniture in the room was an old, wooden rocking chair with another quilt resting on the back, her latest paperback on the seat.

Besides a tiny closet, she had a half bathroom with only a toilet and sink. She used the shared shower downstairs, but did not mind. Just having her own half bathroom made her attic room even more special. It was far from the opulent rooms she had occupied when she was growing up but, for now, it felt like heaven. Safe. Comfortable.

Letting out another sigh, she tried to force her mind to the tasks on her to-do list for tomorrow, but as they always seemed to do at night, when she was feeling like this, her thoughts wandered to that night in the woods two years earlier. Brilliant stars, so much more intense than they were here, sparkling overhead. The rustling of leaves in the slight breeze…and the sight of the handsome man with the beautiful dog, sitting with her until she could be led to safety.

The memory had not faded with time, instead further cementing itself in her mind. His face remained clear, his voice just as mesmerizing. In a world of harsh words and guttural demands, his words had been calming.

Sighing, she turned over and punched her pillow in frustration. Memories of him were all she had and all she would ever have. He was too good. And, even if she were worthy of him, it would be too dangerous to do anything about it. Closing her eyes, she willed sleep to come. *After all, I can dream, can't I?*

Present Day

"Heard you had some excitement last night."

Nathan looked up as he came out of the kennel the next morning, smiling when his gaze landed on Blaise walking toward him, a German Shepard trotting at his side. As the big dog rushed over, Nathan knelt to give the beautiful girl a head rub.

"Grace let you take Gypsy out for a visit today?"

"Yeah. She had her at the nursing home yesterday so Gypsy was indoors almost all day. I figured I'd bring her here this morning and let her have a chance to run around a bit with Scarlett."

They watched the dogs sniff each other before trotting off together toward the house. "Come on in," he invited. "Got the coffee on."

Settling on the front porch chairs with steaming mugs of coffee, their feet up on the rail, the mood between them was relaxed as the they watched the dogs play in the yard.

"So, yesterday?" Blaise prompted.

"Jack called...a little boy staying at Bethany's cabins got lost. Scarlett found him quickly, and he was fine once he was back with his family."

"You do good work."

Quiet for a few minutes, he eventually replied, "I like what I do. My dad always says, 'a man who likes what he does will always be good at it'."

"Is it enough?"

He turned his head and caught Blaise looking at him intently, making him wonder what was really on his mind. "My work? With the dogs?"

"Yeah. If it is, that's great. But, I've sensed a restlessness in you lately, so I wondered if you were...I don't know...stuck in a rut?"

Nodding, he started to catch on. "You're talking about Jack's offer to work for the Saints."

"Not *work* for the Saints, Nathan. *Be* one."

He cocked his head to the side, not sure what Blaise was getting at. "I don't follow you."

Shaking his head slightly, Blaise chuckled, "I'm getting that." Leaning forward, he rested his elbows on his knees, catching Nathan's eyes and holding them. "Look, lots of people do good work, every day, in a lot of different jobs. Help people. Take care of people. Teach our children. Make the world a better place. And they never see the underbelly of society, not like we do. For those of us that do see it? We strive to give society that balance again. The balance they, if we do our jobs right, never realize they're missing. We carve out a bit of that cancer so that everyone else can keep doing their job to make society a good place."

Looking out to the woods he thought on that for a minute. He felt, rather than saw, as Blaise leaned back in his chair again, giving him the time to mull over everything he had said. The Saints protected people in a way that they did not even realize they were being protected. He truly admired them for that. What they did put them at risk, but they did it anyway. He was part of a team that lived that way once…and look lost them. The ensuing silence settled easily as they sipped their coffee for several minutes.

"When I was first approached by Jack to come work for him, he had an idea of what he wanted to accomplish, but it was something most people had never seen before," Blaise eventually added, without looking at him. "At our first team meeting, there was me, Cam, Bart, and Chad. I looked around the table and could not imagine a more diverse group of men. None of us had the same experience. Or backgrounds. I couldn't figure out what the hell we had in common."

Blaise sipped his coffee, then, continued, "By the time the Saints were getting contracts, we had Luke and

Marc on board, and I began to understand. Jack wasn't interested in us being cookie-cutter investigators. He thrived on us bringing totally different skill sets to the team. Sure, we had to learn investigation and security, but he still emphasized that we were all different." Chuckling, he said, "I swear, if it wasn't for Jack's dogged determination that we were going to be a successful company, I think we might have packed it in that first year. But, we persevered. Took the contracts no one wanted and built a reputation. That was about five years ago. Within two years we were growing and thriving."

Once more, the quiet of the morning in the woods was only broken by the dogs at play and the birds chirping overhead. Hearing all that about the Saints…it hit Nathan how exceptional each and every man was— which he already knew, of course. But the pride and admiration with which Blaise talked about them…how hard they worked to fit as a unit, how well they complimented one another…they were a family.

He set his now empty coffee mug onto the wooden, plank porch and admitted, "My parents are simple people. I grew up on a farm down in southwest Virginia. Hard work, but we had good times. First dog I ever had was a coonhound an elderly neighbor was getting rid of. He had dementia, you see, so he wasn't really able to keep up with her. She was old, but I swear I fell in love with that dog. Anyway, one day his son came tearin' into our driveway needing the dog. Seems his dad had wandered off. My dad yelled for me to get the dog and we followed him back to his farm. I watched as that dog tracked the older man through the woods and we found him, safe and sound." After another quiet moment, he confessed, "It was the greatest feeling in the world."

Shrugging, he continued, "I found out all I could about tracking. Got certified and, even as a teenager, started working with the local Sheriff's Department. Joined the Army right out of high school, finished Military Police MOS, specializing in dog handling. Not for drugs or explosives, but for search and rescue. Planned on staying in for my full career."

"What happened?"

Scrubbing his hand over his face, he heaved a sigh. "After four years, we were on a mission...me and five of my buddies and their dogs...at a village that was mostly rubble due to recent bombing by the insurgents. I was over near one of the walls when we were rocked with another explosion. The fuckin' place was still wired. Lost 'em all. All five men. All five dogs."

"Fuckin' hell, Nathan," Blaise said, shaking his head. "I'm sorry, man."

Nodding, his voice scratchy, he admitted, "Me too. My dog and I turned a search and rescue into a search and recovery. By the time our aid got there, we'd found all five. Gotta tell you, finding the bodies of your friends, one after another, is a fuck of a way to live."

Silence moved over them again, each to their own thoughts before Blaise prompted, "So, you got out."

"Yeah. I was done. I'd loved being in the Army but, after that, I had no desire to get that close to another group of friends. I had little time left anyway, so it was easier to just finish my time and leave." Shrugging, he continued, "You'd think, after all that, I'd want to leave everything behind me, do something completely different, but, tracking is still in my blood. It's all I know. The way I do it now, disappearing into the wilderness…it somehow just seems easier. I work alone. It feels safer that way."

That night, he lay in bed and, as usual, turned to stare at the stars through the windows. After explaining to Blaise what he had lost, they had turned the conversation to lighter topics. Now, in the quiet, he couldn't help but think of what he had said. *Alone. Safer.* Instead of those words providing comfort, as they were meant to, he felt the continuing disquiet. Blaise spoke of the Saints like they were family…a brotherhood…could he be a part of something like that again? Did they even need him? Finally, rolling over, he punched his pillow, causing Scarlett to grunt in her sleep. *At least one of us is sleeping.*

3

The sun beamed high over the Blue Ridge Mountains as Nathan made his way to Jack's property. Driving his old truck through the security gates after gaining access, he wound his way along the tree-lined driveway.

Jack had built a huge home on his twenty-six acres that backed to the Blue Ridge Mountains. From the outside, the structure appeared to be a luxury cabin. But, underneath the house and four-car garage, was the command center of the Saints.

Every time he made the trip to the Saints' compound, he was impressed with the size. Parking next to the variety of trucks and SUVs parked along the drive, he alighted from his truck, glad to see that his was not the only old vehicle present.

Seeing the white picket fence surrounding the back yard, he had to grin. Jack had once been concerned that he would not be able to offer his wife a white-picket-fence kind of life, but they had made their relationship work and the fence was a symbol of that—two worlds melding into one. They were one of the strongest couples he knew.

As he approached the front door, Bethany, her dark blonde hair hanging in a braid over her shoulder, smiled widely as she greeted him.

Nodding, he returned her smile, stepping inside. He had been in their house before, but this was the first time Jack had asked him over in an official capacity where he was not tasked for a search. Leaving Scarlett at home and coming alone felt odd.

Before he had a chance to ask her where he should go, Jack entered the room, his hand out, and greeted him with a smile.

"Nathan, glad you could make it on such short notice. Come on down."

He inwardly winced at the idea that Jack might think he was too busy to come. Though he was always active, it was on his own schedule—unless on a search—and he didn't want Jack to think he did not care. Following to a door down the hall, his curiosity piqued as they descended a set of stairs. At the bottom, Jack turned and entered a code into the security panel on the wall before pushing through the door.

Once inside, the door closed behind them with a resounding click. Stepping inside, a quick survey showed a large room with a conference table in the center. White screens lined two walls and another held a bank of computers. He recognized Luke and his wife, Charlie, sitting at the computers, both tossing grins his way.

The other Saints sat at the table, with two empty

chairs at one end. Jack held out his hand, motioning for him to sit. Sliding into one of the empty seats, he greeted the others, Cam, Marc, Nick, Patrick, Jude, Bart, Monty, Chad, and Blaise.

"I'm sure you're wondering why I asked you here," Jack began.

"Well, to be honest, I'm a little in awe of being in your compound."

"Aww, don't worry," Bart drawled. "He just figured if we got you here, then you'd have to join us."

The others chuckled and even stoic Jack grinned. Shaking his head, Jack continued, "Well, you know you always have a standing invitation to join the Saints. But, for today, I've got a special need for information you might have."

Nathan glanced around at the curious faces of the others and surmised they had been unaware of the reason for Jack's request, with the exception of Nick and Blaise, whose faces were hard. Turning his attention to Jack, he nodded.

"Two years ago, you helped us locate Nick's wife, Bayley, and another woman, Agnes Gruzinsky."

His attention was immediately riveted. He was concerned that Bayley, who was Blaise's sister and had married Nick after their ordeal, was involved but, if he were being honest with himself, it was the mention of Agnes, the woman that had remained in his mind for so long, that had him hyper-focused now.

Nick took over, saying, "I was initially with the FBI on that case. Missing women were tied to the Gruzinsky crime family who, as it turns out, were involved in human trafficking and kidnapping women to use as sex slaves. Add in their family connections to the Russian mafia through Gavrill Volkov, and it was a high-profile case. It was suspected that he arranged the transportation of women overseas, but it was never proven."

"Jesus," he breathed, shaking his head at the scope of the crimes.

Blaise added, "If you remember, my goof of a sister ended up gaining the attention of Lazlo Grunzinsky and his sister, Agnes. That's how she met Nick."

"It turned out that Agnes was secretly working with the FBI to bring down her family," Nick continued.

He nodded his head, remembering the basics of the case, as Jack summarised, "We debriefed after that night and the case was closed for us. The trafficking business was shut down and the rescued women were all safe. The FBI had enough evidence to put the Gruzinsky family behind bars. Agnes was taken to Harlan Masten, her contact at the FBI, so that she could testify against her family and go into WITSEC. That was the end of our involvement with the case and we did not continue to monitor."

A sick feeling in the pit of his stomach began, but he forced his attention to stay on Jack's words.

"It turned out that Agnes was not needed to testify against her family because the FBI had more than enough evidence to obtain convictions. But Harlan, not wanting her to be in danger from the Russian mafia, took her under his wing. He arranged for her to have a new identity."

Clearly this was news to a lot of them and Nathan noticed the rapt attention growing around the room as Jack added, "I've received word from both the FBI and a request from the Governor to look into the case again. Agnes' FBI contact, Harlan, was murdered three days ago."

The room was filled with *oh, shit* and *fuckin' hell* as the majority of the Saints reacted to the news of the murder.

Nick sighed, adding, "I heard about it from some friends still at the agency who knew I had been close with Harlan. I was upset, naturally. Harlan was a good agent…a good man. But, it wasn't until Jack came to me late yesterday, needing to talk to Bayley, that I knew there was a connection."

"The reason I had Nick bring Bayley in yesterday was because I needed to know what she and Agnes may have talked about before you found them."

"What'd Bayley say?" Monty asked, his voice a bit choked. The former FBI agent had also known Harlan and the news was clearly hitting him hard.

"She said that Agnes told her that she hated growing up in the family once she realized what they did. She felt powerless for a long time, then slowly came up with a plan. She contacted the FBI and had been working with them for a little while before everything went down. We knew all this, but at least Bayley was able to fill in some of the emotional details."

"Fuckin' brave as shit," Cam breathed under his breath. The large, dark haired man had grown up in gangs and, once out, had become a police officer and then undercover detective. If anyone could relate, in any way, to what she had gone through it would be him.

"There's still a threat against her?" Nathan asked, hating the thought of the slight woman, sharing the stars with him that night as though she were seeing them for the first time, being in danger.

Bart leaned forward, placing his muscular forearms on the table, his face intense. "When we were working a case involving kidnapping a child from a prominent Russian family, I had to interview people who would take over this family's business if they had the chance. One of the people I came across was Gavrill Volkov. Turns out, his cousin is Chessa Gruzinsky, Agnes' mom."

"Fuckin' hell," Jude growled under his breath.

Nathan looked at the others, seeing the same frustration on their faces as he felt, processing the new information. This was quickly adding up to serious trouble.

"He's in prison, but believe me, he still runs his family from the inside. And, he's got a cushy sentence... tax evasion," Jack said.

"You gotta be shittin' me," Cam said. "I thought that piece of dirt's operation out of Norfolk was the one shipping the kidnapped women to places overseas."

"The Gruzinsky's clammed up at their trials and pleaded guilty so they didn't have to testify against each other. Plus, they knew if they turned on Gavrill, their time behind bars would be made hell up until the moment they bled out on the floor somewhere," Nick growled.

"So, while *we're* certain human trafficking is one of the Volkov family businesses," Jack said, maintaining his composure in an increasingly agitated room, "there was no proof and no one to testify against him."

"What about Agnes?" Patrick asked.

"She had no proof, according to Harlan, since she never talked directly to Gavrill. She only knew what her family told her and they wouldn't talk after they were arrested."

"So, they got him on tax evasion? Why didn't we hear about this sooner?" Marc asked, pushing his chair back in frustration.

"Our job was done. There was nothing more for us to do," Jack stated quietly, but firmly, catching Marc's eye.

Nathan watched as Marc held Jack's gaze, taking a deep breath before giving one quick nod to signify he understood. Jack swept the room with his eyes, his gaze landing and holding briefly on each of the Saints to check in with them. With that one, silent gesture the tension started to release from the air.

Clearing his throat, Nick replied, "The FBI had proof that he had money going into the Gruzinsky's hotel business—the legitimate one. Since it was being run alongside the illegal one, and they'd want to keep that one hushed up, an oversight meant he never declared any of the return on his legal investments."

"Sounds like a stupid mistake on his accountant's part," Patrick commented.

Nick agreed, saying, "Seems that the accountant was found dead a week after Gavrill's trial."

"Jesus," Nathan said under his breath.

Shaking his head, Bart surmised, "And Agnes has now cost him plenty."

"Oh, yeah...not only his business, but possibly a longer sentence for him, as well as putting her entire family behind bars."

"And Agnes?" Monty asked. "She still protected by the FBI?"

"I've been in contact with the FBI," Jack explained, "and here's the problem. Agnes Gruzinsky has not been on the FBI's radar. She was not needed for the trial so was no longer a person of interest to them. She essentially disappeared and, as a private citizen, that was not their worry. However, Harlan just retired and his murder points to the Russians, so now she's on their radar again. The FBI is working that angle since they found prints from Johan, one of Gavrill's enforcers, at the scene. Also, Gavrill's brother, Yurgi, is believed to be here in the states now, running Gavrill's businesses. Harlan's murder could be tied into them searching for Agnes...for revenge."

Looking around the room, Jack shook his head as he continued, "Harlan wasn't just murdered. His house was trashed and his computer was stolen. Now, of course, he had no official FBI documentations at his house, but he would have probably kept all the information and notes on Agnes. According to our contact at the FBI, the murder looks like he interrupted someone doing a search. He fought hard but, in the end, was killed. Executed...hands tied behind his back...shot in the back of the head."

"So, you think the Russian mafia is still after Agnes," Nathan stated, the sick feeling in the pit of his stomach now reaching his heart. Not fully understanding why the news was hitting him so hard, he focused on steadying his pounding heartbeat.

"That's what our main concern is. And, what we've been tasked with. Finding Agnes Grunzinsky...before they do—"

"I'm in."

All eyes around the table jumped to him, but he kept his gaze firmly on Jack's face.

Jack's eyes narrowed slightly as he stared back. "Nathan, I've made it no secret that I would like to have you join us on a full time basis, but I called you here to find out anything specific that Agnes may have said to you that night...not to pressure you to join us."

"I realize that," he replied, his voice surprisingly sure and steady. Glancing quickly at Blaise before returning his attention to Jack, he confessed, "To be honest, I've been thinking about going full time with you. I always turned you down because my simple life seemed...uh... well, simple." Grimacing at the stupid way his words sounded, he forged ahead. "I mean, that was what I wanted. Just me, the dogs I raise, and the tracking business."

"Nothing wrong with that," Blaise said, staring at him.

"I know," he agreed, shooting his friend a grateful nod. "But I've come to realize that I've mostly been hiding. The idea of working with, and then possibly losing, good friends kept me to myself." Shrugging, he said, "I've been disquiet lately. Wanting more. Needing more." He pierced Jack with his sincere stare and added, "Been thinking about this, thought if the right time came along I'd know it. Now is that time."

Jack slowly nodded, seeming to appraise his words before saying, "I've never known you to be impulsive."

Pulling himself out of his comfort zone, he admitted, "I've thought a lot about Agnes over the past two years. Something about her was so vulnerable and yet, strong, at the same time. I didn't know her story when we were out in the woods that night, but I respected what she was doing. If she's in danger... she didn't let anything hold her back from doing what's right. I don't want to hold back anymore either."

"Tell you what," Jack said. "I want you but, like all the Saints did, you give us a try and then you can decide if this is what you want as a career. If it isn't, we'll still use you as a tracker when needed. If it is, then you'll have already learned the security business and you can continue as a Saint."

His breath left him in a rush as he nodded, the pain in his chest lifting slightly. "Sounds good."

Jack grinned, "All right. Let's get to work. Tell us what she talked about that night."

He had only been in her presence for less than an hour, but had replayed the event in his mind so many times, he was easily able to recite their conversation. Repeating it for the Saints, he concluded with her quote from Agatha Christie. Looking at Nick, he smiled, saying, "She said it was from Bayley."

Nick rolled his eyes and nodded, shooting Blaise a

slight smile. "Yeah, Bayley adores Agatha Christie and has memorized so many quotes from her and her books. She manages to find just the right time to use them in her life."

Blaise shook his head. "She's done that since she first started reading mysteries. Agatha Christie has always been her favorite."

"Well, it made an impression on Agnes and, in turn, made an impression on me. I actually looked it up online when I got home and printed it out." Shaking his head slightly, he couldn't help but smile a little as he thought of how Agnes looked reciting the words. "She quoted, 'I've had a long life of experience in noticing evil, fancying evil, suspecting evil and going forth to do battle with evil.' She then sighed and said, 'I've got to see this through. Or else evil wins.' I kid you not, it was as though the weight of the world was on her shoulders." Looking at the others, he said, with poorly veiled awe in his voice, "If she can be that brave, how can I be less?"

4

Nathan looked nervously around the table at the other Saints wondering, now that things had settled down, what they thought of his decision to join them, but only found accepting grins shot his way. Breathing a sigh of relief, he offered, "I know the basics of security. I know search and rescue, and I've done my share of search and recovery." Pausing, he sucked in a fortifying breath, "But, I'm willing to learn whatever it takes."

"That's all any of us have done," Chad replied. "None of us came into this knowing much about how to fulfill Jack's vision. We've all learned and are still learning. It's good to have you with us."

The nods all around had him relaxing in his seat and, like the rest of them, turning his eyes to Jack, ready to find out what they needed to do to take care of Agnes.

Jack nodded toward Luke and Charlie, indicating for them to take over. Luke began, "Without having any of Harlan's data, I've still been able to pick up his basic computer searches, emails, etc. So far, nothing. Whoever he contacted to assist him with Agnes' disappearance and probable new identity, must have been top notch and erased any traces from his personal computer. There also has been no email contact that Charlie and I can discern between Harlan and Agnes. But, then again, whoever assisted him really knew their software to erase traces. That's the bad news. The good news is that means the Russians, if they have his computer, also can't find anything."

"So, they've got nothing and we've got nothing," Jude complained, leaning back heavily in his seat.

"Well, we've still got more than they have simply because we already know of some private organizations that are experts in changing identities. Plus, Charlie is scanning other databases to see if we can find anything…and Charlie's much better than what the mafia has."

Chuckles met this statement as they turned to her. Charlie shot her husband a grin and said, "I've been running the records of plastic surgeons who may have given facial changes to any females that were twenty-six-years old in the six months after Agnes disappeared. Of course, there are a lot, but not as many as you might think. Most are boob jobs, so I didn't have to worry about those. I mean, she might have had a boob job," she added, her nose scrunching in thought, but I'm more interested in her face." Giving her head a slight shake, she continued, "Now, we have to throw out her birth-date, since her new identity would have reassigned that, but she would have been somewhat accurate in her age with the doctor."

"What if it was a doctor off the grid?" Patrick asked. "Someone not associated with a clinic."

"I don't think that Harlan would have her use someone not board certified or reputable."

"What about going to Canada or Mexico, or somewhere else? With a false passport?"

Nodding, Luke said, "We thought about that. But we ran her facial recognition through all the flights leaving the country during that time and did not come up with a hit."

Nathan shook his head, awed at the resources available to Jack's Saints. As Charlie sent a picture of Agnes up to the screen on the wall, his breath hitched, seeing her again after two years. Dark hair, bangs swept to the side, dark eyes, pale skin, a Roman nose with a slight bump on the ridge. Her smile was not wide, but still showcased her perfectly straight teeth. The moonlight, while bright that night, had cast shadows on her face, keeping her true beauty from his eyes.

"How hard is it to give someone a whole new identity?" he ventured to ask.

"To do it seamlessly and with no way to trace? Not real easy," Luke admitted. "Charlie and I could have accomplished it if Harlan had come to us, but then, that's not something we've done in the past so it's not surprising he didn't think of us." Shooting a grin at Charlie, he amended, "Well, I haven't. My dearest wife eluded me for a little while as she tried out different identities."

She returned his grin and said, "I didn't completely bury myself, but I did do a pretty good job of going to ground." Looking at Nathan, she explained, "I had some guys after me for a while. I managed to shake them with multiple identities, but they weren't exactly sophisticated in their methods so it wasn't too hard. I expect the mafia would be much more thorough."

"Do we have any idea who might have helped Harlan?" Blaise asked.

Jack rubbed his chin and answered, "I've got some contacts that I'm going to have Luke and Charlie check on. We may have already hit on someone's radar just by what we've already been looking into. I feel like Harlan would have gone to someone reputable so I'll start reaching out to some of them to see if they would agree to work with us."

Charlie explained, "There are security businesses that, like Jack, don't exactly advertise on Google, but then there are those that go so deep underground— figuratively, not literally—that you have to know how to find them. I'll start reaching out to those that Jack knows and see it we can get a hit."

"Until then," Jack said, "you've got your security assignments on your tablets. Nathan, go with Chad and get equipment and then Charlie will set you up on your tablet. I'll have you work with Bart on learning more about Gavrill's operation, now that Yurgi is in the picture to supposedly take over the legitimate side of the Volkov businesses. Then, I'll have you work with Cam and Marc on setting up security for some of our clients. You can learn that aspect until we have something more concrete to go on."

The table soon cleared as the Saints moved to their next activities. Nathan walked toward Chad but was waylaid by Jack's hand on his shoulder.

"Just wanted to say that I'm glad you decided to join us. I think you'll be a real asset."

Pinching his lips, he said, "I don't know how much I can help you, but I don't want to sit on the sidelines anymore."

"Good a reason as any," Jack acknowledged and, with a nod, turned toward the computers where Luke and Charlie sat.

"Come on, Nathan," Chad said, "I'll show you around. Rooms down here are full of equipment needed for our security business. We all live nearby, although we don't meet at the compound daily. We generally hold meetings here twice a week, unless an active case requires us to gather more often. Although lately, as busy as we are, we're meeting more frequently."

He followed the large, dark-haired, former ATF explosives expert into one of the many rooms off the conference room.

"Here's the weapons room. We're all licensed as private investigators now, something Jack'll go over with you. We carry weapons when needed."

Nathan's eyes were wide as he viewed the fully stocked room that not only included firearms, but Kevlar jackets, as well as other military grade equipment.

"Here's the weight-lifting room," Chad said,

throwing open another door. "It's a place to keep in shape, considering most of us don't have time to join a gym." Moving to another door, he stepped inside.

Nathan followed and saw bunk beds and a separate shower facility. "You have to stay here much?"

"Not often, but occasionally when something is going on in the field, we don't like to be too far away, so a few of us'll bunk down and that keeps us close if necessary."

At the end of the hall, Chad pointed to another door and said, "This leads to a second set of stairs that takes you to the upstairs garage. We've got several SUVs with bullet-proof windows and frames. We also have ATVs and snow mobiles. Jack's got about thirty acres here and his property goes up the mountainside. Plus, with Bethany's acres on the other side with her cabins, there's a lot of terrain. We practice, and," he grinned, "we have fun."

Bart came up behind them and said, "Glad to have you with us, man."

"Thanks," Nathan said, looking at the muscular, Nordic man before his eyes slid to Jude, similar in size and mannerism.

"It won't be hard for you to assimilate," Patrick threw out, walking up from behind, clapping him on the back. "I came from California and joined them kind of late. But, you already know everyone, so it'll be easy."

He appreciated the words, easing the slight tension he still had about making such a change to his life. Agnes' face slid through his mind and the knowledge of all she gave up to do the right thing furthered his resolve.

As soon as he was set up with everything he needed, he moved back to the conference table with Bart, near where Luke and Charlie were working.

"You ready?" Luke asked. Seeing his nod, Luke said, "All right. Then let's see what Agnes is facing with the Volkovs."

Agatha slathered mayonnaise on the bread before adding the turkey and ham. Glad to have lettuce and tomato today, she piled them on before placing the sandwiches on the tray. She looked at the woman next to her, filling the glasses with iced tea, and observed the fading bruises on her face.

Smiling, she said, "Did you sleep well last night?"

"Yes, ma'am," Delores answered, her voice hesitant.

Agatha turned and placed her hand on her arm. "Please, just call me Agatha. And, if you didn't sleep well, it's okay to say so. I know how hard it can be to try to sleep your first night in a new place."

Delores blushed, saying, "It's not that I'm not grateful to be here, 'cause I am. I guess, I just kept thinking that I was still hiding from Lester."

"Is that your boyfriend?"

"Ex-boyfriend," Delores bit out, then immediately apologized. "I'm sorry...that sounded rude."

"No...no it didn't. It sounded firm. And that's a good thing."

Tears filled Delores' eyes as she blinked rapidly. "He never liked that. Me being firm...about anything. Said it was sassy and he wasn't going to put up with any sass." She hung her head, sucking in a deep breath. "My mama would be so ashamed."

Giving her a moment, she wondered if Delores' mother had been abused, before finally asking, "What would your mama be ashamed for? The sass, as you call it?"

"Oh, no ma'am—I mean Agatha. My mama was a sweet lady but my daddy always said when she got worked up, she could shake some sass." She sighed heavily, and added, "Daddy always laughed when Mama did, then he'd give her a hug and say she was the best, and Mama always said that made life all better."

She stared at the young woman in the throes of a lovely memory, seeing the smile begin to curve her lips. A sliver of a memory began to worm its way into her mind...one of her father patting her mother's arm affectionately. Swallowing hard, she closed her eyes tightly, pushing the thought away. Smiling, she gazed at Delores and said, "Well, it sounds like your parents had a good relationship. And, thankfully, you got out of one that was not good."

A wider smile spread across Delores' face and she nodded toward the food on the counter, saying, "Let's get this out to the table."

As they walked into the dining room, trays in their hands, others quickly came to assist. After a few minutes, when everyone was settled, Agatha looked around the table at the variety of women and small children taking temporary refuge in the center. Talking. Laughing. A few nervous glances. A few with fading bruises. They came from all walks of life...all circumstances. A few were escaping abusive relationships and some were escaping prostitution, hiding from the men who had ruled their world. All needed a safe place to land until they could figure out the next step in their lives.

Safe Harbor Center. She smiled, thinking the name was appropriate. Over a year ago, Harlan had asked her what she wanted to do with her life now that she was free. Her cosmetic surgeries were over, her new identity was established and, for all intents and purposes, Agnes Gruzinsky was dead. And, Agatha Christel had risen from her ashes.

She thought back to the conversation she had had with Harlan, the FBI agent who had become a surrogate father to her, about moving forward.

Snorting, I quipped, "Taking down a human trafficking ring and putting my family behind bars is hardly the sort of thing I can put on a resume."

Harlan glared, fondly, but glared nonetheless. Knowing he could be relentless, I shrugged, looking down at my clenched hands. "Help. Help women get out of whatever is trapping them."

Harlan was quiet for a moment, before patting my shoulder. "I know of a women's shelter. They always need help. I'm sure the pay isn't good, but I know that won't matter."

I looked up into his face and said, "What about questions?"

"You know your new background. If there's something else we need to add, I'll get it taken care of."

Snorting again, I grinned. "You mean you and the mystery men that are giving me a new life?"

He pretend-glared again, but the corners of his lips twitched. "They're good at what they do. And, if something ever happens to me, they'll take care of you."

Cocking my head to the side, I asked, "How?"

"They'll let you know. But then again, hell, I'm too stubborn to die."

"You'd better be," I rushed. Pondering for a moment, I nodded slowly. "But, in answer to your first question, I think I would like to work at the shelter. Who knows? I might have found my calling."

Brushing off her reverie, she looked up as the Director walked in, a smile on her face as she greeted everyone. Coming to her, Ann smiled.

"Hey, Agatha. Can we meet after lunch is over?"

Nodding, she agreed. Her eyes followed Ann as she continued down the hall to her office. The center was located in a large, old house but they were bursting at the seams and Ann was working tirelessly to get their new facility ready for move-in.

She had taken Agatha last week to visit the new center. Located in a former store that had gone out of business years before, the owner was glad to have someone take it over. Ann Cosner, a social worker with a double degree in business, had worked to create Safe Harbor Center as a safe, halfway house for women in need of a helping hand to get back on their feet. While they were only a temporary place for the women to recuperate, learn employable skills, and find jobs and new housing, they were constantly at full capacity.

She knew Ann had dedicated herself to tirelessly fundraising in order to get the store turned into offices, dorm rooms, a dining room, kitchen, and classrooms. If anyone could have gotten the job done, it was Ann.

As soon as lunch was over and the women assigned clean-up duty had the place sparkling, she walked to Ann's office. Knocking, she entered, smiling her greeting to her boss.

"Come on in," Ann said, returning her smile. "Have a seat. We've got lots to talk about."

As always when someone focused on her, she felt her stomach drop and her palms begin to sweat. It was as though she constantly had the fear of someone looking her in the eye and saying, "I know who you are."

Sitting in the chair, she forced her smile to remain, but it was only as Ann pulled out the files in front of her and began discussing the center's business, that she finally relaxed. *Will I always be looking over my shoulder?* She tried not to think of the answer to that question, afraid pondering too long on the past would choke off all her happiness.

"So, with the added donation from an anonymous source, we will be able to move into our new facility soon," Ann pronounced. "I can't believe that we got the exact amount that was needed to get the place ready for us to occupy. It's like a guardian angel is tied right into us!"

Matching her smile, she said, "You've done so much. You must be proud."

Ann's sharp eyes pierced into her as she replied, "Don't sell yourself short. I may be the public face of Safe Harbor, but I could not have done what I have this past year without you. Before you came along, I had a series of well-intentioned assistants, but each found the work too taxing and the pay too little. You, my dear, have been a godsend."

Shrugging off the compliment, she said, "I like the work. I feel like I'm helping."

"Oh, Lordy, Agatha, you're doing more than helping. You're changing lives. With every woman here that you sit with, talk to, work with...you are changing their life." Closing her file, she said, "I need to let you know that we will be adding a security system to the new building, something we don't have here. We've been lucky so far, but I don't trust our luck to hold forever. The threat of someone coming after one of the women is always present, so security is vital. I've contracted with someone and they'll send men to install the security next week. I have to be here, so I'll send you to the facility to let them inside."

Her heart lighter, she nodded, stood and moved out of the office and down the hall to the computer lab. Stopping in the hall, she pulled out her burner phone, sending a quick text. **Transfer of money successful. Thx.** With a secret smile curling her lips, she continued on.

5

Nathan observed Bart's expression, often jovial, now somber.

"I first came to know about Gavrill Volkov several years ago. In fact, it was on the case where I met Faith. She was working the case with me in an unofficial capacity. She has a special gift for...well, some would call her a seer, but she's just really *in-tune* to people. She accompanied me as we interviewed potential child kidnappers."

Luke flashed a photograph of Gavrill, a man in his forties, black hair with splashes of grey throughout, onto the screen as Bart continued. Though he appeared to be short and heavy, almost squatty in stature, he was nonetheless menacing. It was in his eyes. Dark, intense, focused. *Fuckin' dangerous.*

"We were investigating the kidnapping of one of the old, Russian mafia families' son. In doing so, we had to check out the family's competition. Gavrill was from another Russian family, fairly new to the U.S. They are actually from Croatia, not 'Mother Russia', as he called it. They were described as newcomers, with no elder at the helm, that had muscled into the existing mafia family's territory."

Luke said, "Just think of the Godfather movies. Old family with the head ruling everything. But, as times changed, newer gangs came in and started edging out the established Sicilian mafias. Same thing with the Russians. A member of an old family wanted things to change so he joined forces with Gavrill. Fucked over his family in the process, at a time when they were moving into more legitimate businesses, so they fucked him right back."

He shook his head, saying, "This sounds like some kind of movie script."

Bart agreed, "It's fucked up, all right. Some families were into extortion, money laundering, transporting guns and drugs. Sounds bad, but honestly, not all that crazy. But Gavrill? Man's into everything, especially human trafficking, racketeering, drugs, guns, prostitution, just to name a few things. He operated out of a warehouse in Portsmouth."

"And now?"

"All that was taking place about three to four years ago. Two years ago, when Bayley stumbled into the Gruzinsky family line, we discovered that Chessa, Agnes' mom, is Gavrill's cousin. She married Milos Gruzinsky and they had two sons, Grigory and Lazlo. They continued the family business of kidnapping women, using them as sex slaves in a hotel they had set up for prostitution, and human trafficking. It was suspected that they would send the women to Gavrill's operation and he would transport them to other countries where they would continue sexual enslavement."

"Agnes," Luke interjected, "found out about her family's business and decided to find a way to turn them into the FBI. Smart girl made it happen. Now, we've got Lazlo, Grigory, Milos, and Chessa Grunzinsky all in prison."

"But they couldn't catch Gavrill for it," he confirmed what they had discussed earlier.

"That's where it gets interesting," Charlie said. "They wanted to try Gavrill on trafficking charges but there was no evidence that he had any of the women in his ships at the time. Looking for any way to get him behind bars, they did find evidence for tax evasion. A pittance of a sentence, but enough to make him even more angry about the situation. Now, with his brother here, he's got plenty of help to take down the person who started the downfall of the family."

Which meant going after Agnes. He felt rage building inside at the thought of her in danger. Tamping the emotion down, he vowed to do everything he could to keep Gavrill from finding her.

"I just figured I didn't have no choice," Tina said, slumping in her chair. "My mama turned tricks, but she only did it for the drugs. At least my pimp handled the money and gave me what I needed." She shrugged, "It might not have been much, but it was more than my mama ever made."

"That sounds like a hard life," Agatha said, "but it also sounds like you're a survivor."

Snorting, "I don't know about that. I kidded myself into thinking that I was independent, 'cause I was making the decision to turn tricks. Somehow, my pimp always made it seem like it was my idea, but the reality is, I was letting myself be used. I just couldn't figure out any other way to live. Then, I got beat up and he didn't do nothing for me. I just got tired." Her shoulders drooped as she hung her head. "So sick and tired of being nothing but a body."

"You deserve more, you know. You deserve to be whatever you want to be," she said, hoping she was getting through.

Nodding, Tina agreed, "I know. It won't be easy, 'cause I never finished high school, but I don't want to be like my mama. I want to be more."

The other women in the shelter were asleep, but she had found Tina in the kitchen, sitting alone at the table. Sitting down with her, she did not pry, but let the young woman unburden herself as she needed.

"That's what this place is for," she assured her. "You can find what you need to change your life."

"You sound like someone who knows what they're talking about," Tina observed, her eyes on her.

Nodding, she said, "I was in my own version of hell. But, I found that I had the courage to make a change. Now I try to help others make changes as well."

Tina's lips curved slightly. "Courage. I never thought of it as courage, but that's what this feels like."

"A famous Greek named Thucydides once said, 'The secret to happiness is freedom... And the secret to freedom is courage.' When I first read that, I was struck by how much it meant to me. I wasn't free and now I am. I might not have as much, but I'm happier. And, to become free took a lot of courage."

Tina's slight smile widened. "You're awful smart, Miss Agatha."

Chuckling, she shook her head. "Not really. But, I'm learning. Every day, I'm learning."

As Tina headed upstairs to bed, she followed, climbing the stairs to her attic room. Once in the bathroom, she brushed her teeth and spit out the toothpaste. Wiping her mouth with the hand towel, she stared into her reflection. It was a simple action, one most people did multiple times a day. But, she only allowed herself to stare into the mirror occasionally.

Her face was different...not much, but enough to keep someone from immediately recognizing her. Her nose, which had had a little bump she thought gave her face character, was now slender and smooth. Her teeth, which had been straightened with braces when she was a pre-teen, now had a slightly crooked incisor.

She wondered about the dentist who had given her a crooked tooth, but never asked questions. She assumed he was used to cosmetic changes...no matter what the reason. Her eyes, once a dark, chocolate brown, were now amber with contacts she wore at all times—even to bed. Her ears, which had barely stuck out at the top, now lay close to her head. Her hair, no longer dark, was sandy-blonde with a few auburn streaks. Her fingers reached up to slide through the strands, still feeling as though she wore a wig.

Her eyes continued to rove over her face, seeing her features in parts before stepping back and viewing herself as a whole. The same...and different. And necessary.

Flipping off the light, she crawled into bed, rolling over so that she could peer out at the stars dotting the sky. Star light...star bright...*If I could have a wish, what would it be?* She knew the answer to that question, but to speak it aloud would waste a wish. *I might see the man with the beautiful dog again, but he would not know me. And if he did, he would not want to know me.*

The week passed quickly and Nathan had to admit he was glad for the weekend. He had not worked full time, outside his business, since the military, but assimilating into the Saints had been easy. It was not a nine to five job, therefore it allowed him the luxury of being able to continue with his dog training when not working with Cam installing security systems.

Now, Sunday morning had him preparing for tracking practice with the dogs when he heard a vehicle coming down the gravel drive. Walking out onto his front porch, he spied an SUV coming to a stop just in front. He could see Blaise and Bart in the front seat, but it was not until the doors opened that he also observed Cam and Patrick as well.

Chuckling, he said, "Did I forget a meeting this morning...at my house?"

Scarlett immediately trotted to the guests, rolling over on her back to accept tummy rubs as the men fawned over her. The baying from the kennel could be heard as he walked down the steps.

Bart explained, "Blaise said you work your dogs on the weekends and we wanted to run with you. Figured the trails around here would be good experience and thought we'd help."

"One of you want to be the fugitive?" he asked.

"Not me," Cam joked. "That'd remind me of being chased by the police when I was young." The others laughed and Cam added, "Or, going through the fuckin' Mexican jungle when I rescued Miriam."

He had heard the story of how Cam had been sent to Mexico to rescue a nurse from a drug cartel. Being Hispanic, he was the perfect Saint for the job, being able to integrate into the environment easily. They had to spend days in the wild, trekking across the terrain to get to where Marc, the only Saint who was a pilot, could pick them up. It was hard to imagine Cam joking about the ordeal, but since he was now married to Miriam and they had children, he guessed Cam considered himself lucky.

"I'll do it," Patrick volunteered, grinning eagerly. "What do I need to do?"

"Rub your hands on this towel, so I'll have your scent. Got lots of trails around. Head anywhere you want to go and I'll give you about a ten-minute head start. Get somewhere and you can sit down, climb a tree...whatever. I'll get the other dogs and then I'll let them track you. I'll hold Scarlett back to give the others a chance."

Patrick nodded and, with a wave, started jogging toward the woods at the back of the house.

"Can we come too?" Cam asked.

"Of course. Let me get the dogs." He walked to the kennel and let the other dogs out, laughing as they bounded over to the visitors. "This here's Red. This is Beau and this beauty is Persi."

"Persi?" Bart asked.

"Short for Persephone," he replied. "It's Greek for lovely."

The dogs bounded around, loving the attention, as the men rubbed them. Blaise ran his expert hands over the pregnant hound, offering a comforting nod to Nathan.

"She's in good shape. Everything feels right."

Ten minutes later, he bent to the dogs with the towel and they quickly sniffed, pushing each other to the side as their tails wagged with excitement.

"Okay, let's go," he said, and they immediately started trotting toward the woods behind the house. The guys jogged behind him, watching as he kept Scarlett by his side and let Red and Beau take the lead, with Persi right behind them. Noses to the ground, they deviated occasionally and he laughed again. "Looks like Patrick decided to run in some circles to try to throw them."

When he had bought the property, he loved its thick woods and spent a year carving out trails through the forest, leaving plenty of places for the dogs and a trainer to run.

After a short while, the hounds halted at the bottom of a tall pine tree, standing up on the trunk, baying. Walking to the tree he looked up, seeing Patrick perched on one of the lower branches.

With a jump, Patrick landed deftly on the ground, rubbing the dogs and congratulating them. Nathan pulled treats out of his pocket, giving them to all the dogs.

"You runnin' in circles or you Army types can't figure out which direction to go?" Bart asked, laughing.

"Hell, you're so big, I would've figured you would have sunk like a stone when you were a SEAL," Patrick joked in return.

The group made their way back through the woods, complimenting Nathan on his property as well as his dogs. Once back at the cabin, he invited them in for coffee. As the group settled in his living room, easy conversation ensuing, he realized it was the first time he had a group of friends gathered together in a long time. He wondered if it was worth it...*Letting go of the fear?* Looking over, he caught Blaise's smile and just nodded in return, knowing the answer was abso-fuck-ing-lutely it was worth it.

"You've been a Saint for a week," Cam said. "Got any regrets so far?"

"Nope, not any," he replied honestly. "I guess I'll feel

a little out of my element for a while until I get the hang of the security."

"Once you get the PI course under your belt, that'll help too," Patrick said. "We all had to learn the different tasks to perform."

As they got ready to leave, Cam turned and said, "Don't forget to meet us tomorrow at the address I gave you yesterday. It's a new women's safe house and they want security in place before they move in."

"No problem," he called out, waving as they piled back into the SUV and Blaise turned to head out of the driveway.

He rubbed Scarlett's ears, feeling lighter than he had in years, and said, "Come on, girl. Let's get the others in for a while." He, along with his hound trotting at his side, walked to the kennel.

6

The two men met, shook hands, and sat down at the table. In a different time, a different place, they would both be well-dressed and meeting in an upscale restaurant or exclusive club. But now, while one of them wore a suit, the other was dressed in a plain prison uniform of khaki shirt and khaki pants. Even with their vastly different outerwear, it was not hard to see they had a familial resemblance. The brothers had square jaws, barrel chests, and dark eyes that did not seem to miss much.

"You are well, Yurgi?"

"I am well, brother."

Nodding, Gavrill said, "Thank you for not patronizing me by asking how I am. But let's get down to business."

"I've been in your office, and your lieutenants... assistants, are helping me. Contracts are being fulfilled, shipments are going out." Yurgi's eyes darted to the guards that were standing near the doors.

"Don't worry about them," Gavrill said. "At least the minimum security allows me a chance to have visitors, and not be as scrutinized. Plus," he added, his lips curling, "in here, like everywhere, money talks."

Yurgi returned the smile, his shoulders relaxing slightly. "Is there anything special I need to be working on?" he asked, his voice low.

"I have a concern for my cousin's daughter," Gavrill said. "She has not been heard from in a long time, and I fear for her."

"Would you like me to see if I can assist?"

"Absolutely. I need you to do everything you can to find her, assist her, and make sure she knows that we are here. I would not want her to think that she is alone in this life."

Nodding was the only response Yurgi gave. It was the only response needed. The two men continued to talk over the Volkov business for several more minutes before they stood. Gavrill watched as his half-brother walked out of the room, inwardly seething as he counted down the days until he would be able to do the same.

Agatha sat in her old car in the parking lot of the new facility, her gaze scanning the area. It was non-descript, which was perfect. A small church was down the street. An older neighborhood was behind the building. A discount grocery store was just a block away. She remembered that Ann had already talked to the owner and it appeared he had trouble keeping cashiers, so he would be glad to train any of the women that wanted to work there.

Stepping from her car, she walked to the front, smiling at the curb appeal. The windows had been covered with blinds for now, but she knew Ann's plan was to also hang curtains on the inside.

The front door was still the full glass, original door from when the building was a store. Ann informed her that it would be replaced with a solid, security door by the men who were coming today. Looking at the time on her phone, they were not scheduled to arrive for another fifteen minutes.

Pulling out the key, she unlocked the door and pushed it open, stepping into a welcoming, carpeted lobby. A desk sat in the corner and several chairs were against the wall. In the corner opposite the desk were three small chairs and a toy chest for when women with children came in to talk about the services.

For protection, Ann had another door leading to the rest of the facility put in place. As she walked through it, she was taken aback by the finished project. All it needed was the furniture to be brought from their house.

Moving to the left, she walked down the hall, seeing a few offices, a conference room, and two large rooms that would hold classes. She rested her hand on the wall of one of the offices. The walls had been primed, but the women would paint them once they were moved in. It was a cost-cutting idea for one thing, but Ann was also a big believer that people became more invested if they had a hand in the creation.

Turning, she continued back down the hall, past the reception and into the dorm area. The rooms would hold twin beds, several to a room, including a few that would also contain cribs if necessary. Her imagination ran wild with ideas for decorating. Pictures on the walls. Rugs on the floors. Music piped in through a sound system.

"Ma'am?"

Lost in thought, she had not heard anyone approach until a male voice sounded directly behind her. Yelping, she jumped, turning with her hand clutching her throat. Filling the hall were three large men. "Oh! I didn't hear you," she gushed, stepping backward, certain her face was flaming.

The dark-haired man, said, "We're from Saints Protection and Investigations and will be working on your security today. I'm Cam. This is Jude, and Patrick. We have another person, Nathan, who's unloading some equipment."

Willing her heartbeat to slow, maintaining her distance, she said, "I'm Agatha." She fiddled with her purse strap, glancing between them.

"Ma'am," the tall, curly-haired blond, identified as Jude, spoke, "your front door was unlocked."

Nodding rapidly, she said, "Yes. I unlocked it."

"Why?"

"Uh...," she said, noting their unsmiling faces, "because...uh...you were coming?"

She realized it was more of a question than a statement, but was uncertain what to say. Their other man walked from the front and stood partially behind Cam. Before she had a chance to look at him, the other blond, Patrick, spoke.

"Ma'am, you're a woman alone, in a building with no security, and you left your front door unlocked."

Her gaze shot between them and where the lobby door was, realizing she was cut off from escape. If she needed to run, her only option would be the out the back door.

Pulling out identification, Cam held it out to her, his tone soft. "We are from the Saints, and aren't trying to be jerks, but in our business, we're always looking out for someone's safety. And, this morning, you put your-self in danger."

She wanted to rail against his logic, after all, a woman should be able to move about freely without fear for her safety. *But then, I know more than anyone that they're right.* Pinching her lips together, she nodded. "Point taken." Looking around, she deflected, "I was told to let you in and stay in case there are things you need or information I can provide. Uh…is there anything you need right now?"

"No, ma'am," Cam replied, his smile gentle. "We'll start doing our jobs and will let you know when we're ready to go over information with you."

"Okay, then I'll just be…uh…I was going to sit at the reception desk, but uh…"

"That'll be fine," he assured. Turning, he added, "Oh, and this is Nathan."

The man who had entered the hall, standing slightly

behind the others, moved forward as they turned to go back to the front. He nodded in greeting, then stopped, his eyes widening for an instant, before narrowing, moving over her face.

Her heart pounded, the blood roaring in her ears, as she looked into the face of the man she thought to never see again. *The man with the dog!* She had spent years in her family perfecting a pleasant, blank stare so that no one around her had a clue of her thoughts or intentions. Right now, she pulled upon that experience, giving no outward sign of recognition. Nodding slightly in greeting, she kept her head held high as she moved past him to the lobby, pulling out her laptop before sitting down, for all appearances seeming to not have a care in the world.

Nathan stared at the blonde woman as she walked past him, her head held high, an air of confidence pouring from her. He did not know her and, yet, he had the strangest sense that he might have seen her somewhere before. Her voice, low and melodious, sounded familiar.

Giving his head a shake, he turned to follow Cam back to their vans. He had helped with several home installations of security equipment, but this was the first one with a building this size. Not one to ask too many questions, he was a careful observer. Seeing Cam go for the metal door, he moved to assist.

"First things first," Cam explained. "The glass door they have is pointless against someone wanting to enter.

One hit with a crowbar and the whole thing will shatter." It took both of them to carry the new door to the front and by the time they had, Jude had the old door off the hinges and Patrick had dismantled the door frame.

Patrick and Jude returned to the vans to obtain more equipment and then headed through the back of the building to the stairs that led to the roof. It took a while for Cam and Nathan to refit the opening with new framing and to install the steel door. A shatterproof glass window was in the upper part of the door, allowing visibility.

Agatha watched the process from the desk while appearing to work on her computer. *Well, not the process...more like just the man.* She wondered if he had been working for the Saints when he tracked and rescued her. She cast her mind back to Bayley's boyfriend, Nick. She remembered, when she first saw him, she was sure he was a Fed. *But, maybe he was a Saint as well.*

She tried Googling Saints Protection & Investigations but came up with nothing. No hits. No links. Nothing. Her fingers continued tapping on the keyboard, but she was unable to discover any information.

Cam's phone vibrated and he glanced at the screen. With a chin lift to Nathan, he stepped outside, walking away from the building for privacy.

"Yeah?"

"Someone named Agatha Christel, at your location, is doing an Internet search on us," Luke said.

Cam turned and looked at the young woman sitting at the desk. "It's the woman from the center. Startled her when we got here. She had the door unlocked and was daydreaming. Never even heard us approach."

"Fuck, man. You can walk as silent as a ghost when you want. I wouldn't have heard you either, if you didn't want me to."

Chuckling, Cam shot back, "No stealth...we just walked in and she jumped a mile. I might have groused a bit about personal security."

"Yeah, I bet you did. So, she's clear?"

"Probably just trying to make sure we're legit. I showed her ID."

"Got it. We're here so, whenever you start patching the work through, I'll check it."

"Thanks, man." Cam hung up and put his phone in his pocket as Nathan walked over with the old door and threw it in the back of his truck, which they had agreed he would use to haul unused pieces to the dump.

"Everything okay?"

"Seems our welcome committee has been Googling us while we worked. She won't find anything, but any hits go straight to Luke. He just wanted to know if we needed to be concerned. I told him we startled her and she was probably just checking us out."

"I know this seems weird, but there's something about her that seems familiar."

Grinning, Cam added, "Maybe you should tell her that you're the only single Saint."

Rolling his eyes, Nathan refused to admit to Cam that he'd had his eye on her from the moment he saw her standing in the hall talking to him, her wide, amber eyes taking them all in.

They walked back to finish the installation and he casually glanced over at her, seeing she now had a book in her hands. *Antigone* by Sophocles.

"Interesting book you're reading," he said, smiling as her eyes shot from the page to his. "I haven't read it in a while."

She pulled her lips in, her brow wrinkled, as though trying to discern if he was making fun of her.

He watched the doubt pass across her face and rushed to say, "Seriously. I took an Ancient Literature class in high school. All my friends hated it, but I really liked it." Shrugging, he said, "I never went to college, so it was the last class like that I took, but I kept up with the reading myself. Last one I re-read was *Medea* by Euripides."

Agatha's face relaxed as she realized Nathan was serious and, more importantly, did not recognize her. "I used to spend a lot of time in...um...a library and so I read a lot of different things. When I first read it, I had no idea what it was talking about." Covering her mouth as she smiled, she admitted, "I had to read books on what it was about just to be able to read the actual book."

"Nothing wrong with that," he said, gaze focused on her mouth, making her blush, before catching her eye again. "Well, I'd better get to work."

"Oh, are you finished with the door?"

"Installation. We still have to get it all wired."

She opened her mouth, but then shut it before

saying anything. Nodding, she watched as he tossed a wave and headed down the hall. Sucking in a deep breath, she dropped her chin to her chest, the familiar ache now piercing.

That night, when I saw him come toward me—first his dog, and then he followed—the moon was full and his face, handsome and calm. So unlike the faces of my father and brothers. He had the same dark hair and trimmed beard as now, rugged and manly. Whereas the men in my family could curse and yell, he had spoken softly. The affection for his big dog was obvious and I wondered what it would be like to have him turn that same, kind affection to me. But where I was going, there was no place for someone like him. And now? Even though I did not go into witness protection, well, I'm still tainted with the blood of my family, aren't I?

The lobby suddenly felt restrictive and she jammed her book into her bag, stalking out into the sunlight. A bench was just outside the building and she plopped down onto the seat. With her elbows resting on her knees, she leaned over, placing her head in her hands. *God, what am I doing?*

"Are you all right, miss?"

Jumping, she yelped again, immediately feeling foolish. Looking up, she saw Nathan at the door, staring down at her. "Yes, yes. I was just…um…sitting."

Nodding once, he moved to the van to gather more equipment. As he walked toward the door, she asked, "Are you the only one running back and forth to get the stuff you all need?"

"No," he laughed. "But, I'm the newest to the group,

so as I'm learning the ropes it helps for me to become acquainted with all the hardware."

"Oh, you're new?" she asked, with what she hoped was a nonchalant tone to her voice.

"I've been friends with them for years, but new to this aspect of the job." He looked up toward the roof and said, "I'd better get back to work. Enjoy the sunshine."

Her eyes followed him as he moved through the new door. Leaning her head back against the warm brick wall, she blew out a long breath. Just the look of him sent shivers down her spine, and not the bad kind. For an instant, she allowed herself the luxury of imagining if she were different, what it would be like to be with a man like Nathan. Jumping as the door opened again, this time she saw Patrick move to the van.

Standing, she looked at the grocery down the street and determined to do something besides just pine for a man she could never have. *At least I can do something kind for them all.*

7

Nathan stood on the roof of the building, holding the camera as Cam readied the mount. Movement on the quiet street snagged his attention and he watched as Agatha walked down the sidewalk. His eyes followed her until she entered the grocery store.

"Yep, looks like it's struck."

Startled, he looked down, seeing Cam staring up at him, a wide grin on his face. To the side, he heard Jude laughing. "What?"

"You man. You've been staring at Agatha, who is very pretty so I'm not surprised, and by the look on your face, I'd say you'd like to ask her out."

He opened his mouth to deny it but the words caught in his throat. This woman was the first in a long time to capture his attention. The last few dates he had gone on, he found that as he stared into the face of his date it would morph into the shadowed image of Agnes. Thinking he was losing his mind, he eventually gave up dating and would just occasionally pick up a random woman in a bar, go back to her place and, when he got home, immediately shower, as though to get the scent of her off. Might have been a dick move, but even sex with someone else had not rid him of the image of the woman from the woods.

Sighing, he looked at the others, saying, "Nah. Just admiring a pretty woman."

They got back to work and he focused his attention on the intricate system they were installing and Cam's explanations.

"This'll have cameras on all sides of the building that feed directly into a security service that we utilize at Alvarez Security. They keep employees monitoring the cameras twenty-four-seven. The owner, Tony Alvarez, was an Army Special Forces buddy of Jack's and his business is top-notch. Jude'll wire them so they can't be cut off and if anyone tampers with them, Alvarez will get notified and they'll, in turn, notify us. Same for the cameras inside."

"This is a lot for a non-profit business, isn't it?"

Nodding, he said, "Jack is picky about the residences or businesses he'll agree to service. If their needs are more simplistic, he recommends one of the local security companies. But, this place is special. They harbor women who've escaped domestic violence or a pimp. Whatever they need to start over, this place tries to get them on their feet. My Miriam is a nurse and she heard about what they do and when we heard they needed security, Jack stepped up."

"He cuttin' them a deal, 'cause this shit's got to cost a ton?"

"Actually, when the director came to him, she said they had gotten a large, private, anonymous donation and she wanted to use it on security. Hell, Jack told her that he'd only charge her half and she could use the rest for the women. To be honest, he's only gonna charge for some of the equipment. The rest is just our own *donation.*"

Finishing on the roof, they climbed back down the indoor ladder, securing the flap door above them. Just as Nathan's feet landed on the floor, he turned and came face to face with Agatha. His gaze dropped from her wide eyes to her hands, which were filled with grocery bags.

"I bought lunch for everyone...uh...if you want it," she explained.

Cam's feet hit the floor and he looked at her, his smile wide. "Lunch? Ma'am, you didn't have to do that."

"I thought you'd be getting hungry. I found a card table and some folding chairs in the supply closet. I'll set them up in the kitchen." At their surprised expressions, Agatha quickly turned and walked down the hall, a little embarrassed. Entering the kitchen, she opened the bags and took out subs piled high with deli meat. Not sure if they drank soda, she bought water bottles instead. Quickly setting everything on the wobbly table, she moved to the counter just as the men walked in.

"Aren't you going to eat?" Nathan asked, noticing there were only four subs placed out on the table.

Looking at the bag in her hand, she suddenly shook her head and lied, "I've already eaten something. I bought a few things for the center. I'll go put them in my car." Turning quickly, she hurried out of the room, leaving him staring at the back of her.

"Stop wondering and just ask her out," Jude said, biting into his sandwich.

"She's pretty," Patrick added, "and seems real nice. Go for it."

Cam studied him carefully before saying, "Something about her has got you thinking. What is it?"

Shaking his head slowly, Nathan said, "I don't know. I don't recognize her, but you're right. It's like there is a strange sense of déjà vu. Something about her seems familiar, but I've got no clue what it is."

"She's skittish," Jude said.

He swung his gaze back to the others. "Think she works at the center because she had needed it at one time?"

Shrugging, Cam asked, "Would that matter to you?"

Pondering the question, he shook his head as his protective instincts kicked in. "No. I just think she needs to be handled with care."

"You're used to skittish people when you track and rescue them. You'll be fine."

Track and rescue them. Patrick's words resounded in his head as the memory of the woman in the woods from two years ago slid through his thoughts once again.

The sound of his phone ringing usually had Nathan bolting from bed, but it had taken him a long time to get to sleep, so by three a.m., he was out cold. If it weren't for Scarlett standing on his bed, nuzzling him awake, he wasn't sure he would have heard it at all. Grabbing the offending device, he knew it could only be bad news at that time of night.

Getting the information, he disconnected before jumping from bed, shaking the sleep from his foggy mind. "Come on, girl. We've got a job."

The call from the local Sheriff's office sent he and Scarlett to a campground in the next county. Pulling up to the deputy's vehicle, he noticed a woman talking to the officer. As he approached, the woman rushed to him before the deputy had a chance to speak.

"Please, you gotta find her."

"Ma'am," the officer interrupted, "let me give Mr. Washington the information so he can start looking." He turned to Nathan and said, "Female. Twenty-two years old. Name is Gail Stanton. Wearing jeans, light blue sweater and a navy, hooded fleece jacket. Brown hair, brown eyes—"

"White shoes...sneakers," the woman blurted. "She's got her hair pulled up in a ponytail."

"Ma'am," the officer said again, but the woman was not to be deterred.

"She's got a shiner on her left eye and bruises. She's got bruises."

Nathan's gaze jumped from the woman to the officer, then back to the woman.

"I been tellin' her to leave him. He's mean as a snake and when he comes home drunk, he's even meaner. He got home from his night out with his buddies and started in on her again. She managed to get away and knew me and my husband were here camping with the Boy Scouts." Her head jerked back to a campsite on the other side of the parking lot where a man stood, guarding the tents.

"She got here and was scared shitless. Her car's an old junker and it barely got her here. I told my husband we had to keep her safe. Then Thomas, that's her boyfriend, called and said he was on his way and she'd better get herself back."

"And, did she go with him?" he asked, uncertain why they would need a tracker if she had.

"He never showed up!" the woman shouted. "But she got scared that he was almost here and took off through the woods. I tried to get her to call the police but she was scared Thomas was gonna come and might put us or the boys in danger." She reached out, grasping his arm, her face twisted in fear. "But she ain't come back yet."

"Do you have something of hers? Something my dog can follow."

"That's her car right there," she said, pointing to a rusty, old-model sedan.

"That'll do," he replied, taking Scarlett to the car and opening the door. Scarlett put her front paws on the seat and sniffed the steering wheel. Climbing back out, she put her nose down and began to track.

Turning back to the woman, he asked, "What's your name, and is there something that she will know is just from you?"

"Betsy...Betsy Deater. And, uh...tell her that Betsy

said…," she paused, wringing her hands in front of her, "uh…oh, yeah…the sand is warm but watch out for jellyfish."

Nodding, he turned on his radio and powerful flashlight, moving in right behind his dog and following her into the woods. The night made tracking particularly difficult for him, although Scarlett did not seem to mind. She did not have the same problems dealing with tree roots, low branches, and slippery pathways.

Thirty minutes later, Scarlett stopped and sat down. Shining his light toward the bushes to the side, he called out, "Gail? Gail? I'm Nathan Washington and this is my dog, Scarlett. We were sent by your friend Betsy Deater. She's worried and called the police. We want to take you back to safety."

For a second, the sight of a dark haired, dark-eyed young woman hiding in the shadows of the woods struck him, reminding him of Agnes.

The woman, tucked into the shrubs, held up her hand to shield her eyes. "I aint' goin' back to him."

"I'm not taking you to anyone, Gail. I just need to get you to safety and to let the Sheriff know that you're okay. And, if you want to press charges, then you can."

"No! That'll just make him madder. I just gotta get away." Her voice hitched as she wiped at her eyes. "I'm so tired…so fuckin' tired of livin' this way."

He knelt so that he was next to Scarlett, whose tongue was lolling to one side. He stroked her head and murmured, "Good girl."

After a moment, Gail shifted out of the bushes,

standing but keeping her distance. "How do I know who sent you?"

He swung his light to the badge on his belt, identifying him as a National Search and Rescue Dog Association tracker. "Betsy told me to tell you that 'the sand is warm but watch out for jellyfish'. She knew that would let you know that she was the one I talked to."

A slight snicker slipped from her mouth, and he observed as her hand jumped to her split lip. Anger flooded him at the thought of the young woman running scared for her life due to her jack-ass boyfriend...*hopefully ex-boyfriend.*

"Me and Betsy went to the beach when we were teenagers. Loved it so much, we used to say there was nothin' in the world better than warm sand. Then, on the last day, we were out in the water and we both got stung by jellyfish. Not them big ones like you see on TV. Just little ones, but they hurt so bad. Lord, I haven't thought about that in a long time." Sighing, she said, "I haven't thought of much except trying to survive."

"You know, you don't have to live like this," he said. "I happen to know of a shelter that will take you in. It's safe and I've met one of the workers. They'll take care of you until you figured out what to do."

Shaking her head, Gail whispered, "I never thought I'd be like this. My parents didn't raise me to be anyone's punching bag."

"Then, all you gotta do is let me take you to safety." He watched her eyes drop to Scarlett, her face softening as she gazed at the dog. She slowly nodded and they began to walk back, the light from his flashlight illuminating the pathway.

Once at the campground, after she assured Betsy that she was all right while he reported to the deputy, he led her to his truck. Scarlett sat in the middle and he drove to the shelter. As he pulled up to the house, he hated that they had not moved into the new building yet. The best he could do was to regularly check on the security of this place until they moved in a week.

It was now four o'clock in the morning and he wondered how to let someone know they were there. "Stay here," he said, climbing out of the truck. As he moved to the front door, he noticed a button with a small sign next to it, declaring **After Hours**. Giving it a press, he waited for a few minutes until he heard someone undoing the lock.

The door opened slightly and he spied Agatha, her eyes going wide as she took him in. "What...what are you doing here?"

"You live here?"

Her face scrunched as she asked, "You came in the middle of the night to ask that?"

"No, no. I was just surprised, that's all. I've got a woman...just tracked her for the police. She needs a place to go."

"What happened?" she said, her gaze trying to see beyond him.

"She was running from her abusive boyfriend and got lost in the woods."

Swinging the door open wide, she rushed, "Bring her. Bring her in."

For a second, he stood rooted to the floor. Her sleep tousled hair fell about her shoulders. Wearing blue, polka dot, flannel pajamas, with a pink, fuzzy robe tied about her waist and blue slippers on her feet, she looked utterly adorable. Turning quickly, he stalked to his truck and escorted Gail to the front door, entering behind her, hearing their introduction.

"I'm Gail. He said I could stay here...at least for tonight until I can figure something out."

"Of course. I'm Agatha. Agatha Christel. Come on into the kitchen and I'll fix you some tea."

As the two women walked down the narrow hall, he stood just inside the door, his heart in his throat. *Agatha Christel. Fuck, what a name.*

Once Gail was safely in the kitchen, Agatha turned in the doorway to head back to Nathan looking over her shoulder and smiling at the woman reassuringly before rushing out. She found him in the foyer, hands in his pockets, head bent in thought.

"I'm sorry. I didn't even thank you." He looked up and his intense stare unnerved her, causing her to drop her chin, allowing some of her hair to fall forward, partially hiding her face. "Well, I'll take care of her now."

"Sure," he mumbled. He watched her as she approached slowly, trying to usher him out without being rude...or touching him...but before she moved too far, he blurted, "Would you like to go out sometime? Coffee...dinner?"

Her eyes widened and her mouth opened and closed several times, but no words came. She stood rooted to the floor, her breath caught in her throat.

"Breathe," he whispered, a small smirk playing about his lips.

Her breath rushed out and her chest heaved. "I'm sorry...I wish...but, uh...I don't think so."

His smile faltered a little, a flash of sadness, before he fixed it. "I respect that, but I hope we have a chance to see each other again. I'd like to get to know you better."

"Me too," she whispered before she could stop herself, her face heating with a blush. "Uh...maybe... sometime..." she babbled, backpedaling, before seeing him out and closing the door.

Nathan left the house, listening to be sure Agatha locked the door behind him. As he climbed into his truck, he sat for a few minutes on the street, her face filling his mind. Blonde hair, a straight nose, a slightly crooked front tooth. Amber eyes. Rubbing his face, he chuckled. *Jesus, the guys were right, I really am obsessed.*

Driving, he grinned, looking forward to the next time he would see the her again, glad to be interested in a real woman and not just a memory.

Lying in bed, Agatha closed her eyes tightly, her heart pounding. *Why did I say 'maybe'? This is too dangerous. But, I so want a chance at something normal...something with him...* Opening her eyes, she stared at the stars, sucking in a deep breath before letting it out slowly, a spark of hope igniting deep inside.

8

"Charlie, can you do a favor for me?"

The dark-haired beauty looked up and smiled. "Sure, Nathan, whatcha need?"

"Can you check on someone? Agatha Christel."

Her brow scrunched as she asked, "The woman from the women's center? The one who was checking into us when you were installing the new security?"

"Yeah." Seeing the doubt in her eyes, he said, "Look, I know this sounds ludicrous, but I swear, she seems familiar, but I just can't place where I've seen her."

Shrugging, she replied, "Okay, let's see what we have." Within a moment, she had the information and began to read off, "Agatha Christel. Parents were Dina and Jonathan Christel. Both deceased. Born and raised in Wilmington, North Carolina. She attended college for one year but dropped out and worked in retail for several years. Relocated here four years ago. Got the job at the women's center about a year ago." Smiling up at him, she said, "You want her birthday and social security number?"

"No, no, but thanks for checking." Sighing, he shook his head. "I was sure that I had seen her somewhere before, but none of that sounds familiar." With an embarrassed grin, he walked away.

Agatha bent over a box, taping it securely as Gail walked in to pick it up.

"Some men are here to help," Gail announced as she walked out with the box in her arms. "I think Ann is talking to them now."

She knew that Ann had been hoping to get volunteers to help so they would save on the cost of movers, but as she looked around at the furniture and boxes, she puffed her cheeks and blew out a deep breath. *How on earth will we get all this moved?*

"Nice to see you again, Agatha."

A familiar male voice coming from the door had her jerking around and staring dumbly at Nathan.

"Hi…uh…what are you doing here?"

"Seems like my boss' wife and your boss decided that the center could use the assistance of some muscle to get furniture moved today."

She stared for a few seconds more at the affable grin on his face. Unable to keep the smile from her own, she agreed, "I couldn't say it better myself. I was just wondering how we were going to manage."

He moved closer and said, "How about I take that?"

He nodded toward the largest box and hefted it in his hands.

She picked up a smaller one and moved down the hall, walking out of the front door. The street was filled with trucks and SUVs and the man-candy standing nearby caused her feet to stumble. "Shit," she whispered, as she steadied herself. There were so many large men, she could not count them without being obvious. She recognized Cam, Jude, and Patrick from the other day, but the others were all strangers. *Gorgeous, handsome, big, muscular strangers.*

One of the men, with dark hair and a dark beard, walked forward, a smile on his face. "Ms. Christel, I'm Jack Bryant. Me and my men are here to help today, in any way we can."

Moving forward, she halted suddenly as one of the men turned, smiled and took the box from her hands. *Fuck! Nick! The man Bayley was with two years ago.* Heart pounding in her chest, she mumbled her thanks, turning quickly only to slam into Nathan.

"Whoa, there," Nathan said, his sharp gaze instantly noticing Agatha's unease as she scurried off. He remembered Patrick's assessment of her being skittish—and why that might be. Looking around, he inwardly cursed, realizing that all of the Saints could appear intimidating to a woman who had possibly been abused. He handed the large box he was carrying off to one of the others before following her.

Once inside, he approached cautiously, saying, "I know the crowd can be overwhelming. If you want, you can stay inside and we'll handle the moving."

Plastering a calm façade on her face, her voice steady and void of intonation, she said, "Oh, it's fine. I was just startled, that's all."

He eyed her critically, but her demeanor appeared so composed, all he could do was nod. "Then lead the way and show me what to move."

A grin slipped out as she lifted her eyes to him. "Well, first things first...I guess this table can go."

Four hours later, the last of the boxes were placed in their appropriate rooms in the new facility and Agatha watched as Ann bustled around, making sure the women and children were settled before walking over to Jack and thanking him profusely. Nathan hung back with her and, together, they watched as the Saints waved goodbye, heading to their vehicles. As nice as they all had been, she felt as though she could breathe easier once they left. Glancing up toward Nathan though, she realized she felt at ease with him.

"Thank you for coming today—"

"Will you reconsider going out with me?" he asked. "Just to dinner? Anywhere you would be comfortable."

Sucking in her lips, she considered her response. Peering into his eyes, seeing such sincerity there, she could not help herself. It might be stupid and reckless, given that at any moment he could recognize her, but she did not want to turn him down. Not him. Nodding slowly, she let herself have this one moment, even if it was only for a night. "Yeah, I'd like that."

His smile widened and he asked, "When?"

Pondering, she said, "Well, I've got to be here tonight to help with everything, but I have tomorrow evening off."

Turning more fully towards her, he placed his hand lightly on her shoulder. "Thank you. I'm honored."

"Honored?" she breathed. She could not remember the last time anyone told her they were honored to be with her. *Yes, I can. It was Harlan.* Smiling as she watched him walk toward his truck, she startled when Ann came up beside her.

"He seems very nice. Did I hear him ask you out?"

"Yes, but..."

"No buts. It's about time you had some fun," Ann declared, swinging her arm around her shoulders and guiding her inside.

Agatha tried to keep her eyes off Nathan as they sat in his truck, driving toward the restaurant. Shifting her gaze, using her peripheral vision, she noted his strong jaw covered with a neatly trimmed beard. His hair, slightly longer on top, gave evidence to the natural curl, with one lock falling down on his forehead. He would push his fingers through his hair to get it back, giving the whole thing a slightly messy look, but the curl was not to be tamed. Her fingers longed to touch the silkiness, but she kept them clenched together in her lap.

A date. What would he think if he knew this was her first date? Oh, not the first time she had been with a man, but the first non-chaperoned date. Almost rolling her eyes before she caught herself, she thought about the old ways her parents had raised her. Learn to be a lady. Learn the family business. Get married to a man of their choosing and make more Russian babies...preferably boys.

Her brothers had accompanied her on the few official dates she'd had, keeping the men at a respectable distance. *Well, except for Antoine.* She inwardly grimaced at the awkward, fumbling sex she had in the closet of his parents' house while a large party was taking place on the premises. She had agreed to the impromptu liaison, desperate to find out what all the fuss about sex was. Losing her virginity had been less than spectacular, to say the least, making it easy to keep men at bay afterwards. Her parents thought she was a modest young woman, not realizing she considered herself a prude with no desire for sex.

Casting her gaze sideways again, she wondered if sex with Nathan would be different...more like the romance novels she reads. His shoulders were broad, his muscular biceps showcased in the short sleeve shirt he wore. His dark jeans stretched across thick thighs and as she glanced at the hands holding the steering wheel she became entranced with his fingers. Long, tanned, strong. Sighing, she squirmed slightly at the unfamiliar ache between her legs.

Noticing Agatha shifting in her seat, Nathan wondered if she were comfortable. "Sorry about my truck," he apologized.

"Sorry?"

"Yeah, I know it's not comfortable. At least, not much for humans. I guess I mostly transport dogs."

Keeping her breath steady, she repeated, "Dogs?"

Smiling widely, he warmed to the topic. "I raise Bloodhounds and train them for tracking. They're comfortable in this old truck and probably the reason why I haven't traded up and gotten something newer."

"The truck is fine. Honestly," she assured. "Tell me more about your dogs."

Before he had a chance to respond, they pulled into the parking lot. She peered out the window at the steak and seafood restaurant and smiled.

He turned to her and, seeing her face, breathed easier. "I should have asked what you like to eat, but I figured this place, which is known for both their beef and their seafood, would give you a choice." Suddenly, eyes wide, he said, "Oh, my God, I didn't ask if you were vegetarian...or had seafood allergies!"

She placed her hand on his arm and rushed, "It's fine. No allergies and I love both."

Audibly sighing in relief, he said, "Hang tight. I'll get your door."

Agatha sat, watching as Nathan rounded the front of his truck and came to her door. Opening it, he offered his hand as she slid from the seat, never letting go even as they made their way inside. In fact, following the hostess, he kept hold of her hand until she was seated.

Once they ordered, she turned to him and said, "You were telling me about your dogs." Observing the relaxed expression on his face, she knew she had picked the right topic.

"I was raised on a farm and I got a dog when our elderly neighbor could no longer take care of his. Fell in love with that Bloodhound and they've been my favorite breed ever since. I learned to track, got certified in that, and did that while in the Army with the military police."

Watching the twinkle in his eyes, she sat mesmerized, unable to look away. His eyes were the color of melted, milk chocolate with caramel swirled throughout. Blinking, she held back a laugh at the dessert-like analogy. Covering quickly, she pretended ignorance by asking, "Do your dogs look for drugs or um…what else? Oh, maybe explosives? I read about dogs that do that."

Shaking his head, he said, "No, although my friend, Blaise…one of the Saints you met the other day…his wife, Grace, used to raise dogs that searched for drugs. She now trains them to be companion dogs."

"Is that like service dogs?"

"It can be, but she specializes in dogs trained to be with the elderly or those with dementia. As companions, they can greatly aid in the quality of life for these people."

Giving her head a little shake, she said, "I had no idea there were so many uses for dogs besides just pets."

"Did you have any pets? Or do you?"

Her smile dropped and she stared at her glass, avoiding his eyes. "No…I wanted one, but my parents didn't want…well…" she lifted her shoulders in a gesture of defeat. "No. Not now either."

He watched her face, trying to figure out what she was thinking, but she didn't want to elaborate, couldn't really, without giving away too much.

Their silence was interrupted as the server brought their food. His steak and potato filled his plate and her seafood sampler platter was huge. She smiled as she looked over saying, "Your steak looks amazing."

Visibly glad to see her relaxing again, he said, "I was just going to say the same thing about your seafood."

Biting her lip, she hoped she was not being too forward and chanced, "Uh…we can share some, if you'd like."

The wide eyes he turned to her caused her to back-track. "But, that'd be silly. So sorry, I don't know why I—"

"No, no," he rushed, easing her obvious discomfort. "I was surprised because I was just thinking the same thing, but you got to it first. I'd love to share."

Smiling in relief, she admitted, "I suppose I should tell you that I don't date a lot. It's just that I'm usually so busy and…" She fiddled with her napkin, now wishing she'd kept her mouth shut again. *God, I'm usually so controlled! What is it about him that makes me babble like a fool?*

Chuckling, he said, "Well, if you're being so honest…I should be the same." He waited until her curiosity had her gaze moving back to his before continuing, "I don't do a lot of dating myself. Can't really say why. My life is mostly my cabin and my dogs, and I'm good with that."

She observed him for a moment, seeing both strength and vulnerability in him. "You understand your dogs."

His gaze jumped to hers as his lips twitched. "Yeah.

Dogs I get. Loyal. Trusting. Honest. People…not so much."

A strange ache settled in her chest at the word *honest*. She wanted to know him. Everything about him. But would never be able to give him the same.

"Is your food alright?" the server interrupted.

They both startled and, laughing, admitted they had not tried it. He cut his steak and placed part of it on her plate as she scooped shrimp and scallops onto his. Leaving the heavier topics, they enjoyed the food, wine, and lighter conversation.

9

It was hard for Nathan to keep his eyes off Agatha. Dressed in dark, tight jeans and a pale, blue blouse, she had held his attention from the moment she walked toward him. Her dark, blonde hair was sleek, styled simply. Her makeup appeared skillful...not too elaborate, but playing up her amber eyes. She did not smile often, but when she did, her smile was almost perfect. One incisor was slightly crooked and he found it gave her face character.

She appeared to be enjoying her food and he realized he had been staring for a moment too long. Jerking his gaze back to his plate, he hoped he had not creeped her out.

Over dessert, she licked her bottom lip carefully, probably making sure the chocolate sauce was not all over her face but, for him, it was a test in composure and he struggled, again, not to stare.

"You were telling me about your dogs, earlier," she

reminded. He smiled, thankful for the distraction but also happy to talk about his beloved dogs.

"I'm a tracker. I use my dogs for search and rescue." He watched her face carefully, wondering what she thought. He knew some women wanted more than his simple life. *Might be a Saint now, but I'm still essentially a farmer's son who loves dogs.* As he waited, he noted her attention was still riveted to him, a small smile playing about her mouth, no look of discontent crossing her features.

"It's your passion," she stated, her eyes still on his.

Nodding slowly, he agreed. "Yeah, it is. I love the trust between my dogs and me. I trust them explicitly to find who we're looking for and they trust me to take care of them." Shrugging, he said, "Sometimes, in humans, it's harder to find that kind of trust."

Snorting softly, she said, "Almost impossible, I think."

"Not really," he countered. "You just have to find the right people to trust. I've known for years that the other Saints were absolutely trustworthy. And, I've seen them with their wives...also bonds that're completely full of trust. So, it's there. You just have to find it."

They sat silent for a moment and he asked, "Tell me about your passion."

Her gaze jumped from her empty plate to his face and she immediately replied, "None. I don't really have a passion."

"I can't believe that," he said.

"It's true," she insisted, giving a little shrug.

"You work in a women's shelter. I saw how you took Gail in the other day."

Her brow crinkled as she said, "But, that's what I do. I mean, that's not really a passion, is it?"

"Why the shelter?" he prodded.

"Sorry?"

"Why work there? I mean, what keeps you doing it? If you could change careers, would you?"

Tilting her head to the side, she considered his questions. "I guess that when the opportunity came up, I was glad to help the center. I like working with Ann and feel like I can do a little bit to make the women's lives better. It makes me feel good when I see the women, who have come in beaten down, leave with their dignity intact."

He watched her face soften as she spoke, and he said, "That, sweet Aggie, is passion."

She blinked furiously, swallowing hard. She had never been called by a nickname and the intimacy it implied made her feel warm inside. Quickly looking down, she tried to hide her watery eyes, but he saw them.

Taking pity on her discomfort, he leaned forward, saying, "Let's get out of here. I feel like I need a walk after all that food." He stood and offered his hand, loving the feel of her delicate touch. Adding a slight pressure to her fingers, he pulled her close as they made their way back to his truck. The restaurant was on the waterfront of the river that cut through the area and a sidewalk bordered the bank.

"Wanna take a walk?'

"I'd love that," she agreed. They walked along,

silently holding hands for several minutes, until she stopped by the railing to watch the gulls swooping down to the fishing boats returning to the harbor at the end of the day. "Birds are so lucky, don't you think?"

Uncertain how to answer a question that he had never pondered before, he chuckled. "Can't say as I thought of them as lucky before."

Dropping her head, she grinned. "Okay, I know that sounded really random. But, to be able to just open your wings and take off flying...that would be amazing."

"Are you envious of their freedom?"

Shrugging, she said, "When I was a little girl, I used to have nightmares that someone was chasing me, but just as they were reaching out for me, I'd lift up into the air and fly away." Twisting her head around, she added, "And don't you make fun of me. I actually read that lots of people have that dream!"

Laughing, he stood behind her, his arms reaching to the rail in front, boxing her in with his large body and blocking the cool breeze. Leaning his head down, he whispered in her ear, "I'd never make fun of you."

This time, as she turned her head to the side, his lips were only a breath away from hers. Desiring her kiss more than anything he had felt in a long time, he nonetheless waited, watching as her eyes moved between his and his lips.

Finally, tentatively, he moved in slowly, giving her plenty of opportunity to tell him to back off if she wanted, but instead, she leaned forward. Their lips met and he tried to hold back the desire to pull her into his arms, crushing her body against his.

She tasted of chocolate and light wine, decadent and sweet all at the same time. He felt her uncertainty but as he licked her lips, she opened her mouth and he swept his tongue inside. Intoxicated with her, he slowly shifted her body so that she was facing him, her arms clutching his biceps, her fingers digging in as though she needed assistance to remain upright. His arms slid around her body, one hand pressing into the small of her back, holding her steady, and the other fisting in her hair, angling her mouth as he continued to explore her warmth.

Agatha felt Nathan's kiss down to her knees, as they grew weak. She was not sure she would have been able to remain standing if his arm was not banded around her. His tongue tangled with hers and she had to admit the taste of dark wine, chocolate and something masculine was driving her to distraction. She barely remembered the kiss she shared as she lost her virginity, but she knew for a fact it was nothing like this kiss. Nathan's kiss sent electric shocks from their lips to every nerve in her body and she fought the desire to rub up against him, willing the ache between her legs to cease.

Just when her legs began to quiver, he pulled back, and she instantly felt the loss. Chest heaving, she gulped in air, having no idea what to say. Her mouth opened of its own volition but "wow" was the only thing that came forth. He was peering deeply into her eyes, and she thought she caught a shadow pass through them before it quickly left.

He smiled and pressed her head against his chest,

where she could hear his heartbeat pounding, and the shadow was instantly forgotten. Blowing out a deep breath, he repeated her sentiment. "Wow is right."

She leaned back, a wide smile on her lips and he bent to kiss them lightly. "I'd better get you home."

Nodding, she said, "I'd like to say that I'm not Cinderella and won't turn into a pumpkin, but I feel like I need to be at the center since this is only our second night in the new place."

Giving her a squeeze, he grinned as he linked fingers with her and they walked to his truck.

Once they arrived at the center, he helped her out of his truck again and walked her to the front door. Standing, hand in hand, he said, "I had a great time tonight."

Suddenly nervous, she sucked in her lips. "Me too. I honestly can't remember ever having such a nice evening."

"Can I see you again?"

Nodding, she remained calm on the surface while jumping up and down on the inside. "Absolutely."

Heart warming, Nathan bent to kiss Agatha, touching his tongue to hers before pulling back. "I'll call tomorrow." His gaze shifted to the door behind her and he added, "Let me hear the lock when you get in and don't forget to set the alarm." He watched as she moved inside and waited until he heard the click before climbing back into his truck.

Driving home, his mind swirled with thoughts of the evening, trying to reconcile the unexpected change in him. *How can I be obsessed with one woman, that I can only see in my dreams, for almost two years, and then, suddenly, desire another woman like this? It's all happening so fast. Agnes has meant so much to me for so long, but Agatha...I can't deny what is happening with her.* By the time he pulled into his driveway, he knew that to have held on to the idea of Agnes like he had, a woman he'd only known for an hour and was a dream that had no chance of coming true, was crazy. And it was only because of Aggie, feeling something real with her, something possible, that he could finally start to accept that. *At least, I can try to.*

Having fed the dogs before he went out, he only had Scarlett to greet as he went into his cabin. Kicking off his boots, he moved into the kitchen to grab a beer before plopping onto the sofa, allowing her to climb up onto it with him, her large head lying in his lap, her dark brown eyes staring up at him.

"Scarlett, I've come to the conclusion tonight that I might actually be crazy. I've spent two fuckin' years with my mind filled with a woman that I barely know. We only spent an hour together, but every time I learned something about her, it made me admire her more. All she gave up. All she risked. That alone was enough to block out every other woman I ever met until…"

Rubbing Scarlett's head behind her ears she groaned in pleasure then continued to stare up at him, as though understanding his confessions.

"But, that's all Agnes Gruzinsky was, right? A chance meeting. The proverbial ships passing in the night. A person to be admired, but that's it." Chuckling, he said, "She's sure as shit moved on. The idea of her granting more than a passing thought to me over the past two years, after everything she went through, and especially after Harlan got her to safety..." Taking a swig of beer, he said, "I've been an idiot, staying linked to a ghost."

Scarlett groaned again as she shifted, her eyes now closing with the contentment of his hand rubbing her stomach. He leaned his head back against the sofa, determined to focus his thoughts firmly on Agatha. *Agatha Christel.* Fuck, even her name reminds me of Agnes and how she quoted Agatha Christy that night. *And, Agatha deserves so much more than to compete with a ghost.* For the first time in two years, someone real and tangible, was seeping into his heart.

Moving the large dog head from his lap he walked back into the kitchen and tossed the bottle into the trash, frustrated at his own back and forth. Walking down the short hall to the bedroom, he tapped his leg, calling, "Come on, girl."

Scarlett climbed down from the sofa and trotted toward him. Once he finished in the bathroom, he grinned, seeing her already ensconced in the middle of the bed. "Move over," he chided gently, and she dutifully rolled over to one side.

For a moment, the idea of Agatha sharing his bed at some point gave him pause. Pulling the covers up, he smiled at the thought of Scarlett having to get used to sleeping on the floor.

God, I am crazy...I've been on one date with her and I'm already thinking about her being here in my bed. Rolling over, his gaze automatically moved to the window, the sight of stars in the night sky comforting.

The similarities between the two women stayed on his mind, but some part of him knew that, in the end, what he really wanted was Agatha. The very real Agatha. The very sweet, amazing, beautiful Agatha. It was just going to take some time to fully let go of the woman he had been dreaming of for two years.

Sleep finally came but vivid dreams had him tossing most of the night as the face of the woman in the van as it pulled away morphed into the face of the woman he had just kissed.

10

Bethany welcomed the Saints as they came into the house, waving toward the kitchen counter where two large baking platters of muffins sat waiting to be decimated. Nathan grinned as he grabbed a plate, knowing if he did not dig in immediately, he would miss out.

Cam, already stuffing his mouth with a blueberry and peach muffin, said, "This is the only place I know where getting to the food is a competitive sport."

The others laughed, each filling their plates as well.

"God, this is good, Bethany," Chad said. "I gotta thank you for teaching Dani how to make this. She's been practicing and I'm reaping the benefits at home."

"Practicing?" Bethany exclaimed. "She's an excellent baker!"

Chad grinned. "I tell her it's *almost* perfect and that keeps her making more."

"Damn, man," Jude said. "You better hope she doesn't catch on to your little subterfuge to get more."

Nathan finished his plate and, rinsing it in the sink,

looked around the room, glad for the easy camaraderie of the Saints. He knew their women shared the same bond with each other. The image of Aggie in the room with all of them flew through his mind and he blinked, the realization of just how much he would like that hitting him.

Jack called them all to the meeting and with thanks shouted out to Bethany once more, they headed downstairs. Quickly getting down to business, Jack began.

"The FBI are still working Harlan's murder, and while they have their theories, they have no proof. It seems Gavrill's brother, Yurgi, was in Norfolk at the time and, while they have monitored Gavrill's communications from prison, they can't prove a link."

"It seems that there's a lot of supposition but no facts to go on," Bart groused.

Nodding, Jack agreed. "The FBI is looking into the communications and there's a possibility that Johan was back in the country illegally and has now gone to ground again. He'd be my first suspect for Harlan's murder. Gavrill's allowed much more leniency with his visitations as well. I've had Luke and Charlie working on that possibility to pass on info to the FBI."

Luke said, "The inmates in the minimum security prison—"

"Fuck!" Cam cursed, his face contorted. Sighing, while shaking his head, he apologized, "Sorry. Just frustrated that Gavrill only got in on fuckin' taxes."

"I know…minimum security for tax evasion when in reality he's a cold-blooded killer, mafia ruler, human trafficing, kidnapper, and who the fuck knows what else," Luke acknowledged. "But, anyway, he's able to use email, which he knows is monitored, but not scrutinized. Charlie's been working on seeing if he's using code and, of course, my brilliant wife has discovered some of what he's been saying."

"So far," Charlie said, "he's using a simple code with both English and Russian words, with a mathematical integration. No way is he smart enough to figure this out on his own, so someone in his organization is helping. No surprise there but, even then, it isn't all that sophisticated. Still, he's not saying anything suspicious," she smiled, "at least not on the surface."

"You got something?" Nathan asked, still getting used to the rapid-fire dialog during a Saints' meeting.

Charlie nodded, "Well, yes and no. I'm still working on it, but I'm sure he's giving orders to his organization. I'm mostly interested in what he's telling Yurgi. Now that I understand the code he's using, I'm monitoring him constantly."

Jack turned to Bart and said, "I was going to ask if you'd like to have another crack at him. This time, interviewing him in prison."

Grinning as he high-fived Cam, he replied, "Fuck, yeah!"

Chuckling, Jack said, "I was sure you would." Turning to Nathan, he said, "You want to ride shotgun on this."

"Abso-fuckin'-lutely," he agreed. The chance to move further into the investigation, as well as get his eyes on the man who was responsible for Agnes' necessity to disappear, was exactly what he wanted.

"Nick, I'd like you to go as well. As former FBI, you'll have your own perspective." Jack grinned, "Figured you'd like to drop in on Yurgi. And, as an added bonus, I'll have you talk to Agnes' family in prison also."

"Any luck on finding who assisted Agnes in her great disappearance?" Jude asked.

Charlie shook her head and said, "I've got nothing. I've checked with some of the other security business that, like Jack, operate under radar but, so far, nothing. Or, at least, no one is saying anything."

The meeting continued, but Nathan's mind jumped to planning for the trip...and telling Agatha that he would be gone for a few days.

Agatha moved through the new center, having spent the day making sure the furniture moved from the old center was correctly placed in their new location. Some of the new furniture and supplies that Ann had ordered arrived earlier and she oversaw them being unpacked and taken to the appropriate rooms as well.

There was an excitement in the air as the women at the shelter helped. Most of them had happily discovered the computer lab, classrooms, and the larger dining hall. The mothers with children had relished the playroom and new cribs for the bedrooms.

Ann had declared that while schedules were a good thing to keep, for this week, they would all be working to make the place livable and comfortable.

Hearing the center's bell ring, she moved to the front

to answer. Outside stood a group of women and she smiled politely, waiting for them to speak.

"Hello, I'm Bethany Bryant. I'm Jack Bryant's wife and, I know our husbands helped you move in, but I also talked to Ann and she gave me a wish list of some things you all could use. So, I brought some friends to help out."

Nodding in understanding, she introduced herself and smiled as the women entered the reception lobby of the center, their arms full of bags.

Bethany grinned, tossing her long braid over her shoulder. "I also understand that you and Nathan went out last night."

"Uh..." she stammered, eyes wide at the grins shot her way. "I...uh..."

Laughing, Bethany said, "Don't worry. We're not here to check you out. We're just glad that Nathan took the plunge and asked you."

"You mustn't let Bethany scare you," a pretty blonde said. "Bethany likes to mother-hen all the men who work with Jack. I'm Sabrina, by the way. Jude's my husband and Bart's my cousin."

She stared at Sabrina, perfectly coiffed and put-together, and had a flash of a memory of herself a few years ago. Before she had a chance to speak, Bethany took over once more, explaining that one of the things Ann said the center needed was some professional clothing for the women who would be learning new skills and going out to interview, as well as gaining new employment.

A woman with a vibrant smile and pink, purple,

and teal streaks in her blonde hair introduced herself. "I'm Angel Lytton. My husband is Monty, my brother is Patrick, and I own Angel's Cupcake Heaven. I brought some of my treats for everyone. I'm actually looking for some extra help right now, no experience needed. Please let me know if anyone is interested, okay."

"Oh, my goodness," she said, her smile genuine. "That would be amazing."

A petite, dark-haired woman wearing maternity nursing scrubs stepped forward next. "I'm Miriam... Cam's wife. I work at a nursing home and if any of the women here are interested, there are always some employment opportunities there as well. The director wanted me to give you her card to pass along."

Several more women stepped forward, each warm in their greetings and she tried to keep their names straight. Grace, Blaise's wife, was wearing comfortable jeans, boots, and had her hair pulled up into a high ponytail. She remembered she was the dog trainer. *Blaise is also Nathan's best friend...I wonder if he's talked about me?*

"There are several more of us but, of course, some are working today—oh, here come a few more."

"Sorry, I'm late," came a familiar voice as the young woman bounded through the door, her blonde hair flying out behind her. "You must be Agatha...I'm Bayley, Nick's wife and Blaise's sister. It's so nice to meet you!"

She forced a smile but her insides quaked at seeing a former acquaintance. *God, don't let her recognize me!*

Bayley smiled widely at her, but no recognition

flared in her eyes before she was distracted, handing over the shopping bags she had brought.

The last woman to walk through the door had dark hair framing her face and penetrating, but gentle, eyes, taking in the scene before her.

"Faith, you made it!" Bethany exclaimed. "Come meet Agatha."

Faith walked over, her face serene as she took her hand. "It's so nice to meet you…" Her words faltered, eyes roving over Agatha's face as if they were seeing into her.

She locked her knees to keep from falling to the floor, the jolt of having someone appear to stare into her soul, rocking her being. Faith continued to hold her hand, giving it a squeeze before letting it go and stepping back. Biting her bottom lip, she turned to the others. "So, has she met everyone?"

"All of us except Dani, Kendall, Charlie, and Evie, who are at work. We were just giving her the things we brought," Bethany explained.

Feeling overwhelmed at the crowd of women, all bearing gifts, she was relieved when Ann came from the back and greeted Bethany, offering to give them a tour of the new facility. Letting Ann take the lead, she held back, bringing up the rear.

They passed the dorm-like bedrooms, a few with cribs or smaller children's beds. The women exclaimed over the classrooms and the new computer lab. Angel set her boxes of cupcakes on one of the tables in the dining hall and smiled cheerfully as the women from the center came forward to have a treat.

Finally, back in the lobby, Agatha said goodbye to everyone, her facial muscles hurting from the smile she had forced in order to hide the fear that Bayley might see through her new image. With a last wave, she watched the women disappear through the front door, before slumping into the nearest chair.

Almost immediately, the door opened again and Faith hustled through, shooting her an apologetic grin. "I forgot something," she said, scooping up a sweater lying on one of the chairs.

She quickly plastered her smile on once more but was startled when Faith grabbed her hand.

Leaning forward, Faith whispered, "I sense something with you. I'm not sure...but please be careful. I feel...danger is lurking." With those words, and an almost apologetic smile, she hurried out the door, leaving Agatha staring dumbly in her wake.

"Hey," Agatha said, her voice breathless as she hurried out to Nathan's truck.

He barely had time to park and alight before she was jogging toward him. She skidded to a stop just in front of him, her face smiling up at his, but her hand twisting the strap on her purse.

"Hey, yourself," he grinned in return, not hesitating to pull her into his arms. Hugging her tightly, he felt her relax as her arms encircled his waist. Leaning back to peer into her face, he said, "It's okay to run into my arms, you know."

Ducking her head, a blush rose across her cheeks. He lifted her head with his knuckle tucked under the chin. Her eyebrows lowered and she sucked in her lips, staring up at him.

"I wasn't sure," she confessed.

He nodded in understanding. "I know we're new, but I really want to get to know you better, so as long as you're on board, we're gonna keep seeing each other. And, for the record, while I normally want you to wait until I come get you, it was a real ego boost to see you come blasting out of the building to greet me."

"I didn't come blasting out," she protested, playfully slapping his chest, quickly realizing that, with the hard muscle underneath her fingertips, he probably did not feel anything.

He bent slightly, wrapped his arms around her waist and swung her off the ground and around in a circle. "You did too come blasting out and don't deny it...like I said, it was a real ego boost."

He stopped twirling, but kept her in his arms, her feet dangling off the ground. She gripped his shoulders and rolled her eyes, retorting, "Like you need an ego boost."

He held her tightly, saying, "I love that you wanted to see me so much you couldn't wait," before he lowered her slowly to the ground, her front plastered to his until her feet touched the pavement, her hands still holding onto his shoulders.

"I've been waiting all day just to have you drive up to get me," she said, her voice hoarse with emotion, surprised at her own confession.

Agatha's honesty in that moment, without any hesitation or fear, took Nathan's breath away unexpectedly. Bending, his reply was his kiss, but as his mouth moved over hers, it became clear to him it was much more than a simple reply. It was more like a declaration, but of what, he was not sure. Finally, pulling back, he said, "Let's get you fed, sweet Aggie."

11

"So then, they all came in and I was overwhelmed by their generosity," Agatha said, describing her day as she wiped spaghetti sauce from her lips.

Nathan rolled his eyes, knowing she was being kind. "Look, I know those women and yes, they are super sweet, but I also know they were there to check you out." He watched her eyes grow enormous and hurried to add, "Not to judge, but they've been after me to go out more and even threatened to set me up on blind dates…which I've always refused."

Swallowing audibly, she said, "Oh, my God, now I feel kind of sick."

He grabbed her hand and said, "Don't do that. You're fine and they were just curious. They really are good people, but I wish they hadn't ambushed you like that."

"I know they're good people. I could tell they were. But, just the thought of them wondering about me makes me nervous."

"It's not like that. It's just, once you meet Jack and he

likes you, you're engulfed in Bethany's mothering. She has made sure each addition to their group via the Saints has felt welcome." Shaking his head, he explained, "Jack and Bethany are complete opposites but one look at them together and you can see the love.

"Miriam is a nurse and when she worked for the Red Cross, she was kidnapped in Mexico by a drug cartel. Cam, a former undercover detective, was sent to rescue her and they fell in love there. Bart, a former SEAL, went to celebrate his cousin, Sabrina's, wedding, got involved in a case and ended up with Faith, who was helping out on the same case. Sabrina's husband, Jude, was also a SEAL before he started working for Jack."

Seeing her wide eyes, he laughed as he kept going. "Monty was former FBI, like Nick. Angel is pretty much his opposite also. Hell, Bayley and Nick...total opposites. I've known her for a while since she's also Blaise's sister. She comes across as quirky, but she's really smart.

"Speaking of smart...Dani, Chad's wife, used to work for the ATF as an explosives expert and she now works for an explosive's factory along with Patrick's Evie, who's an engineer. Throw in Kendall, Marc's wife, who is some kind of doctor of biological terrorism, hell, those women are super smart."

Agatha's shoulders slumped slightly, a movement that did not go unnoticed by Nathan. He squeezed her hand, gaining her attention. "What is it?"

She shook her head, but the slight pressure on her hand had her looking up. Shrugging, she confessed, "I never went to college."

He blinked for a second before asking, "Never?"

Remembering her cover story, she amended smoothly, "Well, I started. For a year, but uh...never finished."

Nodding, he said, "Would it make you feel better to know that I never went at all?"

Cocking her head to the side, she repeated, "Never?"

"Nope. Never had the desire to." Chuckling, he added, "And probably never had a chance. Grades in high school were decent but not all A's. Worked my dad's farm and then joined the Army. Got involved in tracking and never wanted to do anything else."

The conversation flowed easily and she relaxed, watching the animation on his face as he talked about his friends.

"Having a good time?" he asked, his gaze warm on her face.

Blushing, she said truthfully, "I haven't had such a good time in...ever."

"Me either," he admitted. "Talking to you is so easy."

"It's usually hard for me to talk to people. Well, the women at the center are easy, but I don't tend to make friends. I can't think of what to say and just sort of clam up."

He smiled, reaching over to place his hand on hers on top of the table. "We're alike that way, but that makes this all the more special." Seeing her tilt her head, he explained, "We click."

She smiled, her chest almost bursting with pleasure. Looking down at their connected hands, she asked, "How did you meet the Saints...become involved with them?"

Gently rubbing her fingers as the server removed their plates and poured more wine, he said, "I've known Blaise for a few years. We met through our love of dogs. He's also a veterinarian, has worked with the government, and we became friends after I heard he had built an innovative kennel. Found out he worked for Jack and, while most of their major cases he worked on he couldn't talk about, he filled me in on the security and investigative business. I was a certified tracker and he called me in on a case they were working on. Actually, it was the case where he met Grace, his wife."

She loved the feel of her hand nestled in his as he spoke. His normally quiet persona took on a spark when he talked about his friends and his work. Smiling her encouragement, she listened attentively.

"Blaise introduced me to Jack and we hit it off. I'm a quiet guy and so is Jack. Our personalities meshed and after finding out I had been in the Army military police, along with my tracking abilities, he asked me to join his team. I initially declined, preferring to just work on my own, but I continued to contract with them over the last few years." Chuckling, he added, "Jack kept extending his offer of full-time work, but it wasn't until recently that I took him up on it."

"Why now? What made you want to work for him full time now?" Shifting in his seat, his affable smile drooped and she tilted her head in curiosity. "You don't have to tell me," she assured. "I was just curious." Grabbing her wine glass, she took a sip, pretending to study the dessert menu.

"No, no, it's okay. Just a little hard to explain."

Blowing out a breath, he said, "Did you ever feel like you wanted something so big, it's not within your reach? Or maybe, if it's in your reach, you'd never be able to hang on to it?"

She stared, not breathing, as she looked into his face, so strong...and yet, so vulnerable at that moment. And, yes...she knew exactly what he meant. Words did not come, so her only response was to nod slowly, never taking her eyes off his.

"I've got plenty of self-confidence when it comes to what I do...what I know." Shrugging, he said, "In a nutshell, I'm a simple farm boy who loves my dogs. Sure, I did investigation in the military, but it was still mostly just me, my team, and our dogs. When I first met Jack, those men seemed larger than life. Smart, confident, and competent. I was honored to get to know them, call 'em friends and help 'em out when I could...but join them? Hell, what could I bring to them?"

Nathan had been staring at his hands resting on the table and finally dared to lift his eyes to Agatha's face, afraid of what he would see. To his surprise, her face held understanding and she reached over to clasp his hands in hers.

"It's hard to imagine you feeling that way. I could tell you that you bring a lot to the table, but...I know all about wondering if you can make a difference," she whispered. "I've felt that way a lot of times."

Her words snaked through him, filling him with the sensation of so strongly connecting with someone it felt like being bound to them. He sucked in a breath before letting it out slowly, the touch of her hands on his as she gave a little squeeze, warming his heart.

"I finally decided to come out of my comfort zone."

"I get it...I really do," she admitted. "Sometimes, it's hard, though. Thinking that there's nothing you can do to help...or make a change." Sucking in a shuddering breath, she attempted a smile, but it wobbled. Visibly pushing past whatever memories were floating around her mind, she added, "But, you did it."

Nodding, he said, "Yeah. I've wanted to do more investigating, besides the tracking. I've been a real loner since getting out of the military, and Blaise finally called bullshit on my excuses. But that's a story for another day."

"Then I hope we have another day...I'd like to hear all your stories."

His lips curved slightly and he gently rubbed his thumb over her fingers. "Me too."

After a moment of hesitation, he added, "I was called to track a subject about two years ago and, gotta confess, that person, who I don't really know at all, has stayed in my mind ever since. Jack had me come in to talk about them a few weeks ago and I found out they might still be in trouble. So, I just realized the time was right. I wanted to help, *needed* to help this person, and joining the Saints was the best thing to do."

Wishing she could revel in the information that she had stayed in his mind, her joy was quickly engulfed by her fear that she could still be in danger. *Could he be talking about me?* Swallowing the lump in her throat,

Agatha prayed her dinner stayed down as she listened to Nathan speak. "Oh...I see." The words sounded trite to her ears but she could not think of any other response. Holding herself together, she forced her face to adopt the serene expression she was so used to giving.

He stared at her for a moment, unblinking, then, shook his head. "You know, Aggie, I swear, sometimes it's like you drop a screen down over your face, hiding what's really going on behind your eyes."

Jerking, her mask slipped as she stammered, "Don't be silly. I...I don't know what you mean."

He kept studying her for another minute, the seconds ticking by interminably. Finally, he nodded, "Sorry. I shouldn't have said that." Leaning back in his seat, he added, "I have to go out of town for a few days. I'm going to Norfolk to interview a few people who might be able to shine some light on the case."

The blood ran from her face as ice crept around her heart. "Norfolk?"

"Yeah. I'll be with some of the others interviewing a few people in prison in that area. I regret that I'll be gone for a few days and can't see you, but I'll be back by the weekend."

Her night ruined, she tried to keep her formal persona from slipping into place so that he would not notice it again, but without it she had no idea how to compose her features. Grimacing, she tried to still her racing heartbeat.

"Are you all right?" he asked. "You look like you're in pain."

"Actually, I've developed a headache and think I should call it a night."

"I'm sorry, Aggie." He waved the server over and took care of the check. Assisting her from her seat, he wrapped his arm around her shoulders and pulled her close. Kissing the top of her head, he said, "Let's get you home."

She remained quiet on the drive, not trusting her voice. At the center, he assisted her down and escorted her to the door.

Holding her close, he said, "I feel bad that I did most of the talking at dinner. I never got a chance to learn more about you."

Burying her face in his shirt, she remained silent, thankful that she had not had to talk about herself. "It's fine," she mumbled.

He lifted her chin and placed a sweet kiss on her lips. Closing her eyes, she wished it was the kind of kiss that he had given her previously...one that stole her heart. But it looked like her past had finally caught up to her, just as she'd feared it would, and now protecting her heart...and his, was of utmost importance.

"I'll call you when I get back," he promised.

She nodded, her smile wobbly, before going inside and locking the door behind her.

That night she lay in bed, having moved the furniture in the small room to where she could look outside the window, and gazed at the stars. They were not bright and what little she could see was often obscured with clouds.

At war with herself, the desire to have a real relationship with Nathan battled with her fear of discovery. *Is it even worth it for him, to put himself at risk for a girl like me?* Finally, she fell into a fitful sleep, the burden of her family's sins weighing her down, casting a pall over any happiness she might have found.

In his cabin, Nathan lay in his bed, his thoughts tangled over the abrupt ending to dinner and his upcoming trip. *The trip is necessary. It's time to make sure Agnes is safe, wherever she is. And lay her to rest in my mind. Then, all my focus can be on Aggie and what's building there.* Once more, his dreams created nightmares where the two women's faces swirled together.

12

Nathan watched as Milos Gruzinsky walked into the room, his square jaw set and barrel chest puffed out. Grey hair neatly gelled back and his face clean-shaven, the grey pants and matching grey regulation shirt appeared incongruent with the image he wanted to project. Still, he moved with the continued air of a man in charge of his life, at the top of his game.

Milos continued, staring at Nick, "There is nothing I would give to you."

"Tell me about your daughter," Nick said, his voice low and even.

Nathan had watched enough police interrogations in the military to recognize how suited Nick was for the task. His FBI background gave him the perfect, almost nonchalant, attitude in talking to Milos.

Blinking, Milos reared back, surprise evident on his face. "My Agnes? Why would I talk to you about Agnes?" He narrowed his eyes, growling, "Wherever she is, may God protect her from you."

Nathan's gaze jumped from Milos to Nick to Bart and back to Milos again. *Protect her?*

"You think she needs protecting? From me?" Nick asked.

Milos' face grew red as he said, "She's the only one who was not caught up in the..." He hesitated, visibly calming himself before continuing. "In the situation."

"Situation? You must be referring to kidnapping and enslaving women to be used as sexual slaves in your hotel."

Milos' lips pinched together as he neither denied nor confirmed Nick's statement.

Since Agnes had not been caught at the scene where the truck filled with drugged, escaping women had been found, and the only person present at the time, the guard, was killed, it looked like the family never knew what happened to her. They must have assumed she escaped and was in hiding somewhere, having no clue that Harlan took her under his wing, protecting her and changing her identity. *They have no idea she's the one who betrayed the family.*

He kept his gaze on Milos, curious as to Nick's next move.

"You think the authorities are the only ones after your daughter?" Nick asked.

At this, Milos' brow lowered and, unable to keep up the pretense of disinterest, he asked, "What do you mean?"

"You tell me. Who else would want to locate her?"

Milos' dark eyes worked, darting between the three men staring at him, his brow still furrowed. "Is this a trick? My daughter's involvement with the family business was nothing."

"It's no trick and we *know* she was involved." Nick let that settle in and added, "But, what we don't know is where she went and how to keep someone else... someone with a lot of power, from getting to her."

Sweat broke out on Milos' forehead as he continued to glare. "Who..."

"Who is the one person, besides your immediate family, that took a fall in your demise? Who got caught up and is now serving time for tax evasion?"

A gasp escaped from Milos's lips as his eyes widened. "No—"

"What the fuck makes you think Gavrill won't go after Agnes? He could kill any of your family while you're in prison with the snap of his fingers and you know that. But, I guess he figures that death would be too quick a punishment, so he'll let you rot in jail. But her? She's out there. Whether you think he's got a reason to go after her, she's free and he's not. You think he's gonna let that ride?"

Nathan watched with fascination as the play of emotions crossed Milos' face, slowly turning the hard set of his jaw into a visage of fear.

"I don't know where she is," Milos confessed, his voice hoarse. "I have not seen, nor heard, from my daughter since the night of the raid. I have no idea what Gavrill thinks."

Everyone sat quietly for a moment, then Milos suddenly pushed his chair back and stood, his face hard. "I cannot help you, but I know she was innocent. Whatever you think of my family, she was innocent." Working his mouth, as if the words he was about to say tasted foul, he finally bit out, "I pray you find her before someone else does." With that, he turned on his heel and walked from the room, his back as straight as when he entered, once more a man pretending to be in charge of his destiny.

The three of them said very little as they sat in the same room, waiting for the guards to bring in Grigory, Agnes' oldest brother. Nathan's mind was swimming with the emotions that had poured from Milos...defiance, anger, fear, and then defeat. Sucking in a deep breath, he let it out slowly, finishing just as the door opened again.

At first glance, Grigory was dissimilar in appearance to his father and as he observed him, he saw glimpses of Agnes instead. *Must take after their mom.* He was thinner, not as square-jawed as his father, and his outward persona was more rumpled, both in clothing and in mannerisms.

His answers were more perfunctory, giving away little emotion. Nick followed the same line of questioning as he had with Milos, but Grigory simply shrugged.

"As I've told you, I have no idea where my sister is. She's been, I assume, in hiding since the raid."

"You haven't tried to reach out to her, find out where she is?"

Snorting, Grigory said, "And just how would I do that from here?"

"You had a fiancé. Portia."

A flash of emotion finally passed through Grigory's features. Shaking his head, he said, "I'm sure you've relished keeping up with my family's downfall. Yes, Portia dropped the engagement as soon as I was sentenced. Her family kept the pretense of loyalty as long as there was a possibility of me being found inno-cent, but," he spread his arms out, "as you can see, I wasn't. Therefore, no engagement. No loyalty." The last word was ground out, as though the taste of it was bitter in his mouth.

"Do you think your sister is in danger from Gavrill?"

Grigory lifted his eyes to Nick and replied, "She could have testified and hung us all, but she didn't. She stayed away. Safe. Smart." His voice trailed off, slightly, as though in pain. "She was always smart. Maybe smarter than we thought."

He refused to talk to them anymore and as the guards led him away, Nathan stood from his chair, stretching his aching back. He had been fighting the desire to punch both Agnes' father and brother, and the tension was causing his jaw to ache from clenching his teeth.

"Hang on, guys," Nick said, eyeing both he and Bart.

Bart, like him, had stood up to stretch. "Gotta tell you, interviewing these pricks makes me want to punch the shit outta them."

Nathan chuckled, nodding his agreement. The idea that Agnes was raised around men like her father and brother caused his anger to ratchet up, but before he could get too riled, a noise at the door had them all sitting down quickly, tapping down their emotions.

Their last interview at the men's federal penitentiary today was Lazlo, Agnes' other brother. As soon as he walked into the room, Nathan was struck by his similarity with Milos. Square jaw, thick neck, barrel chested. Dark hair, combed neatly to the side, his grey uniform was pressed and he wore it like a suit. With a straight back, he walked swiftly into the room as though he owned the place, his dark eyes moving over the occupants before landing on Nick.

A slow smile, bordering on a snarl, curved his lips. "Well, well, Agent Stone." Placing his hands on the table, he leaned forward until the guards stepped up. "How's Bayley? Now that's one woman I wouldn't have minded getting to know better."

His insinuation was not lost on the Saints and Nathan refused to take his eyes off the slime, not giving him the satisfaction of letting him know his words set his blood to boil.

Nick gave no indication that Lazlo's words concerned him. "I'm here to talk about your sister, Agnes."

"Yeah, and you can go fuck yourself."

"Have a seat and let's see if you're smart enough to put two and two together."

Dark eyes narrowed in anger, but curiosity must have won, as Lazlo moved to the seat, jerked it out with a scraping sound of metal over the tile floor and sat down. Cocking his head, the inmate said, "What about my bitch of a sister?"

Nathan's heart pounded, hearing the hate in Lazlo's voice, wondering what he knew.

"Kind of harsh, don't you think?" Bart interjected.

"I'm here. Grigory's here. Father's here. Mama's in prison. And sister is free, living it up somewhere."

"Where do you think that is?"

Scoffing, he replied, "How the fuck should I know?"

"Why the anger? Just because she got away?"

"Got a better reason? She knew the business. Mama saw to that. Used her to help, too. She might have acted meek, but in the end she was the one with the idea that blew up in our faces. All broads are the same…only good if their legs are spread and their mouths are shut."

"The idea?"

"Agnes came up with some ideas that had our father eating out of her hand. Gave her some responsibilities and in the end, she fucked up."

"Grigory didn't seem to have a problem with her."

Sneering, he said, "You think that, then you're an idiot. He had her followed. Don't know what she was doing, but she fucked up. And, when things got hot, she ran."

"So, you're pissed 'cause you were caught and your sister kept her name out of it. Seems she was smarter than the rest of you."

Lazlo glared but clamped his jaw shut, his lips pressed tightly together.

"You know who wants her, and wants her dead," Nick stated.

Lazlo's gaze jumped to Nick's, but he still remained silent.

"Gravrill's sitting in prison right now due to your family's incarceration. I'll tell you what I told your father. He could kill any of your family, at any time, with a snap of his fingers. But, he probably thinks that death would be too quick a punishment, so he'll let you rot in jail. But she's out there. She's free and he's not. We'd like to see that he can't get to her, so you got any idea where she might be?"

Grimacing, Lazlo shook his head as he leaned forward, his dark eyes unblinking. "I'm pissed as fuck that my sister's out there when her shit led to this fuckin' mess. Do I want her dead at Gavrill's hand? No, but I sure as fuck have my own problems to worry about. Don't know where she is and don't care." Standing, he motioned to the guards he was ready to leave.

Nathan watched him stride to the door, still giving the appearance of a man in charge of his world. *Jesus, how did Agnes survive in that world?*

On this trip, Bart had the wheel, Nick was riding shotgun, and Nathan took up the backseat of Bart's SUV. He had been researching Yurgi for the past hour with the information that Luke had sent him.

"From what I'm seeing, Yurgi is Gavrill's half-brother. Luke has been able to dig up that they had the same father but different mothers. In fact, it looks like their father may have had multiple mistresses and therefore there are quite a few half siblings. And that doesn't even include all of the cousins."

Nick said, "We often find with organized crime families, that they have huge families—multiple siblings, multiple cousins. This is going back as far as history goes, with the idea that blood is thicker than water. If you're running a crime syndicate, you want those around you to be family, because you can trust them the most."

After several hours, they drove down a long road, warehouses on both sides. The massive metal buildings were a hubbub of activity during the height of the day. Workers, forklifts, huge crates ready to be delivered onto ships as well as those being taken off, filled the area.

"Seeing those crates make me think of the state of those women that Agnes saved...the ones Scarlett and I had to round up. I hope like hell those crates don't have human cargo."

The others shared his sentiments as they drove along.

Parking outside one of the large brick buildings next to a warehouse, Bart said, "Looks like our welcoming committee is here."

They looked toward the door, seeing four large men standing there, all dressed in black, dark sunglasses, no smiles, and with obvious gun bulges in their jackets. Climbing down from the SUV, the three of them walked confidently forward. One of the guards stepped in front of the others, blocking the way.

"We're here to see Yurgi Volkov."

The man gave a wide smile as the three men behind him chuckled softly. "And what makes you think that Mr. Volkov wants to see you?"

"It's in his best interest to see us," Nick said, his voice firm and steady. "Considering how much we know about the Volkov business and how we will be spending some time visiting with Gavrill in his new residence. I think Yurgi will want to see us. Check with him. Tell him the Saints can easily carry a message back to Gavrill, should he have one he'd like shared."

The sunglasses may have hidden the man's eyes, but the uncertainty that crossed his face was not missed. He turned his head, barked a few guttural commands toward one of the men behind him, then looked back at the Saints and said, "Wait."

Within five minutes the guard was back and nodded for them to follow him. They walked inside the cavernous warehouse, through aisles with large crates stacked five tall on either side. Workers stopped and stared, but Nathan could discern no one else following them as they passed. At the far end, they approached a metal staircase going up the side of the wall. The man they had been following stopped at the bottom and, with a head jerk, motioned for them to go up the stairs, where they were met by another armed guard.

The man at the top of the stairs knocked once on the door behind him before swinging it wide open. He also indicated with a head jerk that they should move through the door. Once inside the room, Nathan could see that it was an office area. The floor was wooden, polished to a sheen. The walls were painted a soft cream and, while the furniture was basic, it appeared comfortable. Two women, dressed professionally, sat at the desks near the windows, both typing on computers, neither looking up as the Saints walked through the room.

At the far end of the reception area was another door. The guard that had allowed them into this area passed by them and knocked once on the inner door before opening it as well. Nick walked through first, followed by Nathan, with Bart bringing up the rear.

Nathan quickly took in the room, a plush rug on the wooden floor, wooden chairs with leather-padded seats, and no windows. He knew he was in Gavrill's former office, which would have provided him with the utmost security. Behind the desk, sat Yurgi. Similar in stature to Gavrill, with black hair and a square jaw, he said nothing, but offered a beady-eyed stare toward them.

Three chairs had been set in front of the large wooden desk, but Nick did not immediately take one, instead stopping, giving Yurgi a chance to invite them to sit. It was a small, conciliatory gesture, that could go a long way in assisting them with what they wanted.

At a curt nod from Yurgi, the guard that had walked in behind Bart motioned for them to take a seat. With nods of their own, they each sat, facing Yurgi.

"Your brother has communicated with you that he would like someone found. We're here to suggest that you not follow his instructions. Right now, the FBI has no evidence of your brother transporting human cargo. We know you are struggling at the helm of the Volkov business. Trying to keep it intact," Nick said.

Nathan noted Yurgi's eyes widened and the muscles in his jaw tightened at the not so subtle jab. Or maybe it was just that they had so much information. *Good job, Luke.*

Nick continued, "The more you struggle and fail to keep this shipping business afloat, the more opportunity you give the FBI to get the warrant it needs to board your ships."

"You assume that I know what you are talking about," Yurgi replied, his Slavic accent heavy. "I assure you, I am doing nothing more than running the business my brother had to give up temporarily when he was falsely charged with the tax evasion."

Bart leaned forward, his large body radiating anger, and said, "Cut the bullshit. We've got the means to discover all the illegal cargo that this business ships, and have no problem turning that evidence over to the FBI. But right now, we don't care about the guns and the drugs. However, if you know what's good for you, you better make sure that none of these containers carry human cargo."

Yurgi grimaced, but said nothing.

"Your brother has managed to keep that part of his business safe from the prying eyes of the authorities, but those days have come to an end," Nathan added. "What we want to make sure of, is that the threat he has made against his cousin's daughter goes unheeded."

Nick finished, "You know Gavrill is keeping an eye on his business and he knows the business is struggling. If you pursue his quest to go after Agnes Gruzinsky, we'll make sure this business fails while you are at the helm."

"I do not take to threats," Yurgi said, his voice like gravel as his eyes bore straight into them.

"Not a threat," Nathan assured him. "Just a promise. Keep to the legitimate business." Walking out, he prayed Agnes...wherever she was...would remain safely in hiding.

Pushing his plate back, Nathan could not help but think of the previous night when he had been with Agatha at a restaurant.

"Jesus, skipping lunch gave me a headache," Bart complain. "Or maybe it was the asinine conversations we had with the Gruzinsky males. Fuckin' assholes."

Nodding, he agreed. "Of the three, Milos is the one who is the most sure his daughter had nothing to do with their downfall. He doesn't suspect at all that Agnes was on the inside, helping the FBI. How the fuck they managed to keep that from them, I can't imagine."

"Harlan would have instigated that and, as lead agent, he had the authority to make that call. Agnes got damn lucky there were no witnesses left, harsh as that sounds. The agents flooded the hotel, found the women chained to beds and it was their testimonies that sent them all to prison. The doctor who was in on it with Agnes turned evidence for immunity, but for some reason he kept quiet about her involvement."

"How the fuck Harlan pulled it off…" he started, his words trailing in awe.

"And now, he's dead," Bart stated, scrubbing his hand over his face.

"Her family?"

Nick shook his head. "If any of those three had knowledge, they would've given something away. They're just not that smart. Plus, I don't think they have the clout they think they have."

He did not like the implication. Making eye contact with his companions, he stated, "Gavrill."

"My money's on him," Nick agreed.

"We'll get our chance at him tomorrow."

"And then mama," Nick added.

"You really think we'll get something from Chessa?" he asked.

Nick pinned him with a hard stare. "Don't count her out. Remember, she was part of Gavrill's family before she married Milos."

"But she's a—"

"Woman?" Nick interjected. "Don't let that fool you into thinking she's soft."

He shook his head. "No, I was going to say she's a mother."

Nick was quiet for a moment before looking at both he and Bart. "I was an FBI agent for a lot of years. Believe me, I wish being a mother kept women from being evil, but it doesn't. If someone's evil, nothing'll get in their way. Not even their child."

Nathan laid in the hotel bed, his muscles more tired from the tension of the day than after a long run with his dogs. Blowing out his breath, he thought of Agatha. He had told her he would call, but his mind was so full...he hated to call when he could not talk about the events of the day.

Climbing from the bed, he walked to the sliding glass door leading to a small balcony overlooking the Norfolk harbor. Stepping out, he walked to the rail, leaning his forearms on the cold metal. He could see the lights reflecting like diamonds on the inky water as it slapped against the boardwalk. Looking up, the stars were shining in the cloudless night sky.

He wondered for the millionth time if Agnes, wherever she was, looked to the night sky to see the stars. *And, if she does, does she remember me?*

Straightening, he stalked back inside, angry with himself. *Why the fuck can't I get her out of my mind? I was supposed to have put this behind me. I thought I had.*

Sitting down on the edge of the bed, he picked up his phone but, instead of dialing, just sat with it in his hand. *I'm so fucked.*

He liked Agatha and hoped they were at the beginning of something special, but it seemed wrong to lead her on if his head was still entangled in the myth of a woman who barely knew him and he would never see again. *Do others do this? Be interested in two women at the same time?*

He tossed the phone to the mattress beside him and leaned forward. With his elbows on his knees, he pressed his face into his palms, grinding at his eyes, trying to force the image of Agnes as she slowly disappeared from his view, staring out of the huge SUV at him, looking small and afraid, from his mind. *And sad. She also looked sad.*

He turned his phone to silent before slipping back underneath the covers. He knew it was not fair to Agatha to call her when his mind was on another woman. Grimacing, he rolled over, wishing sleep would come…knowing it would not.

Agatha paced the halls of the center, sleep not coming. Nathan said he would call but he had not. *Probably just busy.* Her feet stumbled as she walked…*or he interviewed my criminal family and now knows just how truly horrible I am.*

Clenching her fists at her side, she raged against the battle inside. *He doesn't know who I am. I'm Agatha…not Agnes. Agatha…not a member of a crime family.* Leaning her back against the wall, her head slumped forward as Harlan's words came back to her.

"You're not your family. You're not what their crimes are. You're a survivor, just like the other women. The women you saved."

A noise behind her caused her to jump, whirling around. "Oh, Gail, it's you."

"Can't sleep either, Agatha?"

"No. I thought about making a cup of herbal tea, but have just been wandering instead."

"I'll have a cup if you will," Gail offered.

Smiling, she said, "Okay, I'll take you up on that." They walked into the kitchen and she put on the kettle to boil while Gail took two mugs from the cabinet. Within a few minutes they were sitting at the table, steam rising from their tea, with the quiet of the night soothing over them.

"Can I ask you a question?" Gail said, her voice hesitant.

"Of course."

"I was just wondering why you live here and not in your own place. Do you have to?"

Shaking her head, she replied "No. I mean, it's not part of my contract with Ann. It's just, I was new to the area when I took the job and she offered to let me have the attic bedroom in the other house until I found a place. But, then, I liked being there and it was nice to have an employee here, so Ann said I could stay as long as I liked."

"But here...you don't have much privacy. I mean, you've got a room on the other end of the hall from the rest of us, but don't you find that...uh..."

Laughing, she said, "Limiting?"

"Yeah. I mean I've seen you getting picked up by that nice man...Nathan...the one who found me the night I ran into the woods. He's fine looking and I figured if you and he were getting serious, then you'd be looking for someplace more private."

Unable to keep the smile from her face, she lifted her shoulders. "I take your point...but, who knows what'll happen." Her smile slipped with the thought that he had promised to call and then did not.

Gail observed her for a moment before saying, "Relationships are hard. Lord knows, I found that out in a bad way."

Lifting her eyes, she stayed silent while Gail continued.

"My daddy always told me to wait for a prince. Thought I had. Things were so good at first. I've spent the past several days with the counselor who comes here, trying to figure out where things went wrong.

"Thomas was nice at first. Treated me real good. He didn't drink, hang out with the boys too much, make too many demands. But as time went on, things started to change. I got a few promotions, little steps up, one at a time...hell, it was only at the local grocery store but I went from register clerk, to being back in the bakery, to being the bakery manager. Got a raise by the time I reached manager, thought things were good."

"So, what happened?" she asked softly.

Gail sipped her tea before replying, "It's like, for every good thing that happened, he got angrier instead of happier. I got a raise and he wanted to know why dinner wasn't on the table when he got home. I made employee of the month and got my picture on the wall of the store and he got pissed, saying I was flaunting myself to other men." She shook her head and said, "I worked so hard to make him see that he was the center of my world, but nothing I did made a difference."

Gail's gaze settled on her mug as she continued, "First, it was yelling. Then he'd grab my arm and jerk me around. And then, he slapped me. Every time, saying how sorry he was when it happened. Then, one night he punched me. Pushed me down the stairs. My friend kept telling me to leave but I was scared. Scared to stay and scared to leave." Sighing, she said, "What a fucked-up way to live."

"And now?"

A little smile slid across Gail's face. "I think every person deserves to be loved. I know I have worth and value. I'm shy of ever trusting another man again, but I deserve a shot at true love and no way will I ever settle for less again."

Gail stood and rinsed her mug out before placing it in the dishwasher. Patting Agatha on the shoulder as she left the room, her words swirled in Agatha's mind. *"Every person deserves to be loved."* Flipping out the light, she walked out of the room. *Yes...even me.*

Nathan instantly noticed the difference between what they were looking at now and the maximum security prison the Gruzinksy's were in.

"This is a fuckin' joke," he bit out, glaring around at the minimum security facility.

"It's low level," Nick said calmly, although his jaw was tight as well. "Doesn't matter that Gavrill's the head of a violent crime family, he was only charged and convicted with tax evasion."

The three had moved through the gates and down a hall to a large conference room after showing their credentials. As they sat, he felt his heartrate increase, thinking of the man they were about to talk to. Drugs.

Guns. Gambling. Prostitution. Slavery. Human trafficking. There was little this man did not do to rule his kingdom.

Having seen his photograph, he was still unprepared for when Gavrill walked through the door. One look at the guard walking along with him and it was not hard to see that the man was on Gavrill's pay. Nick looked at the guard as well and Nathan was sure he also saw the casual air with which the man held himself.

"We'll interview the prisoner by himself, and have permission to do so," Nick stated, his voice firm.

The guard looked at Gavrill, as though to ascertain what he should do.

"You got a problem following orders, or maybe just who you take orders from?" Bart growled.

The guard shot him a murderous glare but stepped out of the room nonetheless. The sound of clapping drew their attention to Gavrill's grinning face.

"Well played, former Agent Stone." He shifted his attention to Bart. "And you, Mr. Taggart, we meet again." Moving toward the chair, he said, "It's your dime, so I suggest we get down to why you're here."

"We want to know what you know about Agnes Gruzinsky."

Nathan studied Gavrill's expression, but it never changed. No eye blink. No flinch. No twitch. No reaction at all. His heart pounded as he waited to see what he would say.

"Agnes...my cousin's daughter. The only one in that family that is not currently in prison." His dark eyes bore into theirs one by one. "Anything else you want to know."

"Do you know where she is?"

"If she's smart, she's a long way away from here."

"And is she smart?" Nick pressed.

Nathan suddenly figured out what Gavrill resembled. Still. Poised to strike. Eyes pinned on his prey. A snake. *A fucking snake.* Holding his breath, he waited to see what was next. Seconds ticked by and for the first time, Gavrill's jaw ticked ever so slightly. If he had blinked, he would have missed it, but there it was…a tiny reaction.

"She's a woman," Gavrill stated, his shoulders lifting in a shrug.

"That doesn't answer the question," Bart said, leaning forward slightly.

Opening his hands, palms up, on the table, Gavrill said, "It does to me."

"So, Agnes, now disappeared, the only one in the family to not be rounded up, implicated, and currently serving a prison sentence…isn't smart?" Nick asked.

"Also, the only one who's whereabouts are currently not known, isn't smart?" Nathan pressed, unable to stay quiet in the presence of so vile a man. His fists itched to wipe the smug expression off Gavrill's face.

The silence in the room was deafening and he thought for a second Gavrill was going to call for the guard and refuse to answer any more questions.

After a moment that stretched interminably, Gavrill's eyes dropped to his hands resting on the table, saying, "She may be the smartest one of any of them."

"Any of them?"

"My cousin's husband and idiot sons."

"Why would you say that?"

A sly grin spread across his face as he lifted his gaze. "My, my, you must think I am terribly stupid. I, of course, have no idea what unsavory business the Gruzinsky's were involved in. But, according to the news, it seems they were very bad…and very stupid. But Agnes…it has been years since I saw her last, but she did not strike me as a very bright young woman. She knew her place and that was to be quiet and stay out of the way. So, I do not know where she is, but I applaud her that she managed to stay out of prison."

"So, you have no interest in finding her?"

Gavrill hesitated for an instant. "Oh, I would always be interested in family."

"What about Harlan Masten?"

"The intrepid FBI agent, Mr. Masten. Excuse me, former agent. Or should I say, recently deceased former agent?"

"I see you stay well informed."

"I find it is in my best interest to stay informed."

"And Yurgi's sudden decision to return to the US after his extended stay in Croatia?"

"I see you stay informed as well."

As the parrying continued, Nathan felt like he was observing a tennis match, the lobs moving back and forth between Gavrill and Nick.

"The agency will be watching him carefully. Very carefully."

"My brother is merely looking after the family's

business interests while I'm enjoying my vacation here. That's all. And all you'll ever find."

He called for the guard, who hustled in, shooting glares at Bart. The two men left the room, leaving the Saints wondering about Gavrill's game.

Not moving for a moment, Nathan admitted, "Got to tell you, I understand dogs a helluva lot better than people. I have no fuckin' clue what to think about that piece of shit."

Bart looked over at Nick, saying, "You're better at this than I am. When I talked to him with Faith along, she said it was like talking to pure evil."

Nodding, Nick said, "He wants to find Agnes. Lazlo's told his suspicions to him. He's smart. He knows Agnes has gone to ground, but he wants to find her."

"And Harlan?"

"He called the hit…no doubt in my mind. But, he's slick. Manages to get his family's dirty work done without getting caught…so far."

"I want that bastard," Nathan growled, the idea of Gavrill even looking at Agnes making his skin crawl.

1 4

"God, I'm tired," Bart complained from the backseat as they left the Norfolk area and drove to the women's federal prison.

"Come on, SEAL, stop complaining," Nick joked.

Nathan rode shotgun while Nick drove, and had to admit he was wiped as well. "How the fuck did you do this as a career for so long?" he asked Nick.

"Being an agent wasn't all about questioning assholes. Plus, as an agent, I had them over a barrel. Now, they don't have to cooperate if they don't want to. I knew going in that we'd get nothing from Gavrill, but I still wanted to get my eyes on him."

"And the Gruzinskys?"

"They're weaker...easier to read."

They left the subject and the conversation flowed to sports, the new training Jack had set up, and then his dogs. An hour later, they pulled up to a facility similar to what the men were in. After they checked in, they were led to an interview room, the pale blue walls the only difference from the men's prison.

Sitting at the table, Nathan looked up as Chessa Gruzinsky was escorted into the room. His breath caught in his throat as he stared into the dark eyed, slender faced, smooth skinned woman that was an older version of Agnes. Up close, he could see the age lines marring her perfect skin and that her black hair was streaked with a little grey, but other than that, the similarity with the face he'd looked into through the window in the SUV as it drove away was uncanny.

She shot a glare at all three of them before sitting down at the table with the grace of a queen. Placing her hands in her lap, she turned her attention toward them. "I have no idea what purpose this interview has," she began, her voice calm but full of venom. "I believe everything came out in the trial."

"But not your daughter," Nick jumped in, refusing to give her a chance to ponder her answers. "She was not involved. Why was that?"

Chessa's eyes narrowed and he thought she was going to snarl. Her eyes jumped to his, briefly, before she relaxed. "My Agnes? What does she have to do with any of this?"

Nodding, Nick said, "Your husband's in prison. Your two sons are in prison. And here you sit. But Agnes… she's off somewhere. Doesn't that bother you?"

She worked her mouth for a second before shrugging. "She had nothing to do with anything. She is a mere girl."

"She's a grown woman who has not been seen since

that night your family's businesses were raided. Have you got any idea where she is?"

"No. I haven't seen or heard from her."

"That seems kind of odd. I mean, wouldn't a devoted daughter come visit? See you at the trial?"

Chessa's mouth worked more, as though a bitter taste had passed her lips.

"We just visited with your sons—"

"Bah, my sons are stupid," she bit out. "They have no idea what women are capable of. We hold the family together. We make things happen. They think they rule us?"

"So, you do think that Agnes is smart. Smart enough to get somewhere she can't be found."

"The women in my family are smart, but as to where she is now? I have no idea."

"And Gavrill? Do you think he knows where she is?" Seeing her eyes widen, Nick pressed, "Does he have a reason to go after her? After all, she was the only one to come out of this unscathed."

Chessa sat quietly for a minute, her eyes focused on her hands, now clenched on the table in front of her. Lifting her gaze, she finally said, "I have no idea where my daughter might be. But, I'm not stupid. If she turned on us, then my cousin is welcome to her."

Nathan blinked, fury pouring through him at her words. Before he had a chance to speak, she stood and called for the guard.

Just before walking through the door, she looked back over her shoulder, and added, "Maybe she is smart. Smarter than all of us."

Agatha picked up the phone, seeing Ann's number on caller ID. "Good morning."

"He...hello," Ann croaked.

"Oh, you sound horrible!"

"Laryngitis," Ann whispered. "No fever, but my throat is raw."

"I've got everything under control here, so stay home and rest."

Continuing to whisper, Ann said, "Magazine reporter is coming today. Article."

"Oh, that's right. Do you want me to cancel until you're feeling better?"

"No, please, no. We need the exposure for more donations. Please, can you do it?"

"Me? But, Ann, you're the director," she protested. "You should be the one to do it. What if I say something wrong?"

"Agatha, please, don't be silly," Ann continued to croak. "I really need you to do this and you know the center as well as I do. They won't be asking for any financial information...just about the center...who we serve, what we do. But remember, don't let them get any pictures of the women's faces. We must protect their identities."

"Absolutely," she agreed. Heaving a sigh, she said, "I'll take care of it. You just stay home and get well." Disconnecting, she leaned back in her chair, blowing out a long breath. *God, I hope I don't mess this up. Ann's really counting on the exposure in order to get more money for the center.* She jerked, suddenly realizing she would be the one talking to the reporter and looked down at her clothes. Wearing an old shirt because it was cleaning day, she jumped up and hurried down the hall to her room, needing to change and fix her hair.

Tina walked around the corner and yelled, "Where you going so fast?"

Skidding to a stop, she turned and said, "Ann's sick today and we have a reporter coming to find out more about the center. Remind the others that'll be happening in about an hour. And they're not to worry... no one will be taking their pictures. I'm going to get presentable!"

"You're beautiful just as you are, but don't worry. You get prettied-up and I'll let the others know."

Waving her thanks, she hurried into her room.

"Ms. Christel, thank you so much for all of the wonderful information you've given us. We're sorry that Ms. Cosner is ill today, but you have certainly given us an excellent tour and interview of the Safe Haven Center."

Smiling, Agatha relaxed, glad to have the interview over. "We appreciate anything you can do to get our center more donations. Obviously, monetary assistance is always welcome and we are a non-profit center, so donations are tax deductible."

"Are there any specific requests that you would like to mention?"

Looking around for a few seconds as she thought, she said, "We can always take toiletries, paper products, non-perishable food donations, and since some of the women who seek our shelter have children with them, diapers and baby wipes are also needed at all times."

"Our readers will be particularly glad to see the classrooms and computer lab that you have for the women."

"It's very important that we help them get back on their feet. Most of the women have been systematically cut off from others. It's what many abusers do to control them. So, we want to make sure they have the skills to get back into the workforce."

The reporter smiled as she stood. "I know that we have to protect the women's privacy, but can we take a few photographs that will not include their faces?"

Glad that they understood the parameters, she nodded. "We can walk back to the classroom if you like."

Walking down the hall, they entered the computer lab. As the reporter stood in the back, Agatha moved to the front to speak to the teacher and women.

"Ladies, just keep facing the front while we have someone taking a few pictures from the back to get a feel for our center and what we can offer." She moved to the side and observed as the reporter took several shots.

"And how about the dining facility?" the reporter asked.

"Sure." Leading her back down the hall, she walked into the kitchen and saw a few women preparing lunch. Telling them to look down, with their backs to the camera for a moment, she smiled as the reporter called out that she was finished.

At the front door, she held out her hand to say good-bye, when she was pulled into a hug.

"I'm sorry to be so emotional. I know that it's not professional, but I just have to say that I fought to get this assignment from my boss. If my mom had had a place like this, well, her life…and the lives of me and my brother, would have been so much better." Holding Agatha's gaze, she said, "Don't ever think that what you're doing here isn't important. You're saving and changing lives…every day."

Stunned, she watched as the perfectly coiffed woman walked out of the center, seeming to all as a woman in complete control. Blowing out a huge breath, she turned and saw the volunteer sitting at the reception desk.

"She's right, you know," Betty said. "I watch you with the women. They like you, but more than that, you seem to get them. Get the fact that for so long they felt like they had no choice in how life treated them. Or that they had no worth. And nothing beats down someone's feeling of worth like having a loved one treat them as valueless."

She stood, rooted in place, her breath ragged as a tear slid down her cheek.

Betty walked around her desk and said, "I've watched you. There's something in you that also holds you back. Something, I'll bet, from your past, which makes you think that you don't deserve happiness. But, Ms. Christel, no matter what happened way back when, you're doing wonders here." Leaning forward, until her face was directly in Agatha's, she drove her point home. "You are worthy and deserve to be happy." Reaching down to squeeze her hand, she smiled and walked back to her desk, as Agatha walked on unsteady legs back into the center.

Grateful for the empty halls, she hurried to her room and shut the door. With her arms wrapped tightly about her middle, she stood at the small window that overlooked the alley in the back, but still allowed sunlight to come through. Closing her eyes, she repeated, *I'm worthy and deserve to be happy.* Wondering if she really could, she thought of Nathan. He had not called but was due back town tonight. Letting out a shuddering breath, she felt the sliver of sunlight on her face. *Please, let him think I'm worthy too.*

"See you tomorrow," Nathan called out as Nick dropped him off at his cabin. They had already taken Bart home and, while he'd been happy to see Faith, and their son and daughter, come out to greet Bart, his heart had panged with longing. An unexpected sensation, he had pushed it aside as they walked over to greet him as well.

Faith had moved toward him, her mouth open as if to speak, but she snapped it closed again before anything could come out. He had cocked his head but she had merely smiled and said, "Glad you're all home safe."

"I understand you had the horrible experience of

meeting Gavrill several years ago. Bart'll fill you in, but I can assure you, he's just as rotten as Bart described."

A visible shiver ran over her and she grimaced. Opening her mouth again, she closed it once more, her eyes boring into his. In a move uncharacteristic of her, she placed her hand lightly over his heart. "Please be careful," she whispered, before turning around quickly and walking back to Bart, who was tossing their son into the air.

Now, back home, he greeted Scarlett and headed straight to the kennel. Grace had come over to care for the dogs and he knew the place was fine, but even so, he could not wait to see his animals. The baying ensued as he opened the door and grew louder as he walked in, calling out his greetings.

Taking them for a run, he let them into the house afterward and watched as they immediately piled onto the rug in the living room. Grinning, he grabbed a beer from the refrigerator and followed the dogs, plopping down onto the sofa.

His mind would not settle, filled with a swirl of thoughts, all calling to him. The prisons...Agnes' family...Gavrill...wondering where she was...Agatha... knowing she was waiting on him to call.

The desire to be with Agatha pulled at him. His heart beat stronger when he was with her. Beautiful, kind, caring. *She looks at me as though I hung the stars in the sky. Stars...fuck.*

That brought Agnes back to mind. Her haunted face. Her possibly being danger. The way his heart still warmed when he thought of her.

Dammit, I thought I was moving on. I've never been the kind of man to lead a woman on. Hell, my daddy'd whoop up on me if he thought that was the man he raised.

Not one to date often, it had never been an issue before, but the indecision he was now facing made him angry with himself.

Standing, he called the dogs and put Persi, Beau, and Red into their kennels for the night. Stalking back inside, he picked up his phone and sent a text.

Know it's late. I'm back. Can I see you tomorrow?

A few minutes later, his phone vibrated an incoming message.

Of course! Is everything alright?

It's fine – just wiped.

Ok – talk to you tomorrow.

Tossing his phone back to the counter, he stomped into the bedroom, Scarlett trotting at his side. She jumped up on his bed, but instead of closing her eyes, she stared at him with a soulful gaze.

He looked at her and dropped his chin to his chest, standing in the middle of the room, his hands on his hips. "I know, girl. I'm fucked. No matter what I do, I'm fucked."

Finally drifting off, dreams overtook his fitful sleep.

He stood in the dark, Scarlett at his side, watching Agnes approach the SUV. This time, though, she turned and looked at him, a smile on her face, and said, "Be happy." As the SUV pulled away, Agnes looked at him through the window, her black hair framing her pale face, and lifted her hand, waving goodbye. He waved in return, watching her fade into the night. Looking down, his hand moved to Scarlett's head to scratch her ears before he turned toward the woods again. The sun was rising, sending sunbeams through the trees, illuminating the forest. A noise caught his attention and he looked up, seeing Agatha walking toward him, a beautiful smile on her face as she waved in greeting. The sunlight glistened on her blonde hair, creating a halo about her face. His heart leaped at seeing her, warmth flowing through his entire body. She was here. Now. Real. Just as she reached him, arms outstretched, he awoke.

Blinking in the morning light, he jumped from bed, rousing Scarlett. Grinning widely, he said, "Come on, Scarlett. Let's get going. We've got chores to do, reports to give to Jack, and I've got a girl to get to."

15

Parking outside the center the next day, Nathan watched as Agatha walked toward him, a rare, wide smile on her face as she approached. Her jeans fit her hips and her sky-blue t-shirt was modest, but it could not hide her perfect curves. His heart zinged as he hustled to greet her, thrilled when she walked straight into his arms.

Wrapping her tightly to him, he caught a whiff of her floral shampoo and buried his face in her hair.

"Are you sniffing me," she asked, merriment in her voice.

"Guilty," he confessed, leaning back to peer into her face. All night, he had wondered what to do and by morning's light, he knew. Agnes was a case. A woman from the past that he had connected with, but that was merely a blip on the timeline of his life. Agatha was a woman that was real, here and now, giving herself to him. *And I'd be a damned fool if I let her go just to waste my life thinking about someone I'll never have, and who I didn't really know in the first place.*

"So…uh…how was your trip?" she asked, her eyes not meeting his.

He lifted her chin with his finger and said, "The last thing I want to talk about is interviewing the worst of society with a beautiful woman in my arms." He felt her knees buckle and tightened his arms around her, as all the blood drained from her face.

"Aggie…you okay?"

Agatha gasped as she jerked to a stand, forcing her knees to lock in place. "Sorry…yes. Uh…just…uh…"

"Let's get you fed, okay. If I know you, you probably skipped lunch again."

He settled her into the cab of his truck, but noticed her complexion was still pale. "I had an idea, but now, I'm not sure if it's a good one."

She turned toward him, waiting.

"I was going to grab some Chinese on the way out of town and take you back to my place for dinner. I hate being away from the dogs, since Persi's expecting, but—"

"No, no, that's perfect," she rushed to say. "Please, let's do that. I'd much rather have something at your place than in a restaurant right now."

He leaned across the console toward her upturned face and halted a breath away. "I really want to kiss you right now, sweet Aggie."

She swallowed the lump in her throat and said, "I'd like that too."

His lips devoured hers, firm against petal soft, and

she moaned into his mouth, unable to harness the delight his touch sent through her whole body.

Pulling back, he looked at her hooded eyelids and kiss-swollen lips with longing. "I gotta stop for now. 'Cause when I take your lips again, I want to give them the time and attention they deserve."

A shiver ran over her body as she stared into his face. Nodding, she settled back into her seat as he drove to the nearest Chinese restaurant and ran inside to get their food.

As she sat in the truck waiting for him, she sucked in a huge cleansing breath before letting it out slowly. *I'm not Agnes...not related to the monsters he just met. I'm Agatha...and I'm worthy to be loved.* Repeating that a few more times, she breathed easier as she watched him jog to the truck, his arms full of bags. *Lord, what that man can do to a pair of jeans.* His biceps flexed with the bags on his arms and she wondered how the t-shirt could contain the muscles. Before she knew it, he opened the door and set the bags behind his seat.

"What all did you buy?"

"Cashew chicken, sweet and sour pork, beef and broccoli, egg rolls, wonton soup, and crab rangoons."

"Holy moly, Nathan!"

He grinned widely, his eyes twinkling. "I like to eat… and after you nearly passed out on me a few minutes ago, I want to make sure you eat as well."

Not wanting to pursue that line of conversation, she nodded and said, "Then you'd better get me home and feed me!"

Twenty minutes later they turned onto a gravel

drive taking them deep into the woods. She stared, wide eyed, at the beautiful forest surrounding them. "This is lovely," she exclaimed. "I haven't been out in woods since…a long time ago."

He smiled and said, "You can hear our welcoming committee."

She cocked her head as he turned off the engine and the sound of baying hounds could be heard easily. Clapping her hands, she said, "Oh, can I see them?"

"Absolutely," he agreed, climbing down from the truck. Leaving the bags for a moment, he took her hand and led her to his kennel.

Once inside, she squealed in delight. "Oh, my God. They're beautiful."

He let go of her hand and moved to the food counter. Fixing their bowls while she wandered to the dogs, she knelt and let them lick her hands.

"You must be Persi," she said, staring at the obviously pregnant dog. "When is she due?"

"In another couple of weeks," he replied, bringing over the food for Persi and setting it in her cage.

Moving to the next ones, he introduced, "This is Beau and this is Red." Placing their food in as well, he went back to the table and picked up the last bowl.

"Hey, Scarlett," Agatha said, kneeling at the last run, scratching the ears of the beautiful hound.

Nathan turned around and looked at her in surprise. "How'd you know her name?"

Without skipping a beat, she continued to pet the dog and said, "You told me, silly."

Shrugging, he walked over and set Scarlett's bowl down, watching in satisfaction as the dogs gobbled their food.

Taking her hand, he gently pulled her to a stand, and said, "Now, I need to feed you."

Smiling, she walked to the truck and waited as he retrieved the bags, the steam still rising from the contents.

"Oh, that smells so good," she moaned.

He looked at her, the moan reaching straight to his cock. The thought passed his mind to swoop in and kiss her like he had promised. *Damn, man. Get her fed first and stop thinking like a caveman.*

Entering his cabin, he was hit with nerves, wondering what she would think of his small house. It suited him, but he had never brought a woman here before. Suddenly unsure, he placed the bags on the table and said, "I guess my place seems kind of simple—"

"Stop," she ordered, her fingers pressed to his lips. Her face was soft in the light and she rose on her toes to place a kiss on the underside of his jaw. "It's you...so it's perfect."

They stood, toe to toe, staring at each other, a slight smile crossing both of their faces. He bent to kiss her forehead, saying, "Have a seat, sweet Aggie. I'll get the plates."

He brought over plates and she placed the container boxes onto the table, opening them to allow more steam and delicate scents to rise.

Sitting, Agatha helped herself to a little of everything, immediately moaning over the taste. She opened her eyes to see Nathan staring, his amber eyes dark with lust. Licking her lips, her gaze dropped to his mouth.

"Keep eating, Aggie. The temptation is killing me."

She wondered what the heroines in her romance novels would do. Bat their eyes coquettishly? Shoot off a rapid-fire quip? Sexy banter? Her eyes dropped to her plate, the realization that she did not know how to do any of those things making her feel inadequate.

"What just happened?" he asked, having seen her face drop.

Shrugging, she looked over at him. "I'm not very good at this."

Jerking slightly, he asked, "This what, Aggie?"

"You know. Flirting. I read about it in my romance novels. I even watch other women do it, but I'm clueless." Snorting, she said, "There's a young cashier at the grocery, and you should see her whenever a good-looking man goes by. She practically drools, bats her eyes, jokes with him, tells him he's sexy…even if his wife or girlfriend is right there." She scrunched her face and said, "She makes it look so easy. But, when I'm with you, I feel like I can't think of anything witty to say and it makes me feel kind of stupid when it comes to men." Heaving a huge sigh, she said, "There. I got it out. But now feel like a total idiot."

Laughter erupted from him and she immediately pinched her lips together. "Don't laugh at me!"

"No, no, babe," he said, reaching across and taking her hand. He pulled gently and she followed, standing and moving toward his chair. He drew her down to his lap, settling her close. "First of all, Aggie, I'd never laugh at you. But, you need to understand that sometimes I feel the same way that you do."

She was quiet, but peered closely, seeing sincerity in his eyes. "How?"

"Born and raised on a working farm, I didn't have a lot of time for anything other than school, sports, and helping my folks. It was a good life, but partying and hanging out with girls wasn't exactly how I spent my weekends. I joined the Army right after high school, so, there were no frat parties for me. Sure," he admitted, "we would party some to let off steam, but the female soldiers I worked with were just that—co-workers, and I was never going to go there. Too many headaches."

She reached up and held on to his wide shoulders, loving the feel of his muscles underneath her fingers.

Trying to ignore the feel of Agatha's touch, Nathan continued, "I've been friends with the Saints for about four years now, and would get invited out to the bars with them when some of them were still single. You should have seen Bart and Cam...they'd flirt with every pretty girl they saw and end up taking them home. I can't imagine how many women they...uh...well, were with before Miriam and Faith came along. Monty was high class and came from money. He never lacked female attention either. Marc was always the outdoorsy type and from, what I hear, had plenty of company to share his tents for a night."

Eyes wide, she said, "Wow. Isn't it kind of weird, now that they're all settled?"

"Not really. I mean, every one of those guys is now a one-woman man. They live and die for their mates."

He lifted his hand and tucked her hair behind her ear. "What I'm trying to say is…that wasn't me. I'm not a partier. I'm not a monk, either, but I didn't pick up women very often and none recently. I've never brought a woman to my house. It was always just physical, and honestly, not a lot of those."

Staring up at the handsome face that was filling her thoughts during the day and her dreams at night, Agatha wondered aloud, "Why not?"

Shrugging, he said, "I think I've always longed to have what my parents have and knew I'd never find that in a bar hookup." Holding her gaze, he finished, "So, you don't need to try to be coy, or flirtatious, or try to say a certain thing. Just be you. 'Cause I sure as fuck don't know how to turn on the charm to get a woman. All I can be is just me."

"So, if you're just being you, and you say that the temptation is killing you…what's happening?" By now, her hands had moved up from his shoulders to cup his strong jaw, the feel of his stubble rough underneath her fingertips. "I guess I kinda need things spelled out, plain and simple."

He grinned as he slid one hand up her back to cup the back of her head, drawing her closer. "Plain and simple is all I got, babe. I need to get you fed because the temptation to drag you to my bedroom and find all the ways I can make you moan with my mouth on your body, is hard to fight. Every time I hear you make those little noises, my dick gets harder. But, you're hungry and my daddy raised a gentleman. So, you eat first and then—"

"I'm no longer hungry for Chinese," she whispered, her eyes boring into his. "I just want you."

"Thank fuck," he growled, slamming his mouth onto hers.

16

Nathan stood and Agatha wrapped her legs around his waist, clinging to his shoulders with her hands. His chair fell backward, but they gave it no notice as he stalked down the hall to his bedroom. He made it to his bed, turned and fell backward, her body landing on top of his, an "umph" leaving her lips.

With a deft flip, he rolled her under him, planting his forearms on the mattress beside her to keep the pressure of his heavy weight off her. He stared at her for a moment, the air heavy with anticipation between them. Slowly, he lowered his mouth to hers, this time the kiss languorous. Nibbling at her bottom lip, he tugged it with his teeth before soothing it with his tongue.

She squirmed underneath him, feeling his thick cock pressing into her thigh. Her fingers dug into his shoulders again, pulling him closer even though their bodies were pressed together from toes to lips.

His kisses trailed down her jaw to the underside of her chin, continuing in their path until finally landing on the pulse point at the base of her neck. The fluttering of movement under his lips was the sign of her heart, beating for them.

A sound left her lips and he kissed his way upward again, wanting to hear every moan and capture them in his mouth.

"Tell me what you want, sweet Aggie," he begged, shifting his weight to the side, freeing a hand to slip underneath her shirt. Moving upward, the feel of her soft skin under his fingertips was a siren's call straight to his cock. His fingers grazed the underside of her breast and he halted, waiting for her reply.

Agatha sucked her lips in, desire pooling between her legs, her breasts heavy with longing for his fingers to inch higher. Her body, primed and quivering, lay in wait for his ministrations.

At her silence, Nathan lifted his head, peering into her face, uncertain of what he saw. "You want me to stop? Just say the word, babe, and this stops now."

"No," Agatha whispered, her voice hoarse with need. "I...I...don't know what to ask for." Seeing his eyebrow lift, she felt the heat of blush rise from her chest to her hairline. Her eyes slid to the side as embarrassment flooded throughout her being.

"Look at me," he ordered gently. Waiting until she shifted her gaze back to him, he asked, "We do this, it means something. And for it to mean something, I want us on the same page. So, you gotta talk to me." Waiting for a few seconds for his words to sink in, he asked, "Where did you go...when I asked what you wanted?"

"I..." she hesitated, her mind swirling and body

stiffening.

Feeling her muscles tense, he moved his hand from underneath her shirt and rolled to the side, pulling her with him. Shifting them on the bed, so their heads were on the pillows, he lay with her cuddled in his arms.

"Can I ask you something?"

She nodded, trying to hide the fear of what he was going to ask.

"Did something bad happen to you?" He watched as her wide-eyed gaze jumped to his. "Did someone hurt you…during sex?"

"No…I…no…" she stammered.

"Okay…" he acknowledged, his voice soft as his arms continued to hold her closely. "Are you a…?"

"I'm not a virgin," she blurted, her gaze on his chin and not his eyes. Heat infused her body and she knew she was ruining what should be a perfect evening. *He deserves honesty…well, as much as I can give him.* Clearing her throat, she said, "I'm not very experienced. In fact, I've only had sex once…uh…several years ago."

The idea of her being hurt or not being treated right, especially during her first time, sent anger throughout Nathan and he fought to steady his voice. "Did he hurt you—"

"No." Seeing the doubt in his eyes, she pinched her lips together. "This is so embarrassing," she whispered, mortified.

"For me to make this good for you, I need to know. There's nothing you could tell me that would change how I feel about you…how I want this to go."

Agatha held his gaze, knowing that giving all of the

truth would destroy them, but she wanted this with every fiber in her being. To be held. To be kissed. To have his body in hers...just hers...just Agatha, not Agnes, who was tainted with the sins of her family. Nodding, she answered, "I had just turned eighteen and was at a...uh...family gathering. A young man I liked took me into a closet and...I don't know...we sort of fumbled around. It didn't feel good, but he didn't hurt me on purpose. I wasn't forced, or anything like that...I just didn't know what I was doing and I'm not sure he did either."

"It hurt?" Nathan growled softly, forcing his voice to lower even though he wanted to roar.

She nodded, but rushed, "It was over quickly, so it wasn't too bad. After that, I...uh...didn't really want to. I just figured some people weren't made for sex." Sucking in a deep breath, she blew it out before adding, "When you asked me to tell you what I wanted, I didn't know what to say. I don't know the words to use. I mean, I know...from reading books. But," she shrugged, "I just felt stupid and awkward."

"Oh, babe," he groaned, pulling her closer while leaning over her, his hands now cupping her face. "I didn't mean for you to tell me exactly what you wanted me to do to you...I'll take care of that. In fact, taking care of you...in all ways, and that includes sexually, is my job. Or at least, I want it to be my job. And that fuckwad, who took you in a closet, pisses me off, because a woman should always be treated with respect and care. If he was any kind of man, he would have wanted your first time to be special and he should have taken care of you first. He didn't do that and your body wasn't ready. That's why it hurt. Babe, it should never hurt."

Agatha stared into his eyes, her fingers clinging to his biceps, as his words moved over her.

"But, I needed to know that you want this...us. I didn't want to make any assumptions based on lust. That's what I meant when I asked what you wanted. I just needed to hear that you wanted this tonight."

Her mouth opened but no words came out, so he continued. "I meant what I said earlier...we do this, it means something. I need to know if you're on the same page."

Her heart pounded with all that he said, both thrilled and terrified. He desired her and she had never felt desire from a man before.

Not finished, he added, "I also know you work with abused women, so you know how men can fuck up a woman. You gotta know, I would never take a hand to you. I would never let anger come between us. I plan on taking care of you, but I'm not a man who demands things go my way. If we disagree, then we discuss. I won't use sex as a way to control you. In fact, I don't control you. I might be bossy at times, and I'm sure you will be too," he smiled a little at that, "but your needs will always be first on my mind."

She nodded, understanding flooding her. Closing her eyes, she forced thoughts of her family to the background. *I'm not Agnes, daughter of abusers. I'm Agatha... rescuer of the abused.* Fighting to hold on to that thought, she nodded again, blurting, "I want this. I want you. I don't know what I'm doing, but if you show me what to do, I'm a fast learner."

A beautiful grin spread across his face as he leaned down, halting a breath away from her lips. "A fast learner...I like that."

Kissing her, he moved his mouth over hers, plunging his tongue inside, tasting her delicate flavor. She gave herself to him, letting him take the lead, but mimicking his movements. Tangling her tongue with his, she explored his mouth, enjoying the tingling sensation that his kiss sent to her core.

Once sure that she was right there with him, Nathan once more moved his hand to the bottom of her shirt, slipping upward along the soft skin of her belly, resting underneath her breasts. His thumb grazed her bra-covered nipple, feeling the hard bud beneath the soft material. Capturing her moan in his mouth, he cupped her breast, the weight heavy in his hand.

She began to squirm, heat pooling between her legs. His hand continued its path upward, taking her t-shirt over her head, exposing the green satin of her bra. Holding her gaze, he watched as she nodded permission, then, slid the bra strap from her shoulder as she unsnapped the front closure. Her breasts spilled out, the dark rosy nipples budding for him.

He took one in his mouth, sucking deeply before nipping with his teeth and soothing with his tongue. The delicious sensations caused her to moan once more, this time her hips writhing in need. Moving between breasts, he laved each one, his beard abrading the sensitive skin, leaving his mark.

She clutched his head as he kissed his way over her belly. Mewling in discontent when his lips left her body, he grinned as his fingers made their way to her jeans. Within a minute, he divested her of the rest of her clothing, laying her bare for his heated perusal.

"Fuck, sweet Aggie, you're beautiful," he said, his eyes roaming over her body, blinking as his gaze reached her lower abdomen. "You've got a tattoo," he said, surprise in his voice.

Bending to get a better look, the ink was done well but, while he was glad she had gone to a reputable place, a bolt of jealously shot through him at the location of the artist's work, just at her bikini line on her lower abdomen. A small lighthouse was inked into her pale skin, beams of light shooting from the top. "When did you get it?"

"About a year ago. I desperately wanted to do something that was so unlike what anyone would have expected," she replied, a little smile playing about her lips at the memory.

"A lighthouse?"

Nodding, she explained, "I had no idea what to get, but a friend suggested the lighthouse...I suppose the light in the darkness analogy. It was kind of a lark to get it, but, I'm glad I did. Of course," she laughed, "I was so afraid of it hurting, the tattoo artist gave me something that took the edge off, and before you get upset thinking I was roofied, my friend was with me the whole time. I was completely awake, but didn't feel any pain."

"Well, I have to admit they did a good job.".

Agatha leaned up, staring into Nathan's eyes, seeing honesty there. Her father had always said she was his little beauty. Her mother was gorgeous and people always said she looked like her. She had even noticed the eyes of other men following her...until they realized who she was and their eyes dropped in deference. Her father's men never looked at her as anything other than someone to guard. But that was as Agnes.

As Agatha, she avoided places where she might be noticed...recognized. Harlan had assured her she was still pretty, with her shorter, blonde hair, amber eyes, altered nose and teeth. She had always told him that her looks no longer mattered. Living life, her way, was what was important.

But, right now, right here, as this man she respected stared at her in unabashed desire, she smiled, her heart lighter. Opening her arms, she invited him in.

He bent, kissing the inside of her thighs, before gliding his hand through her damp folds. She gasped at the unfamiliar touch, but as he inserted a thick finger into her sex, her gasp turned into a moan. With his thumb pressing against her clit, he moved his finger deep inside, discovering the motions that made her moan even louder.

It only took a moment before she grabbed the sheets with her fists, her hips jerking upward as the sensations wound tighter inside. Just as he increased the pressure on her clit, she erupted, a volcano of molten heat searing her core, sending shock waves throughout her body. Crying out, she shook from the inside out as her core squeezed his finger. After what seemed like an eternity, her body relaxed, exhausted and sated as she floated back to earth.

Opening her eyes, heavy with lust, she gazed at his satisfied expression, watching as he brought his finger to his mouth, sucking off her juices.

"Oh, my," she breathed. "I've never..."

He kissed her and she tasted the unfamiliar essence of herself on his lips where he had sucked his finger. Blowing out a breath, she wondered if she would have the energy to finish what they had started.

"Give me a minute and oh, yeah, you will, babe. But don't worry, I'll do all the work."

She realized she had spoken out loud and grinned, too sated to be embarrassed.

He stood quickly, jerking his shirt off his body, exposing the muscles in his chest and arms as they flexed. His fingers made short work of unfastening his jeans and they soon found their place on the floor along with the other discarded clothing, including his boxers. Grabbing a condom from his wallet, he rolled it on.

His cock, long and thick, stood out from his body and he fisted it as he crawled over her. Centering the tip at her entrance, he pushed in gently, an inch at a time, giving her a chance to become accustomed to him. Once seated fully, he waited, sweat beading on his forehead.

"I didn't think you'd fit," she confessed in a whisper.

"Oh, babe. I fit like we were made for each other."

She squirmed in need, and, taking the hint, he began to move. Thrusting slowly, he allowed her juices to ease the movement, and soon he was plunging deeply, hard and fast.

Deep inside, Nathan's cock felt like it had slid into a perfect glove, one made just for him. He was truthful when he told her he was not a man who sought out a lot of sex, but he had enough experience to know what was happening was far beyond the physical, far beyond his expectations of what it would feel like to be with someone you truly cared about. The realization that he had wasted time chasing after a dream woman, almost casting this woman away, had him clenching his teeth. Agatha was everything...her body, lush and ready, accepted his like they were made to be together, matching his movements perfectly. Wanting her to come again, he forced his plunges to slow, dragging along the inside of her slick core, building friction.

Agatha's hands clutched his shoulders as she brought her feet up to press against his hard ass, urging him on. The ride was taking her places she never knew existed. Mountaintop high...soaring with the birds...heading to the sun. Her eyes closed, the light bright behind her lids as she felt her body tighten inside. How would she ever survive this? It was too good.

Exploding again, she jerked upward as her nails dug into his skin, her core firing in all directions. Every nerve of her body tingled and, for a second, she wondered if this were normal or if she were dying from sexual pleasure overload. Before she had a chance to ponder that idea any longer, she felt his muscles stiffen against her fingers.

Nathan roared as his head jerked upward, the veins

in his neck standing in stark relief to the thick muscles, tight with strength, as his orgasm blasted from him. No thoughts came to him, his mind engulfed in the pleasure of claiming her body. He continued to thrust slowly until every drop had been expelled from his body, finally falling to the side, making sure to take her with him.

They lay, bodies entangled together, heat pouring off each other, as their racing heartbeats began to slow. He held her close, her head tucked under his chin and wanted to pound his chest in a primal show of pride. He was beginning to understand she had a past that scarred her, one that she had only begun to divulge, but still, he wanted all of her...her past, secrets, dreams, desires, and her future.

The night sky outside the window was cloudless, the stars shining bright. Facing the window, tucked against his chest, Agatha loved how she could see above the tree line into the sky.

"The stars are so bright tonight," she said, barely whispering, not wanting to break the spell weaving between them.

He nodded, his chin against her hair. "I love laying here, staring at them in the night. I once told someone that they are brighter here, where we are far away from the city lights. It allows the stars to illuminate more."

Her hand that had been traveling along his arm jerked to a halt for a second, before continuing its path. "Was she someone important?"

Chuckling, he asked, "Who said I was talking to a woman?"

"I hardly think you'd be talking about the stars to a man," she said, her calm façade firmly in place.

"Yeah, she was special. We weren't involved…not like you're thinking. But someone who I met in tragic circumstances and spent a little time with."

They continued to stroke each other and she hoped if he noticed her heart racing, he'd just attribute it to the sex.

"Did you care for her?"

Wondering why she was asking, Nathan inwardly cursed bringing up the subject, thinking she was probably self-conscious.

"Yes and no," he replied honestly. "She was very special and I admired her. I confess that for a long time, I thought of her and wished that we could see each other again. But, that was not to be. She left and I have no idea where she is. But, that was all it was ever meant to be. I only spent an hour with her, just talking. She wasn't…real…for me, not like you are. You, sweet Aggie," he said, rolling her over so that her face was illuminated by the moonlight and he could peer into her eyes, "are here, in my arms, in my bed, in my life. Just where I want you to be. There has never been anyone in my heart the way you are."

A tear slid from her eye, dropping to the bed below, and he leaned over, kissing its wet trail.

"Thank you," she whispered.

"Oh, babe, you don't have to thank me. You've given me the gift of you and I'm humbled to receive it."

Wrapping their arms around each other, their lips met, once more consuming them in flames.

17

An hour later, they climbed from bed at Nathan's insistence. "Aggie, I still haven't fed you. I know you have to be famished."

She slid into her panties and jeans, but before she could reach for her shirt, he stopped her with his hand on her hip.

Looking up, he handed her one of his t-shirts. She stared at it for a second, then her gaze darted to him.

"I've never had another woman wear my shirt. I'd like to see it on you." She grinned, silently taking it and pulling the soft material over her head, letting it settle over her hips.

He pulled on his boxers and jeans, leaving the top button undone. Seeing her stare, he tilted his head in question.

"That's the sexiest thing I've ever seen," she confessed.

His features softened and he opened his arms, gently ordering, "Here, babe."

She willingly went into his arms, loving the feel of being held tightly against his body. Closing her eyes, she felt washed clean, as though his care had erased her past. Breathing deeply, she squeezed his middle. "If you keep being this sweet to me, you'll spoil me."

Nathan wondered about her comment and leaned back to peer into her face. "Aggie, being sweet doesn't spoil. But, if it does, then you can expect to be spoiled." Giving her a nudge, he said, "Let's go heat some Chinese."

They walked into the kitchen, placed the containers into the microwave, and re-heated the food before they sat at the table to finish their meal. Scarlett lifted her head from the sofa and stared at them for a moment before going back to sleep.

"She probably wishes we'd take the food over to the sofa where she is," he laughed.

"Do you always eat at the table when it's just you?"

Chewing and swallowing first, he said, "Yeah. My mom always said that meals should be eaten at the table. We never sat in front of the TV when eating. She was a real stickler for that."

"Were you happy growing up on the farm?"

Nodding, he replied, "Of course, I didn't know any different. All kids just know whatever environment they're brought up in. It's not until we get older that we analyze our upbringing." Looking back down at his food, he missed her blink, long and slow, before she schooled her face again.

"But, yeah, I liked it. Hard work built these muscles. My dad knows about weather, crops, animals, trees, soil…he's smarter than a lot of other people I've met in my life who have fancy degrees. Mom, she's the salt of the earth. Hardworking, knows how to pinch a penny, but will give to anyone in need."

No longer eating, Agatha stared at the open admiration he had for his parents, so plain on his face. "I think that sounds wonderful," she said. "Truly wonderful."

Her voice sounded wistful, which reminded Nathan that Charlie's search had discovered her parents were deceased. He wanted to know more but did not want to ask unless she felt like sharing. Immediately contrite, he now hated that he had searched into her background. "You finished?" he asked, observing her empty plate.

"Yes, I'm stuffed." Standing, she began to clear the table, rinsing the dishes as he placed the leftovers into the refrigerator.

Closing the door, he turned to her, his brow lowered. "I know you're a grown woman without a curfew, but is it okay for you to be away from the center at night? I want you here, all night with me, but don't want your job to be in jeopardy."

She looked over her shoulder and smiled. "You're sweet, Nathan, but I'm fine. Ann's been trying to get me to go out more anyway." Blushing, she added, "And, when she found out you were picking me up today after having been gone for several days, her exact words were, 'don't come back tonight!'"

Relaxing, he smiled wide. "Well, all right, then. You want a beer or some wine? I thought we could pile up with Scarlett and see what's on TV."

"Wine would be great," she replied as she moved into

the living room, kneeling to scratch Scarlett behind the ears.

The large dog groaned and he laughed. "You keep doing that and you'll have a friend for life."

Grinning back at him, she asked, "And what about you? What do I have to do to keep you a friend for life."

He walked into the room with a beer and her wine in his hands, setting them down on the coffee table. "Oh, sweet Aggie. You keep doing just what you're doing to me and you've got me, babe." He bent to kiss her lips, the taste of Chinese spices on her tongue exploding against his. Pulling back, he adjusted his cock, knowing she might be sore and needing a break from sex.

"Find something on TV, babe. I forgot I've got a couple of Angel's cupcakes for dessert."

"Oh, God, I thought I was full, but the thought of one of her cupcakes... I'll make room for that!"

She looked at the sofa but the large dog was taking up all of the space so she perched on the edge of the coffee table, with the remote in her hand.

As he returned with the two cupcakes on saucers her eyes grew large. "I can't eat all of that. Can we share one and save one?"

"Sure," he replied, noticing Scarlett, lounging on the sofa. With a whistle, her head shot up and she climbed down from the furniture, settling on the rug. Giving a hand to Agatha, they sat next to each other, the plate of dessert held in his hand as he fed her bites of the delightful confection. Watching as her lips closed around the fork, he felt his dick stir again.

"Fuck, girl. Watching you eat is sexy. I might have to turn away or I'm liable to carry you back to my room for more than sleep."

Laughing, she licked the frosting off her lips before sticking her finger into more from the plate and smearing it on his lips and kissing it off. The movement took him by surprise and he tossed the empty saucer to the coffee table with a clatter. Flipping her underneath him, he latched onto her lips, taking over the kiss. Wet and with full tongue, he tasted wine and confection, intoxicated with her essence.

Finally breaking apart, his cock aching as it pressed against his jeans, he panted. "Damn," he breathed, staring into her face. Shoving his arms into the sofa, he lifted his body off hers and stood. Scrubbing his hand over his face, he grinned. "I'm gonna go out and let the other dogs in for a while while you find something on TV. I'm determined to do this right and not make tonight all about sex. Although, fuck girl, this is a test to see if I can control my urges."

She giggled, sitting up and straightening her shirt. "Yes, you go get the dogs and I'll find something non-sexy on TV."

Kissing the top of her head, he jogged out to the kennel, Scarlett on his heels. Not wanting to keep her waiting, he hustled letting the others out of their runs. "All right, you all. You're my chaperones for a while, but just don't completely cock-block me."

Slapping his leg as he whistled, he opened the kennel door, all four dogs jumping happily around his legs.

Inside, Agatha flipped the channels, not finding

anything interesting to watch. No chick-flick. No action film. No stupid TV sitcom. Blowing out a deep breath, she continued to channel surf. Finally, an old movie popped up on the screen.

A noise at the door sounded and she stood, observing Nathan and the four dogs trotting in, excited to be part of the date. They bounded into the room, immediately sniffing her. She laughed as she petted each one and nodded toward the TV. "Look what I found! Scarlett's namesake."

Walking into the kitchen, Nathan looked over to see *Gone with the Wind's* Scarlett O'Hara filling the screen. His gaze shifted to Agatha's smiling face, focused on rubbing the dogs in front of her. His feet slowed as he watched her carefully.

"Your grandmother would be so proud of you, watching this movie on your date," she said, rising to her feet with the dogs circling her, her smile now beaming at him.

Heart pounding as the blood rushed through his ears, he turned, taking a step forward, his hands landing on the counter, needing the support to hold up his legs. "What did you say?" he asked, his voice like gravel.

Agatha tilted her head slightly, staring at Nathan as the smile slowly slid from her face. Confused at his tone for a second, it finally dawned on her that she had just carelessly given herself away. The air in the room suddenly felt thin, and she gasped, trying to breathe. Panicked, she scanned the room for an exit. With the dogs creating a barrier between she and the kitchen, Nathan wouldn't be able to follow her too quickly, which gave her a head start. In a flash, she dashed toward the still-open door, flying down the steps and running toward the woods. She had no clue where she was going, but Harlan's words were screaming through her mind, "don't ever tell anyone who you really are", "be safe at all costs." She had to get away, as fast as she could. Away from him. Away from her past. Away from the woman he now saw in front of him, the old her, blocking out who she was now.

18

———————

"Fuck!" Nathan yelled, his feet tangling with the excited dogs, thinking the ensuing game was fun. After stumbling, he whistled and the dogs immediately obeyed, trotting beside him as they poured through the door.

With bare feet, there was no way Agatha could get very far but, looking around, he spotted her flying down the driveway anyway. The dogs keeping pace, he ran as fast as he could after her.

"Agnes! Stop!" he yelled, his commanding voice booming out.

She obeyed, skidding to a stop, but stayed facing away. The dogs bounded to her but this time she did not bend to rub their ears. He whistled and they trotted away from her, coming to stop at his side. Her arms wrapped around her waist, holding on tight, as though she were afraid that, if she let go, her body would fly apart.

He stood several feet behind her, his chest heaving not with exertion, but with incredulity. *How can this be?*

The woman I've dreamed of, standing in front of me...the woman I let go of, because she wasn't this woman...my match...the woman I just made love to. The woman I would protect with my life...the fuckin' woman we've been looking for because she is in danger *and I need* to protect her. And *she's been right here all this time.* Heat coursed through his blood, frustration turning into anger.

"You got nothin' to say to me...Agnes?" he bit out.

Shaking her head, she turned in slow motion, eyes closed, silent tears sliding down her cheeks. "Don't call me that," she choked. "Agnes died that night. Agatha was born in her place."

Hands on his hips, he fisted them, the desire to grab her shoulders and shake her was overwhelming.

"You lied to me," he accused, ignoring the peevishness in his voice.

Snorting, she dared to lift her gaze to him, wincing slightly as the anger in his face sliced into her. "You know why. You...of anyone...you, who has sat across from my family...you know why." A sob broke free, but she swallowed it back, her chest heaving with the effort.

"You knew who I was the first time you saw me...at the center?"

She nodded.

"And this?" he ground out, throwing his arms back toward the cabin. "What was this?"

"You have to ask?" Agatha's heart ached so much she feared it would burst, leaving her to lie in the gravel, decimated, cast off and alone.

"Yeah, I have to ask, Agnes...Agatha...whoever the fuck you are."

Lifting a shaking hand, she pointed to her chest. "You know who I am. You called me your Aggie. No other names matter. No other name is really me." Choking on a sob, she said, "I tried to stay away, but when you've thought of someone for two years... someone you barely know but you felt something with them and they saved your life, then finding that someone again...it makes you reckless. And then, *then*, getting to know you and realizing you were so much more than that whisper of a dream, that you were real, and here, and *mine*... Being here with you might have been a mistake but only because it was reckless...not because it wasn't right."

He dragged his hand through his hair, frustration pouring from every fiber in his body. Turning from her, he sucked in a ragged breath, before facing her again.

Without breaking eye contact, he pulled his phone from his pocket. Pressing buttons without looked down, he lifted it to his ear. "Gotta meet. Now. Can't wait till morning. Need everyone. Keep Bethany away." Silence as he listened. "Right. Thirty minutes."

He disconnected and she stared, horrified at him. "You...you're turning me in." Chest heaving, she backed up a step.

"You got nowhere to go. You run, I'll be on you instantly. Let's go."

She stood, under the stars that were no longer brilliant in the sky, and didn't move.

"You're safe. I promise," he vowed.

"Don't make promises you can't keep." Her voice, a raspy whisper, cut through the night.

Finally, on wooden legs that moved of their own volition because she was sure that she no longer had control over her body...or destiny...she walked unsteadily toward the cabin, passing him without giving him a second glance. Once inside, she headed to the bedroom, feeling his presence directly behind her.

Bending, she picked up her shirt off the floor. Jerking his t-shirt over her head, she immediately pulled her shirt on. Walking past him again, she moved to the living room and sat on the sofa, putting her shoes on before picking up her purse.

"You need to put the dogs in the kennel," she said, her voice flat, emotionless. "I'll sit here and wait. I won't try to run." Her steady voice suddenly broke, as she said, "I'm so fucking tired of running."

Nathan almost pulled her into his arms, promising to hold her forever, but the words choked in his throat. Turning, he whistled and led the dogs back to the kennel. A man at war with himself, he stood, for what seemed eternity, in his yard, his fists at his hips, before sighing and walking back into his house. She still sat, as she said she would, on the sofa waiting.

As soon as Nathan returned, Agatha stood and walked to the door, silently passing him, not stopping until she had climbed into the cab of his truck. It hit her then, that everything was different now. He had once told her that his dad told him a man always opens the door for a lady. This time, she had opened the truck door herself, proof that he no longer considered her worthy of that respect. *He sees me as Agnes...no longer Agatha.*

Hopping in, Nathan sat in the driver's seat for a moment in silence, before saying, "I didn't mean for you to get into the truck by yourself. I'm sorry."

She nodded her acknowledgement but did not reply. He started the truck and pulled out down the long driveway, the forest on either side of the gravel path passing by in the darkness.

Neither spoke...neither knew what to say.

It wasn't long before they pulled up in front of a massive, luxury log home, the security lights on the outside illuminating the entire area. Though stunned at the size and not knowing where they were going, Agatha refused to ask any questions. Harlan had taken her places she didn't know for reasons of his own, and she had learned to trust where they were going. Things might be messed up with Nathan now, but she still trusted that he would protect her. As soon as he had parked among the other trucks and SUVs, she placed her hand on the door, but he reached across the console and halted her movement.

"Please, allow me."

His voice sounded pained. She did not turn to look at him, but she stilled her hand. He sighed and climbed down from his truck, rounding the front and opening her door. Escorting her up the wide steps to the over-sized porch, the front door opened before he had a chance to ring the bell.

Jack stood in the doorway, his sharp gaze shifting

between the two of them, but he only said, "Come in. We're all here."

Nathan propelled her forward with his hand now resting on her back, his fingers burning through her shirt, but as soon as she stepped into the house, she forgot all about his claiming hand on her. Coming to a sharp halt, she took in the massive living room. It was overwhelming, with a two-story stone fireplace that continued up to the vaulted ceiling. Floor to ceiling windows flanked the wall facing the mountains, and oversized furniture that would appear crowded in any other house felt welcoming in the cavernous space.

There were three, long sofas, forming a U, each able to seat four large men, with two overstuffed chairs flanking the fireplace. The space would seem masculine but for the colorful throw pillows and afghans tossed on the furniture. A large toy chest in the corner gave proof that a family lived here.

She could almost fool herself that she was wanted here, invited, but instead of feeling calmed by a welcoming committee, she stumbled at the sight of the eleven men and one woman in the room. Sucking in a quick breath, she dropped her eyes, not wanting to see the censure on their faces. Nathan took her elbow, offering a steady hand as he pulled her closer, and looked at the others.

Jack crossed the floor and said, "Most of you have met Ms. Agatha Christel, one of the employees from the Safe Harbor Center. We recently set up the security and helped them move." He looked at her and introduced everyone, even though she'd met most of them before, save Charlie, the only woman in the room, standing close to Luke, and it dawned on her that they didn't know who she was yet.

Turning, Jack's sharp gaze passed through her to Nathan, and he said, "So, what's going on?"

Nathan looked down at Agatha's pale, rigid body. As much as she had to hate him right now, he knew he needed to do this to make her safe. Looking at the other Saints, he said, "I'd like to introduce Agnes Gruzinsky."

19

Perched on the edge of one of the large sofas in the room, her hands primly clasped in her lap, Agatha kept her eyes down, refusing to look at the expressions coming from the Saints in the room.

As soon as Nathan had introduced her by her birth name, they had all visibly startled and *'what the fucks'* resounded. She imagined that Jack was not a man easily caught off guard, but by the look on his face after Nathan's pronouncement, the Saint's iconic leader had been stunned.

Jack had stood, silent as stone for a moment, as the others looked to him for direction. He finally spoke, saying, "I suggest we sit down and you tell us what you know, Ms. Gruzinsky."

"Ms. Christel, if you don't mind," she said, her words stilted with no intonation.

"All right…Ms. Christel…if you please," Jack agreed, his hand waving toward the seating.

She hesitated, but it appeared everyone was waiting

for her, so she moved toward one of the chairs. Nathan's hand rested on her back again, propelling her toward a sofa instead. Desiring to sit alone in a chair, she was uncertain if there were special seating arrangements, so she allowed him to guide her to the sofa, but chose the end and perched on the edge, her back ramrod straight, refusing to sink into the cushions. Nathan had sat next to her, leaning against the back of the sofa.

Jack spoke now and she lifted her head. "Bayley gave us her rendition of the conversation the two of you had in the woods that night, but we'd like to hear your version."

Swallowing against the lump that had taken permanent residence in her throat, she asked, "Why? What could it matter now?"

Jack's gaze shifted to Nathan, who offered a shake of his head. Sitting slightly behind her, she was unable to see the movement, but she felt it all the same. Jack explained, "We're working a case and it would assist us to hear what happened that night…and since then."

She sucked in her lips, wondering what case they could be working on that involved her. *Why hasn't Harlan told me about this?* Granted, she and Harlan rarely spoke now since she was entrenched in her new identity but, if he knew, and whatever it was put her in danger in some way, she felt certain he would have contacted her. Time stood still and she heard every breath taken in the room as they waited for her to speak. Swallowing deeply again, she clenched her fingers tighter together as she steeled her spine.

Lifting her eyes, she focused her gaze on the stone fireplace, gathering strength from its solid surface, ignoring the expressions she knew she would see if she dared to look at the others in the room.

"I was the little sister in my family, treated like a princess. But as I grew older, I noticed that my brothers had respect, simply because they were men. My mother appeared to have...clout in the family, but I was supposed to be quiet, demure, and never cause waves. My brothers were learning the family business, but I was expected to stay pure, marry into another Russian family, and make more Russian babies...preferably male." Shaking her head, she added, "So draconian...but it was my life."

Licking her lips, she continued, "Our family business was running the hotel and when I was old enough, my mother decided that I could help...in the way that a *woman* could help. I learned a bit about the hotel, but it was the rooms in the back that fascinated me, because they were off limits which, of course, made me curious. The other rooms held guests, but there were back rooms that only some men were led to. Always escorted. When I was fifteen, my mother allowed me to visit with her to check on the occupants. I had no idea anyone lived back there. She said that the men couldn't be trusted to take care of the occupants, so it was our duty to see that all was well, for the business. I couldn't wait to see what was inside."

She felt Nathan's fingers warm on her back, but ignored the burn of his touch, knowing it was the last touch from him she would experience. Sucking in a deep breath through her nose, she let it out slowly.

"The first room we entered was just a plain bedroom with a small bathroom. And the only occupant was a woman. Pale. Thin. Her face looked...empty. She barely looked at my mother, keeping her eyes down the whole time we were there, but when my mother placed the food on the table and turned away, I caught her looking at me. Her eyes were...haunted." Chest heaving, she added, "We left the room, my mother locked the door, and we walked away."

Closing her eyes, she hated the images passing behind her eyelids. Giving her head a shake, she cleared the cobwebs from the memories she had tried to shut away in her mind. "I was young, naïve, I had no idea why the girl was there, but I knew, instinctively, it was not good. I tried to ask my mother, but she only said the girl was an employee. And Mama's voice and mannerisms let me know that if I continued to question, I would be punished." A rueful snort sounded, as she added, "My mother loved her children but her punishments were swift and harsh."

Nathan's fingers twitched on Agatha's back and, as he listened, his jaw tightened until he thought his teeth would crack from the pressure. He knew what the Gruzinsky's business had involved, but he had never thought of what it would have been like to grow up in that family. What she had suffered. *Fuckin' hell, how did she handle that?* Keeping his eyes on her, he realized she handled it by doing exactly what she was doing now... keeping her emotions in check.

After a moment of silence, Charlie rose from her seat and moved into the kitchen, returning with a glass of water and handing it to Agatha. Grateful, she took a long sip, the cold liquid refreshing her parched throat.

"I couldn't get that girl's eyes out of my mind. I was sheltered, so I admit it took a while to learn that the girls were there to serve the men who came specifically for them." Sighing, she squeezed her eyes shut, the grimace she could not hide indicating her pain. "When I was older, I once saw Lazlo coming out of the same room, zipping his pants and laughing. He was followed by one of his friends and they were laughing about her. By then, I was old enough to know what was going on."

Nathan opened his mouth to speak but, trying to understand the world she had lived in, he doubted any words could suffice. He offered his comfort by sliding his hand to hers, finding them cold to the touch. She did not open her hands for him, keeping them clenched together, her knuckles white, so he enveloped her hands in his larger one.

"I kept quiet...but I watched...learned. I was smart and soon realized that I was smarter than either of my brothers. I watched my father, mother, and brothers run a family *business* that included the buying and selling of women. And if you wonder how I lived with that knowledge, I'll just say that I learned early the price of going against the family." Shuddering, she explained, "While I was treated as a princess as a young girl, as I got older, I realized that it was not just my mother that doled out punishments for wrongdoings. My father had several men that were always around...I suppose you could call them enforcers. While I was sheltered from that aspect for the most part, I knew what happened at their hands from listening to my brothers talking about the broken bones and bodies of their enemies or those who had displeased my father. I'd never been the recipient of my father's anger, not like that, but just the thought that he could order something like that to happen..."

Agatha heard the intakes of breaths around the room, but continued to stare at the large grey stones of the impressive fireplace.

"For a long time, I had no idea what to do with the horrible knowledge. It haunted my dreams...like living in a nightmare, only one in which I could not awaken from. In my family, women were second class. Oh, believe me, my mother was revered for her honored place as wife and mother, and I was certainly treated as a favored child." Shaking her head, she added, "I was not allowed to go to public school, instead was home-schooled. They would have never allowed me to attend college." Shaking her head again, she whispered, "Most people would never believe that the old ways still exist."

Sucking in a fortifying breath, she continued, "I lived at home...trapped in a gilded cage. Please don't mistake me...I'm not asking for pity...that should go to the women they abused." She continued to stare ahead at the stones, "But, I had to get out, and I had to get them out, so I plotted and planned. I discovered that there were basement rooms where they brought in new girls, keeping them there until they could be checked out by the doctor, made a little hungry, a lot scared, and then moved them upstairs. When they were ready to replace the upstairs girls, I heard they were shipped off to our relatives in Norfolk, who used them however they wanted.

"I had no problem getting the doctor to help me when I finally realized he hated what he was doing. I came up with a plan to sneak the women out in the laundry truck, but had to figure out how. I was struck with the idea that if they were all sick, they couldn't be around any clients. So, he started giving them some drugs that induced nausea and then we claimed that we had no idea what was happening but that they needed to be quarantined. My family was scared they might get sick so they stayed away. That was the easy part. Then I had to play the part of the ultimate bitch...the planner of a scheme that my family would go along with. Claiming to be uninterested in the women, I suggested we kill them and then ship them off. Our cousin in Norfolk was pissed to not get live women, but he was willing to take them out to sea to dump them."

She heard the audible gasps from the others in the room and felt Nathan's hand grip hers tighter. It was almost painful, but she did not flinch.

"Over time, as I became a young woman, I perfected the cold bitch persona and made it no secret that I wanted more of the family business responsibility. So... they believed it. Plus, Lazlo was screwing up and my parents were willing to take a chance on my idea. Of course, as I now know, they sent someone to follow me." Shrugging, she added, "The doctor drugged the girls to slow down their respiration, we got some of the family's hired men to take them to the truck, and the doctor and I drove away."

"And Harlan?"

For the first time in her recitation, her lips curved. "Harlan, my savior," she whispered, her face softening at the thought of him. "I made contact with an FBI agent." Giving a rueful chuckle, she said, "I was so naïve, I can't believe I wasn't caught. I actually called from a payphone, managing to get hold of someone who believed me. He was in on the plan. We were to meet at a warehouse and he would have medical personnel waiting to assist with the women. But an accident, shutting down the highway, made them late. And, of course, we didn't expect anyone, certainly not Bayley, to be following. Or the man my family sent."

Sighing once more, she whispered, "We knew it had risks, but it devolved quickly into a huge mess. After Harlan took possession of the women and got them to safety, he was going to take care of me. I was going to go into witness protection and testify against my family. I had to. I couldn't live with myself knowing that the very clothes on my back...the very food on my plate, came from the buying and selling of women against their will." For the first time, her voice cracked and she blinked furiously to keep the tears at bay. "I loved my family...and I hated them."

Nathan felt the strength begin to fade in her as her shoulders sagged. His mind raced with all she was saying. Her childhood compared to the loving family he grew up in. Her choices that bordered on life or death. He tried not to think about the confusing emotions he had been experiencing, caring for two women and now knowing they were the same person. When he first found out a few hours ago, he had been angry at her deception, but now he felt irritated with himself that he had reacted that way. She was right in a lot of the things she said to him back at the cabin, but she wrong about one thing...Agnes Gruzinsky did not die that night. Her strength of character still lived on in Agatha.

"I had to get to Harlan and that was when Nathan found me. He was kind enough to respect my wishes to get hold of him. Agents were sent to take me to him."

"And Harlan?" Jack asked carefully.

Her lips curving once more, she said softly, "He became everything to me. My surrogate father, mentor, friend. He had been shot, but it was not a serious wound, and he hid me until he was released. Then, he found out that with all the evidence against my family, I did not have to testify. In fact, they thought the FBI just raided them and I had been caught up in the escape. So, no witness protection program for me. Harlan knew I needed to escape and took care of everything. New contacts, surgery for my nose, new hair color, and dentistry. He had...uh...friends give me a whole new identity. Name, background, birth certificate, everything." She smiled slightly and her gaze left the fireplace for the first time, moving to Nick's face. "That night, in the woods, Bayley quoted Agatha Christy to me. The quote fit my life and I remembered it, so when they asked if I had a preference in a new name, I chose Agatha and told them why. They suggested Christel to go with it."

Shifting her gaze to Jack, she said, "I owe Harlan my life. He knew of the women's center and spoke to Ann about hiring me. She and I hit it off and I've been with them for a year. He said that I had no penance to pay but since I felt like I did, it was a good place for me to land."

"When was the last time you spoke to him?"

Her face soft with the memory, she said, "It's been over a month. He told me that I needed to learn to live without him, but I told him he would always be my best friend. I never wanted him to get in trouble for what he did for me, so I only called him occasionally. In fact, his birthday was early last month...that was when I last talked to him."

Charlie asked, "Who did he use to give you a new identity?"

Looking at the pretty dark-haired woman, sitting with Luke's arm around her, she replied, "I have no idea. I just know they did a good job because I've never had a problem with the new information they gave me. Harlan assured me that they were the best and would take care of me. He said if I ever had problems to let him know and he would have them get in touch with me."

"And now?" Jack asked.

"Now? I live my life. I try to not think of my parents or brothers in prison. I go to work and help other women, so that at the end of the day, I can look at myself in the mirror and see Agatha Christel, not the daughter of monsters."

Jack pressed on, "What do you know of Gavrill

Volkov?"

For the first time, she blinked, startled with the question. "Gavrill? He's my mother's cousin. I know he's powerful...runs a large shipping business from Norfolk. When Nathan mentioned you guys were going there, I'll admit, it freaked me out that you might be dealing with him in some way. My mother always spoke of him in reverent terms, almost like he was a god. When she was angry with my father or brothers, she would remind them of her connection with him."

"You mentioned him taking the girls. What can you tell us about that?"

Sucking in her lips, she winced. "Uh...well, I heard that he would take the older girls, the ones Lazlo used to hatefully say were..." She fought the bile threatening to rise in her throat, " 'used up'." A visible shiver crossed her body and she clenched her hands tighter and tighter together, until she thought her fingers would crack.

"I assume he would transfer them overseas to whatever horrible destination lay in wait for them. I based my plan on that concept, knowing that even if he were pissed at my family for costing him money, he would agree to the disposal of the bodies."

The room was deathly quiet, the ticking of the clock the only sound heard. Exhausted, she felt cold and longed to run away to hide once more. Feeling a squeeze, she looked down, seeing Nathan's hand still holding on to her gripped hands.

Swallowing deeply once more, she said, "I have no idea what case you're working on, but I need to talk to Harlan. I need to leave here and may, perhaps, need to assume a new identity. He'll know how to help me...he would want to help me."

The air in the room changed, electricity filling the space between the occupants. She noticed it but did not understand the reason.

Nathan's grip became tighter and he wrapped his other arm around Agatha's shoulders. His heart pounded and uncertainty filled him as he looked over at Jack, whose gaze was fixed on her.

Jack finally spoke, "Agatha, our job was *you*. To locate you, which we were unable to do since your new identity was so superbly arranged. But, we needed to find you...to protect you."

"Protect me? From what?" Her gaze jumped to his, confusion on her face.

"We're not sure, but are fairly certain that someone is after you. Our assumption is that it is Gavrill Volkov—"

Her gasp caused him to halt for a few seconds before continuing. "It appears that he is looking for retaliation for being caught in your family's raid and ending up in prison."

Her wide eyes showed fright and she croaked, "I need to talk to Harlan. Please let me call him."

"Aggie," Nathan said, his heart aching.

At the sound of her nickname from his lips, Agatha jerked her head around, finding him staring at her, sympathy in his eyes. "What is it?" she whispered, her voice barely heard.

He held her gaze and said, "Harlan is...I'm so sorry, Aggie, but he's dead."

She leapt to her feet, a scream tearing from her chest. Wild-eyed, her gaze jerking around to the Saints in the room, she backed away a few steps, crying, "No, no, no."

Nathan followed her up, the sound of her scream still ringing in his ears, and moved forward, his hands out in front of him. "Aggie, come on babe. It's gonna be okay, I promise."

Not hearing him, or unable to, she continued to shake her head in agony, still crying "No," over and over.

He advanced another step but she backed away from him. The other Saints had risen to their feet as well, their faces marred with concern, tension flowing from them.

Agatha threw up one hand as to fend off the wall of testosterone in the room. Her eyes unseeing, she reacted instinctively, doing everything she could to keep space between her and Nathan, who was slowly advancing on her.

"Take it easy, man." Blaise said, his voice soft. "Give her some space."

"Fuck that," Nathan said under his breath, "she's had enough of being on her own."

Ignoring the people in the room, she wrapped her arms around her middle, squeezing tightly, feeling the blood rushing from her head, making her woozy. All thoughts fled her mind, other than the desperate realization that she was all alone in the world, the one person who had saved her and risked so much dead. Her chin dropped, the weight of the world bearing down upon her, another sob ripping from her chest.

"Aggie," Nathan said again, his voice as gentle as he would use to speak to a skittish, rescue dog. "Please, babe, come here."

Through tears, she managed to ask, "How did he die?"

No one spoke and she lifted her hand to swipe at her tears still falling. Her stare penetrated each Saint as she gazed from one to the next. Not stopping on Nathan's face, she settled onto Jack's. "Tell me. Tell me how he died. He was fine the last time I talked with him."

Nathan, not taking his eyes off her, warned, "Jack."

"She's got to know."

Before he could protest again, she screamed, "Tell me!"

Charlie's eyes filled with tears as Luke pulled her closer. The others' faces were carved in stone, but frustration and anger filled their eyes.

Jack finally offered, "Ms. Christel, I'm sorry...he was murdered. It looked like an assassination...a hit that was ordered. The FBI are investigating, but have not made an arrest yet. They suspect Russian mafia."

What little blood was left in her face drained away. Gasping, she began chanting, "No, no, no," as she stumbled further away until her back hit the wall.

Nathan stepped forward again, his hands out, and said, "I promise...promise you're safe."

"You promise? Are you crazy?" Her eyes were still wide and wild, but now focused on his face, before she slumped to the floor, her legs no longer able to hold her upright. "Nobody can keep me safe. And don't you see? If someone does try, they'll get to them. Harlan promised." Another sob caused her to hiccup, but she kept going. "He promised I'd be safe...and look what happened to him!"

20

Cold…to her bones. Curled up on one end of the sofa in the now empty room, a blanket draped over her, Agatha shivered. The Saints had moved to the kitchen, but she could still hear their low voices, murmuring amongst themselves. For the past hour, she lay, weary but not sleeping, listening to them discuss her situation. *Situation.* She wanted to laugh out loud at the ludicrous description of someone killing her rescuer and now wanting to kill her.

Suddenly, a woman was kneeling in front of her, but her eyes refused to focus.

"Agatha? Sweetie, do you remember me? I'm Miriam…Cam's wife. I'm also a nurse. I want to take a look at you, okay? Will that be okay?"

She felt her arm being pulled from the blanket and, as though viewing the scene from above, she watched the dark-haired beauty take her pulse. She felt a blood pressure cuff expand but did not remember it being placed on her arm. Closing her eyes, she hoped that she could wake and the nightmare would be over. *It'll never be over.*

"What was that, Agatha? What'll never be over?" Miriam asked.

Realizing she must have spoken her thoughts aloud, she kept her eyes closed, not wanting to see the sympathy...*or disgust*, on the kind woman's face.

She felt a gentle hand brush her hair back from her face. She remembered her mother's hand on her face when she was ill as a child, singing a Russian lullaby to help her sleep. Before...long before her life fell apart. Now her mother was in prison...*by my hand. And the man who saved me is dead...killed in retaliation.*

Miriam moved away from Agatha and walked into the kitchen where everyone was gathered. Bethany, awakened by the screams, had come down and insisted on making coffee for everyone.

"Thanks for coming in the middle of the night," Jack said.

Leaning her weight onto Cam's sturdy body, she waved him off, "It was no problem. We live so close to both our families that my mom was more than happy to come stay in the house with the kids. I doubt they'll even wake up, but she's there."

Nathan, his heart in his throat, asked, "And...Aggie?"

Sighing, Miriam said, "Her blood pressure is actually low and so is her heartbeat. She needs rest for now—"

"I'd like to go home, please. Can someone take me back to the center?"

Agatha's robotic words came from the living room where she was now standing, the blanket still wrapped around her shoulders. Nathan broke away from the others, walking slowly to her side, not wanting to startle her, and grateful when she did not pull away.

"Babe, as soon as I find out what Jack's plan is, I'll take you back to my home—"

"No," she said, her voice firmer than she looked like she felt.

"Babe—"

"No, Nathan. No 'babe' and no to your home." She dragged her gaze to his face and shook her head. "You were right to be angry earlier. I recognized you right away, when you first came to the center, and didn't say anything, so what we had was built on a lie. And, I don't want to be at your cabin, hiding away. I have a job to do and need to get back to it."

"Agatha," Jack began, "we need to provide security for you while we work to find a connection between Gavrill and the threat on you."

"Can that be done at the center? All the cameras and alarms you all installed are secure, right? So I should be safe."

Sighing, Jack nodded, "Yes, we'll have eyes on you."

"Jack," Nathan began to protest.

"Nathan," she called, her voice low and laced with sadness. Lifting her hand to his arm, she said, "I want to go. I need to go."

"Aggie, please. You've been through a lot in a short amount of time. You need rest. You need a chance to—"

"I need a chance to grieve," she cut in. Sucking in a deep breath, she slid the blanket off her shoulders and folded it neatly, her movements slow and measured.

Turning to face the gathering, she looked each one in the eye, her calm façade sliding back into place. "Thank you for your care and I'm very sorry for all the trouble you're going through. I can't repay the costs for your protection, but I'll accept whatever you can offer just the same. I'm not stupid. I know I need it."

Jack stepped forward, his eyes kind as they rested on her. "Agatha, I'll have Nathan take you back to the center tonight. First thing in the morning the Saints will be working to see if we can determine how to neutralize the threat against you."

"Mr. Bryant, if the threat is coming from Gavrill, then the only way you'll get the connection is if he tries to get at me. Even in prison, he has a long arm. I trust in your protection, but you won't get him if I hide away."

Nathan, stunned silent, realized she was offering herself as bait. He placed his arm around her stiff shoulders, pulling her into his side.

"I promise, Agatha, you'll be safe with us," Jack said, his eyes gleaming with a firmness she clearly understood.

Nodding her thanks, she stiffened, but accepted a hug from Bethany and Miriam before turning to walk toward the front door. Halting suddenly, she turned back and faced the crowd. With her hands clasped together in front of her, she swallowed deeply. "I really am sorry...about my family."

"You can't help the family you were born into," Nathan assured, stepping close.

As his eyes penetrated the cold she felt around her heart, Agatha pinched her lips together.

"Agatha," Jack called out, pulling her eyes to his. "None of us are responsible for the actions of anyone other than ourselves. You are not your family. You are you. Agnes...or Agatha...you are you. And that's someone the Saints are proud to serve."

Unable to keep a tear from sliding down her cheek, she nodded stiffly, turned and walked out the front door with Nathan's arm around her shoulders.

The drive in the wee hours of the morning was silent, each lost to their own thoughts. Finally, Nathan broke the quiet, saying, "I thought about you. A lot. Over the past two years. While your face was always in the shadows, I could see you in my dreams. The last view I had of you was your face pressed to the glass of the SUV as you were driven away. I carried that vision with me always."

She listened, but did not respond. She was all talked out, no words forthcoming.

"The Saints' women would sometimes try to set me up with a friend of theirs, but I was never interested."

She considered all the women who would have been interested in this handsome man, with quiet strength, and wondered why he never went for one of them.

"Bart once told me that it takes a special woman to capture the eye of a Saint. Said we're wired differently. I didn't see myself as one of them for a long time...they seemed bigger than life and I felt like the odd one out. But, coming together to find you has made me see that I am one of them. And he was right…no ordinary woman would do. But you…your strength…the lengths you went to protect yourself and, then, protect all those women. I'm in awe of that strength."

She turned her head to look out her window, the heat of his eyes, gazing intently at her, too hot for her to endure.

"But, I figured I would never have a chance to see you again. I assumed you went into witness protection and were long gone. I began to give up the idea that I might see you again, tried to anyway, but you still filled my dreams. I have no idea if I recognized something in you the day we met at the center, though there was this strange sense of déjà vu I couldn't shake. What I know for sure is I was interested in you, as Agatha, from the moment we met. The crazy thing is that for the last couple of weeks, I've had an inner battle. The Saints were looking for Agnes, and she began to fill my mind again, but Agatha was filling my days, and beginning to fill my heart."

Hearing how he was torn between two women, not knowing they were the same person, she sighed heavily, realizing how difficult the past weeks must have been for him. "I'm sorry."

Silence swirled between them, before she admitted, "I also felt torn. For the past two years, I have thought of you endlessly. Thought of the man who came to rescue me. Thought of the man who helped me get to Harlan. Thought of the man who taught me to look up at the stars, and to see the brightness. You know, I try to look at the stars every night, and am reminded of you. When

I saw you in the center, I could not believe my eyes. It was a dream come true to see you again, and a nightmare that I could not tell you who I was. Harlan emphasized over and over, that I should have moved far away. But, I couldn't."

"Why not?"

She stayed silent, the truth too painful, tearing through her. Finally, recognizing he deserved to know it all, she whispered, "Because I always hoped that one day I might be able to see you again. I knew I could never have you, but just to see you again would have been worthwhile."

"And when you did?"

"I tried to stay away, but as you continued to come around and then showed interest in me, I could not help myself. I knew it was a risk, especially a risk to my heart, but I so wanted to be with you. I knew it couldn't be forever…but, then again, maybe I thought it could be. Maybe you'd never need to know who I was, would never figure it out. It was selfish, I know, but I couldn't let you go."

Pulling into a parking space in front of the center, he turned off the engine and twisted in his seat to look at her. As much as she knew it would hurt, she turned to look at him as well. His beard, usually neatly trimmed, was now scruffy. The lines around his eyes were deep with fatigue, but, his eyes, still burning with intensity, managed to penetrate the cold around her heart. She could only hope that he could find it in himself to forgive her.

"I'm so sorry—"

He sighed as he lifted his hand to cup her jaw. "Aggie, you don't have to apologize. I reacted badly and I'm the one who's sorry. When I had a chance to think about it, of course you had to keep your identity a secret. Harlan was right to drill that into you."

She closed her eyes, the touch from his warm hand on her face something she wanted to remember.

He leaned forward, his fingers at the back of her neck gently pulling her forward. His lips touched hers in a kiss as gentle as a whisper.

She melted under the sweet assault, his kiss sending warm tingles throughout her body, which now felt alive once more.

"You need to get inside, and get some sleep. I'll see you tomorrow," he said, pulling back reluctantly.

She blinked in surprise. Tilting her head to the side, she repeated, "Tomorrow?"

"Yeah, babe. I'll be over tomorrow as soon as I know all of Jack's plans."

Heart aching, she nodded. "Oh, yes... Jack's plans. Uh, it's okay, you know. I don't want you to feel like you have to watch over me."

"Why the hell would I not want to be here?"

"I don't want you to feel awkward," she began.

His brow lowered and he said, "Babe, you aren't making any sense."

"Jesus, Nathan! Do I have to spell it out for you? I know last night was special, before everything fell apart. I just don't know what we are now. And I know because you work for Jack, you have to be involved trying to protect me. But I don't want you to feel obligated."

Blowing out his breath, he said, "Okay, sweet Aggie. You're exhausted, you're grieving, and I can see that everything is muddled in your head, so, let me break this down for you. We've been building something for weeks and tonight, or rather last night now, we finally came together in a way that means something to me and I hope like hell, it means something to you too. It wasn't just sex, but a true joining of two people who I think are destined to be together. The only difference now is I know that both Agnes and Agatha make up my Aggie. And, darlin', you are my Aggie."

She started to speak but he continued over top of her.

"You know, deep inside, that you're not your family, but it still haunts you. I know you, I understand you, Aggie. You think you're not worthy, but what you've gotta hold on to is that you're more than worthy. And, if I have to remind you of that every day for the rest of your life, I will."

With a tear sliding down her cheek, her chest quivering, she bolted forward, slamming her mouth against his, pouring all her emotions into the kiss, letting it speak for her.

Undisclosed Location

"She's with the Saints."

The man standing by the conference table in the middle of the cavernous room nodded. "I noticed that."

"Do you think she's secure? Should we bring her in?" A third man, sitting at the table, swung his gaze to their leader.

Stoically, he replied, "I know them. Well, I know Jack Bryant. They've got an excellent reputation, but we made a promise to Harlan. I think we need to keep a close eye on her."

"I can do that without them knowing I'm checking."

Chuckling, he replied, "I would expect nothing less. Keep me advised." Walking away, he thought of his old friend, Jack, and how the case with Harlan had their businesses unexpectedly converging. With a slight smile, he moved through his cavernous compound.

21

Agatha hit the snooze button when it went off at seven a.m., but knew she needed to get out of bed. Attempting to open her eyes was difficult, considering they were still swollen from the tears the previous night and, as the light hit them, she felt like sand was embedded under her lids. Having promised one of the new women in the center, who was a mother, that she would help her children get on the school bus, she knew she needed to get out of bed.

Groaning, she pushed up and swung her legs over the side. Staggering to the sink, she grabbed a washcloth, wet it with cold water, and pressed it to her aching eyes. After a few minutes, she could finally open them and look around.

Her stomach threatened to revolt as Harlan's death hit her. Sucking in a deep breath, she willed the nausea to quell. Memories flittered through her mind, like flipping through a photo album. His smile. His eyes that twinkled even when he pretended to be grumpy. How he made strong coffee each morning. Watching sports on TV in the evenings with him...something her family never did. *Oh, God, Harlan...did you die trying to protect me?*

Finally, loosening her grip on the counter, she continued to breathe deeply until she was sure her legs would hold her up. Dressing, she headed down the hall, grateful to find the woman already in the kitchen feeding her children breakfast.

"Good morning, Ms. Christel," Beverly said, smiling at her over the heads of her two daughters. "The girls are almost ready. They're finishing breakfast now and then you can show us to the bus stop."

Forcing a smile on her face, she said, "Good morning to you, too. You'll like your new school. We've had several children who have attended and they were very happy there." She knew the staff and administration at that school were particularly aware of the children who came from the center's situations.

Within a few minutes, she and Beverly waved goodbye to the girls as the yellow school bus left the parking lot.

Beverly turned to her, and commented, "I hate to mention it, Ms. Christel, but you look worse for the wear this morning. Are you okay?"

Lifting her hand to smooth her hair back from her face, she nodded. "Yes, I'm fine. I just didn't get a lot of sleep last night." Using her well-practiced façade, she smiled at the other women as they walked back inside.

Ann walked into the center not long after she was

done checking on the women in the computer lab, and motioned for her to follow. They went into Ann's office and sat as she said, "Agatha, I wanted to talk to you about something, but you look ill this morning."

"No, no," she lied once more. "Just a bad night."

Nodding, Ann said, "Okay, I've got something that I want to talk to you about and I've been thinking about it for a while, but needed to get the move completed before I could focus on anything else."

Curious, she sat calmly waiting to see what Ann was going to say. Her palms began to sweat, though, as she considered whether or not Ann could possibly know about her other identity. *Is she going to ask me to leave?*

"Don't look so nervous!" Ann laughed. "You look as though I'm going to send you to the firing squad." Tapping her pencil on the desk before she stuck it behind her ear, she said," I really like the work you've been doing here. You've taken on the role of so much more than just an assistant and, since I'm spending more and more time with fundraising, making sure the center has the money and donations it needs to continue to run, I need someone to be a manager. I wondered if you would step into that role. I would so much rather you take the position, than me have to find a manager while you stay on as the assistant. Of course, it would be a raise in pay."

Blinking, she stared at her boss. Incredulous that she was being offered a promotion instead of getting the sack, she continued to stare mutely, with her mouth hanging open.

"I take it I've caught you by surprise?"

"Uh...yes, to be honest...yes."

"I know there are things in your past you have close to your heart and," throwing her hand up quickly, she said, "I have no intention of asking about them. But, whatever it is, it's made you a wonderful advocate for the women that come here seeking shelter. You truly help them to find their worth as a woman. I need a manager and cannot think of anyone more qualified than you."

"But, Ann, I don't have a college degree."

"You don't need a college degree to take care of the work that needs to be done here. We have counselors we rely on for their psychological needs. I need someone who works here on a daily basis, who under-stands the working of this center. Quite frankly, the job you do now is already managerial work. But, you will finally get the raise that you deserve." Giving her a minute to think over the idea, Ann smiled, before asking, "So, what do you think?"

Unable to believe that a day that had started out so terrible had a silver lining like this one, she smiled openly. "I would love to be the manager!"

Ann leaned forward, sticking her hand across the desk, and she reached over to clasp hands, shaking on the deal. "I have one more thing I want to talk to you about."

She tilted her head to the side, waiting to see what her request was going to be.

"Ever since you've worked for me, I've allowed you to have a room at the center." Seeing her eyes widen,

Ann hurried to say, "That's not changing. You may certainly have a room here if you need one. But, it's important, for your mental health, to have a division between work your personal life. My fear is that those two are intertwined for you. Becoming the manager at the center means that you need to be able to be mentally rested and healthy. If you need to continue to stay here, that's fine. But, I would like to encourage you to look for a place on your own. That way it will be easier for you to separate your work and personal life."

"Okay," she replied slowly, her thoughts swirling with the uncertainty of how to find a place of her own. Nathan's cabin flashed through her mind, but she pushed it away. "I'll start looking."

"As far as I'm concerned, the managerial job starts today. I do have to put it in front of the board but, as I've already mentioned it to them, I can tell you they're thrilled to have you take the position."

Ann stood and walked around her desk, her arms out to engulf Agatha in a hug. "Congratulations, sweetie."

Tears threatened to spill again but she blinked them back, knowing her eyes would never stop swelling if she did not gain control over her emotions. Walking out of the office, she thought of Nathan's words from hours before. *"What you've gotta hold on to is that you're more than worthy."* Moving to her room, needing a few minutes to pull herself together, she could not keep the hope from her heart, remembering Harlan so often saying the same thing. *Maybe, just maybe...he was right.*

"This sucks!" growled Nathan. His jaw ached from the tension as he stared at the other Saints. "How can things keep going so bad for Agatha?"

The Saints, despite little sleep the night before, had arrived early to talk about the security measures for her. At first, they'd felt at ease, since they now knew who Agnes Gruzinsky was and were sure of their ability to protect her. Then, Luke had reported communications between Gavrill and Yurgi that could indicate they were calling in all markers to get to her.

"The thing is," Luke said, "to anyone else, their communication would look like nothing more than two brothers discussing the family's *legitimate* business." He flashed the deciphered communication onto the white board for the others to peruse.

G: All is well. Continued interest in locating missing subcontractor.

Y: Still looking. Their business is difficult to determine.

G: Ask managers for that information. We want our business to continue. They will let you know who can assist.

Y: Will do.

G: Was anything found with new property search?

Y: No. There was an infestation problem. Could not get the details. That avenue closed off.

G: Unfortunate. Still, satisfying to close the door on that opportunity. Keep working sub-contractor problem. Time, money, freedom all tied up in busi-

ness. Would like subcontractor whereabouts known.

Y: Will talk soon.

"It doesn't take a genius to figure out that subcontractor is Agatha, and the search refers to Harlan's apartment and computer. 'Close the door on that opportunity'? Yeah, they're fuckin' responsible for Harlan's murder. The good news is, at least it appears that Harlan, and whoever helped him with Agatha's identity, set up his computer to release a virus if someone else tried to log on."

"I'm still working on trying to figure out who assisted with Agatha's identity," Charlie said, her frustration showing as she chewed on a fingernail. "Whatever security group Harlan used, it would be good to know them...hell, I'd like to collaborate with them."

"Professional jealousy?" Chad asked.

Shrugging, Charlie nodded, admitting, "I guess so. Their work is spectacular and I would like to learn more from them."

"Agreed," said Jack, "but for now, we focus on trying to link Gavrill with intent to harm Agatha, and determining how best to protect her. I've talked to Alvarez Security to let them know what's happening. Since she lives at the center, that makes it easier." Looking at Nathan, he said, "When you're involved with someone on a case, you've got to stay objective. You've got to stay levelheaded. If your relationship with Agatha goes south, you still owe her your loyalty as a Saint."

He opened his mouth to object to the idea that he would not be with Agatha, but Jack jumped in again. "Don't take offense. Just had to be said."

He nodded, irritated, but knew that Jack was right. "So what do we do now?"

"The FBI do not know that Agatha is Agnes. We corroborate with them if we find Harlan's killer, but I do not trust anyone to know that we have Agnes."

"You think a Fed could be dirty?" he asked, his focus intense.

"We hope not, but it wouldn't be the first time. We just don't know all the players," Jack explained.

"Plus, it appears Gavrill's reach is long," Luke added.

Monty jumped in with, "Both Nick and I have an FBI background and, while we hate to think of another agent being a mole for the mafia, it would not be the first time that money has tempted someone to stray. The Russians have a fuck-ton of money to throw at trying to find someone they want. We talked with Jack before everyone came today, and agreed that no one other than us, right now, should know that Agatha is Agnes."

Luke confirmed, "Charlie and I are continuing to work the computer aspect of this case. We're going to keep following the trail from Gavrill to Yurgi and out to anyone else he might be contacting."

"She's been lucky so far," Nathan admitted, "with the change in identity and all that Harlan put in place to protect her. It makes me nervous, but as long as no one recognizes her, we should be able to find the connection between Gavril and Yurgi's orders before they get to her."

"What about our women?" Nick looked at Jack, and then to Cam. "Obviously, Bethany knows about Agatha and, of course, so does Miriam. I'm assuming none of the other wives know, but I wanted to make sure. Bayley was the one who knew her when she was Agnes. I didn't say anything to her this morning, but wanted to know what the protocol is."

Jack nodded, "I appreciate your discretion. While all of our wives have been involved, in one way or another, with a case, at this time I'll ask that you not let them know. Bethany and Miriam won't say anything either. I know that Bayley will be disappointed but, hopefully she'll find out soon enough when there's no more risk to Agatha."

———

That evening Nathan went by the center to see Agatha. She met him in the lobby, a tremulous smile on her tired face. As he wrapped her in his arms, he noted the dark circles underneath her eyes. Breathing in the scent of her shampoo, he took her weight as she leaned into him.

"I can't believe you're still standing, babe," he said. "You've got to be exhausted. I know you got very little sleep last night."

"You're right. I didn't get much sleep last night and had to be up early this morning to help one of the women get her children on the school bus." With her arm still wrapped around his waist she leaned back and looked up into his face. "My heart aches with grief over Harlan but, I did have something positive happen today, that I know would have made him happy."

Grateful to hear the hope in her voice, he tilted his head, waiting to see what she would say.

"Ann has asked me to be the manager. I'll be doing much of what I'm doing now, plus a little more paperwork, but there's a pay raise involved."

"Whoa, babe. That's fabulous!" He leaned down and kissed her, light and sweet.

"And, she talked about something else with me, but I don't know how I feel about it. I wondered if we could talk about it over dinner?"

"Sweet Aggie, whatever you need from me, you got."

Smiling shyly, she slid her hand down his arm and linked fingers with him. Walking out together he assisted her up into his truck. Giving her a quick kiss, he drove to a restaurant, choosing a place where they could have a private conversation.

Once inside the tiny, Italian restaurant, settled in a corner booth, he asked, "So, what is it that you want to talk about?"

Agatha fiddled with her napkin, suddenly unsure about the discussion. Nathan reached across the table and placed his large hand on hers, giving it a little squeeze. She opened her hand, palm up, allowing him to slide his fingers through hers, the warmth moving from her hand to her heart.

"Well, one of the things that Ann talked to me about today was separating work and personal life. It's not really something I've ever thought about, but she says it's very important with the added responsibilities that I'll have as the manager."

"Sounds good, so far," he replied.

Plunging ahead, she continued, "She's never minded me living at the center. After all, it was her idea. She says that it's been good to have someone there with the women. But, now she feels that I need more of a personal life. To be honest, until recently, I didn't have anything other than Harlan that was outside of the center, so staying there made sense."

Sadness clouded her eyes at her mention of Harlan. Rubbing his thumb over her hand, he asked, "And now?"

She bit her bottom lip, revealing her nerves, as her eyes met his. "I feel kind of lost without being able to pick up the phone to call him. But I know he wanted more for me." Sucking in a deep breath, she added, "I guess now I'd like a chance to have a personal life."

His lips curved slightly and he leaned forward, whispering, "Can I hope that involves me?"

A tiny smile curved Agatha's lips, brightening her entire face. Nathan realized it was an expression he had rarely seen from her and hoped to see more of. Reaching into his pocket, he fingered the medallion that Charlie gave him that morning. Sucking in a fortifying breath, he drew it out, saying, "I've got something to give to you…I hope you'll wear it."

She cocked her head to the side, her gaze dropping to his hand, now turned up with the silver medallion lying in his palm, a silver chain attached. Lifting her eyes back to his, she waited for his explanation.

"Charlie had this St. Francis medallion fitted with a tracer and I'd like you to wear it. It allows the Saints to know where you are at all times." He tried to still the shaking of his hand, but she did not seem to notice.

Reaching out, she tentatively took the necklace, her fingers tracing the relief of St. Francis. Blinking, she whispered hoarsely, "It's beautiful."

"My real name is Francis Nathaniel Washington. My mom loves animals and wanted me named after St. Francis, the patron Saint of animals." He chuckled, adding, "My dad wanted me named Nathaniel, but he let Mom get my first name."

She smiled, her fingers still clutching the necklace.

"All of the Saints' women have one…uh…I mean with their Saint's name on it, not mine. Uh…this one is for me…well, for you. But, it has my…"

Her trembling smile stopped his stammering and he released a sigh of relief as she slipped it over her head, letting the medallion settle on her chest.

"Thank you, Nathan. I love that you gave this to me." Her fingers continued to move over the medallion, as though memorizing the shape and feel.

He met her smile, loving the fact that she was wearing a part of him.

After a moment, she sobered and said, "I still have to think about getting an apartment. The problem is, I've never lived on my own. Ever." She looked down, the delicate silver resting on her chest. He nudged her and she lifted her eyes to his. "I don't even know if I want to, but everyone seems to think I need to. It's embarrassing, but I was never allowed any freedom…I have no idea how to even look for an apartment. So…" she shrugged, holding his gaze, "will you help me?"

He opened his mouth several times, snapping it shut each time. He knew he wanted to help her find a place to live, but wondered how to let her know that he would prefer for her to live with him.

22

For the next week, Agatha settled into a new routine. Her days were spent at the center, much like they had been before, but now her duties were managerial, while Ann worked on finding an assistant for her. Several of the women were taking over assistant duties, learning office skills at the same time.

Nathan picked her up in the evenings for dinner and they cruised around looking at apartments, or just had fun, which was something she realized she rarely had before he came into her life.

By the end of the week, Ann walked into her new office, smiling. "I think this job suits you," she said. "You look much happier than I've ever seen you. Or, perhaps it's the young man you're spending time with?"

Blushing, she admitted, "I think it's a little bit of both."

"Have you found a place to live yet?"

Scrunching her nose in distaste, she shook her head. "Every place we visit, Nathan finds something wrong with it. Either it's in a dangerous neighborhood, or he doesn't like the size, doesn't like the parking, thinks it's too expensive, or maybe too cheap. I never knew it could be so complicated to find a place to live."

Lifting her eyebrow, Ann surmised, "Perhaps, it's not that it's so difficult to find a place but, that he'd rather you stay with him."

Eyes wide, she exclaimed, "But we've only known each other for a short while. Do people actually get together so quickly?"

"Oh, my, I know you once said that you were raised in a sheltered environment, but many couples do move in together after knowing each other for only a short while. I'm not sure it's the length of time that you have known each other that makes the difference, as much as how you feel about each other."

Biting her lip, she nodded slowly, not saying anything. Before Ann had a chance to speak again, Gail came running in, excitedly waving a magazine in her hand.

"Miss Ann, Miss Agatha! Have you seen the new magazine? The one that talks about the center? It just came in the mail and I wanted to show it to you!"

They both jumped up and hurried over to Gail, peering over her shoulder as they looked at the article. As Ann read aloud, Agatha grinned, loving how the interview sounded.

"Agatha," Ann said, "you did such a great job! This is a wonderful article, and should help our fundraising tremendously! I like how they did the pictures, obviously not showing the outside of our building nor showing any of the women's faces."

Continuing to peer at the article, she saw a picture of herself in front of the classroom of women. She had never seen herself in an article before, and almost burst with pride. As the other women walked out, she continued to stare at the article, thinking how much she wished she could share it with Harlan.

Her heart ached as it always did when she thought about him. The older man had been a widower for several years and never had children. In the short time that they were together, he treated her like a daughter. *A respected daughter, unlike my own parents.*

She sighed, knowing how proud he would have been of her. Tucking the magazine into her purse, she was glad, at least, she could share it with Nathan.

Chessa walked through the prison library, bored and angry, a state that she found herself in on most days. Never one to read much, she passed the books and walked over to the magazine stand. Flipping through a few, she glanced at the fashion sections, but then tossed them down in disgust. Glancing derisively at her own orange jumpsuit, she knew she would not be wearing anything fashionable for years to come.

The unfairness of life ate at her as she pondered her new station in life. The idea that she, cousin to one of the most powerful men she knew, had ended up in prison, wormed its way through her like a poison. She never considered the plight of the many girls that passed through their hotel as slaves before being shipped off. No one's situation concerned her other than her own.

Her eyes moved over the other inmates and she buried the grimace desperate to slide onto her face. Disgust that she was locked away with these lowlifes caused a slight shudder to pass over her and she turned her eyes away. Moving to the computers, she considered trying to send an email to her husband, but knew that their correspondence would be scanned closely. She wondered, briefly, how her sons, Lazlo and Grigory, were doing, but she did not dare send a message to either.

She turned to walk out of the library, when her eyes landed on the table near the door, where the newest magazines had been brought in and displayed. The Virginian caught her eye and she picked it up, desiring to see some pictures that might seem familiar. She perused the articles on various cities, restaurants, vacation spots, before her gaze landed on an article about a women's shelter for women who had suffered from abuse. Not caring about the shelter or the plight of the women, she stared in stunned silence at one of the pictures showing a woman, in the front of a classroom, facing a group of women sitting at computers.

The picture was not very close. The woman's hair was blonde, her eyes were light, and her nose appeared straight. But, a mother knows.

Her heart pounding, she stared in disbelief at the woman helping to run the center, knowing she was looking at her daughter. Her face twisted into an ugly sneer, bile threatening to choke her. The idea that her daughter had changed her identity and was living a life outside the family infuriated her. Tossing the magazine down, she moved over to an empty computer. Sitting for a few minutes, until she calmed down, she opened her prisoner email, and began to type.

"I've searched online and I have a new place for us to take a look at tomorrow."

Nathan grimaced, his arms twitching at the news as he held Agatha. He had been relaxed and her words made him want to find a way to get her mind off of moving so he could relax again.

She twisted around in bed, lifting her head above his chest and peered down into his face. Scrunching her nose, she said, "You don't seem very excited to help me find an apartment."

Deciding to distract her with a kiss, he flipped her underneath him, planting his lips on hers. Grasping her hands in his, he lifted them above her head, their fingers locked, as he continued his assault on her mouth. She moaned, turning her head to allow him to take the kiss deeper.

Plunging his tongue inside, he tasted the wine and chocolate from their dinner and dessert. Intoxicated with her heady scent, his cock swelled, pressing against her stomach.

As she was swept away with the feel of Nathan's

body on hers, all thoughts about apartment searching flew from Agatha's head. A groan escaped her lips as sensations zinged from her nipples to her core. Throwing her head back, she clenched her thighs together to try to appease her body's desire for friction.

Determined to make the night last, Nathan moved his mouth slowly over hers. Needing to take some weight off her chest, he pulled one hand from hers and held himself up on one forearm. She used her free hand to grasp his shoulder, feeling the play of muscles underneath her fingertips.

Throughout this exquisite torture, he held her lips, taunting and teasing them with his tongue as he explored her depths. She spread her legs wider, allowing him to settle between them, his cock nestling into her wet folds, beckoning him.

He grabbed a condom from where he had earlier tossed several onto the bed and rolled it on quickly. Sliding his cock into her waiting body, he slowly pushed in, inch by inch. Their earlier coupling had been fast and hard, fun and creative. But, this time, he wanted to feel every twinge of her body. He worshiped her mouth as he memorized each sensation as her body accommodated him.

The friction built just as quickly as if he had been rocking into her. Still holding one hand over her head, her breasts pressed against his chest, their eyes never wavered. Over and over he moved until Agatha thought she would go mad as the coil tightened inside.

Squeezing her eyes shut, flashes of light burst behind

her eyelids and she gripped her fingers on his shoulders as her orgasm rushed through her body. Tightening her legs around his waist with her heels against his ass, she pulled him in as he emptied himself into her. Eyes opening, she stared, mesmerized at the corded muscles in his neck as he threw his head back, groaning out his release.

Moments later, as they lay, arms and legs tangled in the sheets, she rested her head on his chest, feeling his steady heartbeat against her ear. "You know, I'm aware that you just used sex to distract me."

"It appeared to work well."

A snort-giggle erupted from deep inside her and she playfully slapped his chest. "You should not get used to using sex to distract me," she said. "It definitely works too well!"

Nathan grinned at the truth in her words, even though she was joking. "I want you to be happy," he sighed, "but, I also want you with me. Is that such a bad thing?"

She lifted her head, staring into his eyes, and smiled. "No, not really."

"Do you want to live on your own? I need to know how important it is to you."

"Why?"

He rolled to his side, his arms still tightly around her, pulling her with him, and said, "I know you've felt as though you haven't had any freedom your entire life. I don't want to take that away from you. So, if living on your own is what you want to do, then that's what I want for you. But if living on your own is simply what you think you're supposed to do, then I'd like us to talk about it."

She considered his words carefully for a few minutes, her head on his shoulder. "I suppose the truth of the matter is, I don't really feel a need to live by myself. Maybe that's being a coward." He opened his mouth to speak and she pressed her fingers on his lips to silence him. "Please, hear me out."

She waited until he nodded his acquiescence. "To some people, living on their own is the ultimate freeing experience. I know that many would expect that from me since I lived with my parents and then lived with Harlan and now at the shelter, never having my own place. But, for me, it doesn't feel that way. I already budget my money so, unless I get a place that's furnished, I have enough to buy furniture. I tend to eat at the center, so I don't really need much of a kitchen. But, while I've learned to enjoy my freedom over the past two years, I like being around people...nice people. I was always alone growing up, even though I was surrounded...Dad's enforcers were everywhere. I was given little freedom unless I was inside the house."

His jaw ticked with anger at the thought of her gilded cage and her world limited to her family.

She continued, unaware of his ire. "The center gives me good people to be around. And I sort of feel that my own apartment would feel very empty and lonely."

Blowing out a breath, the corners of his lips curved and he lifted his hand to brush her hair behind her ear, slowly drawing his thumb along her jaw. Resting his thumb and fingers on her chin he drew her forward for a kiss. "I'm nice people," he said, with a smile. "And I would love for you to move here with me."

"It seems so fast," she whispered back. "I guess I always thought that people dated for a long time, then maybe moved in together, before getting married." Blushing, she added, "That never would have happened to me. It would have been expected of me to be married before moving in with my husband. My oldest brother, Grigory was engaged, but they never lived together. He was still living in the family home, having dinner with all of us together at night."

"I'll leave it so the invitation is always open, but I respect your decision. If you want to keep living at the center for a while, I think that's fine too. But, I do agree with Ann...I think you need to learn to separate your professional life and your personal life."

"I never realized it until just now, that my family never did that. It was always about the family. The family business was still the family. There was no delineation...no getting away from it...no escape."

"It sounds like moving into an apartment is more than you want to do right now. If so, then I would wait until you're sure. Just keep in mind, I would love for you to be here with me."

2 3

The morning sun shone through the window, landing on Agatha's closed eyes, the brightness causing her to jerk awake. Looking over at the time on her phone lying on the nightstand, she jumped up. A strong arm banded about her waist and pulled her back into the warm comfort of Nathan's embrace.

Mumbling, he asked, "What's the rush?"

"Ugh," she replied, squirming against his hold. "You might not have to get up early, but I need to be at work."

He leaned forward nuzzling her hair, sliding his lips over her neck to her jaw, and she twisted to meet his mouth with hers. After a long, wet kiss, he reluctantly let her climb out of bed. With his arm tucked behind his head he smiled, watching as she, shy about her nudity, grabbed his T-shirt, pulling it over her head quickly.

"Babe, I love seeing you in my shirt, but as gorgeous as you are, I prefer seeing you in nothing at all."

Blushing, she slid her eyes over to him, the sight of him lying in bed, reclined against the pillows with the sheet barely covering his lower half...it was all she could do to keep moving to the bathroom.

When she finished with her shower and dressed for work, she walked toward the front, the scent of bacon and eggs drawing her to the kitchen. Looking down at her purse laying on the table, she exclaimed, "Oh my goodness! I forgot to show you the magazine article that came out yesterday. I'm in it!"

Nathan's brow knit in confusion as he set the frying pan over to the side, turned off the heat, and moved to peer over Agatha's shoulder as she flipped open the pages of the magazine. He smiled, hearing the pride in her voice as she told him about it.

"Babe, I'm so proud of you." Before he had a chance to say anything else, his eyes landed on the picture with her in it. Startling, he reared back. "Aggie! What the fuck?"

"I was a little worried about that," she said, her eyes darting from the magazine up to his. "But, I look different than before, and my name is listed as Agatha Christel. Plus, the picture isn't very clear."

He had to admit she was right, but it still made him nervous to have her picture, as changed as she was, in a national magazine. He looked down at her, seeing the nervousness in her eyes. She had stopped wearing the contacts around him and he loved peering into her deep, chocolate brown eyes. Best of all, he could see emotion in them now.

Pulling her in tightly to his chest, he held her. "I'm sure it's okay, babe, it just threw me seeing your picture there. I'll take it in today and let the others see it, just so they know it's there."

Agatha breathed easier and leaned against Nathan's heartbeat. *Maybe...I could have this always, if I move in with him. I just don't want to make a mistake.*

Undisclosed Location

Scanning the magazine article laid out in front of him, he heaved a sigh. "How'd we miss this?"

"I don't know. But there it is, right in front of us. All our work, changing her identity, and she ends up in a fuckin' magazine."

The other man at the table asked, "What are we going to do about it? Do you think we need to make a move?"

He sat, fingers tapping on the table as his eyes drifted back to the photograph of Agatha's altered face in the magazine, staring back at him. Sighing again, he said, "I'm on it." Pushing himself up from the table, with a chin lift he left the room, his heavy boots sounding as they went down the hall.

Nathan walked into the conference room at the Saints' compound and tossed the magazine on the table in front of the others that were already seated.

"What's this?" Bart asked, looking down at the Virginian magazine. "You decide we need a new design for the room?"

"Very funny," he said." How about you look on page eighty-seven."

He stood with his hands on his hips, looking at Bart as he flipped open the magazine, Cam, and Chad leaning in to have a look as well. By now, they had attracted the attention of the others in the room, who peered over their shoulders to see too. Soon enough, sounds of, "oh, shit", were heard throughout the group, just as Jack entered.

"She showed that to me this morning," he continued. "She didn't ask to have her picture taken. The photographer knew the other women were not supposed be facing the camera, to protect their privacy, but I guess they assumed that it was all right to have Agatha's picture in there. Granted, it's not a close-up, and she certainly has her altered appearance, but I hate like hell for her to be out like this."

As the others grumbled their agreement, Jack's lips were pinched and his jaw tight. "Well, it's out. Nothing we can do about it, but we need her to be extra vigilant when she's going and coming from the center."

"She still living there?" Nick asked, his eyes lifting to Nathan's.

Nodding, he said, "Yes, for now. To be honest, we've looked at apartments for her, but she's unsure if she wants to go that route. Personally, I'm trying to get her to move in with me." He saw the grins on the faces of the others around the table and was unable to keep the smile from his face as well. "Hey, she hasn't said yes, yet. She's still thinking about it."

Monty piped up, saying, "Maybe she just doesn't want to share all that space with your dogs."

"Hey, don't rag on the dogs. It didn't hurt me any," Blaise quipped.

"That's 'cause you found the only woman who loves dogs more than you do," joked Jude.

Charlie interrupted the laughter, saying, "Hate to interrupt your fun, guys, but I've got a hit on something interesting. I'm still working on trying to pick up chatter between Gavrill and Yurgi. They communicate by email, cryptically, but it's nothing that the FBI isn't also monitoring. I did see where Chessa sent something to Gavrill for the first time, though. It might not be important, but it caught my eye because she's been so silent."

"What did she say?" Jack asked.

"She mentioned being bored, missing him, and then she added that she missed *all* their family. That caught my eye because she hasn't been in contact with Lazlo or Grigory since they all went to prison. It made me wonder if she was alluding to Agnes."

"Did he reply back?" Nathan asked.

"Not yet, but prisoners are not allowed to go to the library every single day. They're only allowed a couple of days per week. I've tracked their correspondence, and he will not be allowed computer access to receive his email for another day."

Luke had his back to the rest of them, working on his computer. Suddenly, twirling around in his chair and grinning widely, he said, "We just might have a link that tells us how they may be communicating!"

All eyes turned toward him, and Nathan leaned forward, his forearms on the table, eagerly awaiting what he had to share.

"It appears Chessa had a visitor a few weeks ago. Kalina Popov is listed on the prisoner visitor record as being her cousin. What's interesting is that she has also visited Gavrill, as his fiancée."

"So is she their cousin or his fiancé? And doesn't the Bureau of Prisons keep a database of who visits who?" he asked.

"They do, but it's not unheard of for someone to have more than one relative in prison at the same time. So, she could be legitimately visiting two people in the same family who happen to be incarcerated, especially since Gavrill is in a minimum security prison."

Charlie turned toward him, and said, "She would be a perfect person to take messages back and forth between the two of them."

Luke flashed photographs onto the white board and everyone turned their attention to them. Yurgi's and Gavrill's pictures were at the top. Lines drawn from them included Chessa and Milos, Lazlo and Grigory, and another line went to Agnes. Other lines showed another branch of the Volkov family, but they were all underlings. There were also some photographs of others that worked for them but weren't blood relations. The picture of Kalina Popov was there as well. A gorgeous, dark-haired beauty, it was easy to see the family resemblance.

"So, is she really a cousin or his fiancée?" he repeated.

Luke replied, "From the records I can find on her, she's a cousin. Of course, that doesn't mean that she isn't also engaged to him, but my guess is that she uses the title fiancée to gain easier access to him."

"The FBI is focused on Harlan's murder," Jack said. "While we're focused on the threat to Agnes…Agatha, assuming the two are linked. Gavrill is probably feeling desperate, because Yurgi is not smart enough to handle the family business. He was only supposed to be a figurehead. If it comes out from Agatha that Gavrill was to transport the women, it would tie him into human trafficking, and he would no longer see the light of day other than through a prison window. Right now, he'll be out in two more years on the tax evasion sentence."

"Why now?" Patrick asked. "Why is he after her now, and not when all of this first went down almost two years ago?"

Jack leaned back in his chair, and said, "My guess, right after the raid of the Gruzinsky's hotel, when the FBI found some of the women and the others that Agnes had saved, it was too hot for Gavrill to do anything. He had to stay quiet and go underground, to stay out of the FBI's investigation. By the time he could focus on finding her, Agnes had already undergone her identity transformation and was well hidden by Harlan.

By then, the FBI had him for tax evasion and he had other things to worry about."

Frustrated, Nathan said, "I gotta tell you, this is killing me, just waiting to see if something happens to her."

"It makes me wonder what Harlan's plan was. When they didn't need Agnes to testify against her family, he took her in, kept her safe, and arranged to change her identity. I just don't know if that's all he had planned. With no other tie to the trafficking, the FBI had no probable cause to search Gavrill's ships or warehouse. But, it seems like Harlan assumed that at some point, Gavrill would want to come after Agnes, to assure that the last connection was severed. He should have set her up with ongoing security."

"Maybe he did. We can't find out who helped them, so perhaps they're still watching her," Charlie wondered aloud.

"So, where does that leave us, besides just Luke and Charlie trying to follow the communication trail of the family?"

Jack pierced Nathan with his serious stare, and said, "You know how these things work, man. Just like when you're searching for someone, it can take time. Right now, she's safe with eyes on her."

The group continued to discuss their active cases, but Nathan's mind was solidly on Agatha, unable to think of anything other than her safety. He wanted her and he wanted her free of the threat that followed her.

"I've got a favor to ask you and, I swear, there's no ulterior motive," Nathan said, early the next morning, standing in the parking lot of the center, his arms around Agatha.

She leaned back, smiling, and said, "Sure. Whatever you need."

"I've got to go out of town and won't be back until very late and I'd really like it if you could stay at my place. Blaise or Grace could easily come over and take care of the dogs while I'm gone, but it would be easier if—"

"Of course, I'll come! I'd love to take care of the dogs."

"I have to admit, the idea of you being there when I get home will make returning all that more special."

He reached into his pocket and pulled out a newly minted key on a circular keychain with a metal figurine of a bloodhound dangling from the circle. "For you."

Grinning widely, she accepted the gift. She wanted to ask where he was going and why, but knew that, as a Saint, there was much she could not know about his work. Deciding not to worry whether or not it was about her or another case, she gave his waist a squeeze.

"I brought some magazines that I thought you might like," Kalina said.

Gavrill had greeted his *fiancée*, Kalina, before settling back into the chair. Allowed to visit without a guard nearby, he had nonetheless adopted the expression of a man in love. Now, he glanced down at several business, financial, and sporting magazines before lifting his gaze back to her.

"I visited our dear cousin, Chessa, and she thought that this one would be particularly interesting," she continued, pushing the Virginian on top of the others and across the table to him.

His eyes narrowed as he looked up at his visitor. "And what does Chessa suggest I do with this?" he said, holding back a growl. He was still livid that her family had fucked up the last shipment of women, causing their business, and his office, to be caught in an FBI raid. Staring at Kalina, he dared her to explain.

"She thought that the article on page eighty-seven would be of interest to you."

Curious, he flipped to the page indicated and his eyes wandered over the title. Just as he was about to ask, Kalina tapped the page and continued, "This woman is doing good work, isn't she?"

He stared for a moment, not recognizing what he was looking at. The woman in the photograph did not appear familiar. "Is this a fucking game?" he snarled, his patience at an end.

Kalina smiled indulgently. "No, no, my love. Afterall, a mother will always recognize a daughter."

His gaze darted back to the magazine before looking back at her, understanding dawning on him. Sucking in a calming breath, he let it out slowly. Chessa had always been smart...much smarter than her husband or sons. *And, it appears she passed her intelligence on to her daughter.*

Closing the magazine, he smiled at the beautiful

woman sitting in front of him. "Well, done, my dear. I'm sure my brother would love to read this as well. He'll know what to do to help her with her cause." As Kalina left the visitor's room, he leaned back, confident in the knowledge that the last threat to his empire would soon be eliminated.

24

With excitement, Agatha waved goodbye to Ann and climbed into her car. She had called Blaise to let him know that she was on her way, and promised to call him as soon as she arrived at Nathan's. As she turned down the gravel drive, she looked at the thick woods on either side. Green and lush. Absolutely beautiful. When they drove together, she was usually focused on him, but now, with no other distractions, she enjoyed the beauty in his property.

Pulling up to the front to the house, she could hear the baying of the dogs, and grinned. Hurrying to the kennel, she entered the building, laughing as she saw the beautiful bloodhounds standing on their hind feet with their large paws on the sides of their runs. Ears hanging, tongues lolling, dark eyes bright, as they anticipated their dinner.

Following his directions, she fixed the bowls of food, placing them in their runs for them to eat. Letting Scarlett out first, she kneeled to rub the large dog, scratching behind her ears. Beau finished next and she let him out, followed by Red. Giving each dog special attention, she turned and opened the last run, letting Persi out as well.

Staring at the dog's large pregnant belly, she hoped that tonight was not the night she decided to have her puppies. Remembering she promised to call Blaise, she grabbed her phone from her purse and dialed him quickly.

"Hey, I'm here."

"Everything okay?"

"Absolutely. I've just fed the dogs, let them out of the runs, and I'm heading into the house. I'll bring them with me and keep them there until Nathan gets home."

After saying goodbye, she patted her thigh and called the dogs to follow her. On the front porch, she smiled, pulling out her new keychain. Fingering the bloodhound bauble, lost in thought, she was soon reminded what she was doing when Red and Beau bumped into her legs. Opening the front door, she and the four dogs entered and she carefully locked the door behind her.

The dogs, used to their routine, headed into the living room, flopping onto the floor. Scarlett took the queen's position on the sofa. Beau and Red sprawled on the rug in the middle of the room, while Persi found her large pillow placed near the fireplace.

She laid her purse on the kitchen counter and stood for a few minutes just looking around. Uncertain what she should do, she decided to fix a dinner that would heat easily when Nathan got home. After making spaghetti, she placed it in a casserole dish, covering the spiced tomato sauce with mozzarella cheese. Sticking it in the refrigerator, she walked around the counter, smiling at the four dogs piled up asleep.

There was very little snooping to do, although she looked around his house for a little while. Finding an old photo album, she sat cross-legged on the floor next to Red and began to flip through the pages. Pictures of a dark-haired little boy sitting next to a man on a big tractor caused her lips to twitch happily. Studying the album, she could not help but see the difference between his upbringing and hers. Parents laughing with their children. Him playing outdoors. Standing at a creek with a fishing pole in his hands and a small fish dangling from the hook. Trees, ponds, farmland, sunshine. And love.

Closing the album, she leaned back against the coffee table and wondered aloud, "Did I ever feel that kind of love?" Images ran through her mind of formal meals, but no picnics. Her father's heavily ornate study, but no family room. A rare walk in a park, but no adventures outdoors.

A memory of one of her dark nights when she was staying with Harlan came to mind.

Depression threatening to choke me, the feeling that I would never find love or be worthy of love, had me crying softly in bed. Harlan must have heard me, because he knocked on my door. Calling for him to enter, the light behind him cast a glow about him as he walked in.

Moving into my room, he sat down on a chair, clasping

his hands together. "I could hear you crying," he said, then quickly added, "and don't say you're sorry."

"Hmph," I groused lightly, realizing how well he knew me.

"Listen, I'm not too good with feelings, but you wanna tell me what's going on?"

Shrugging slightly, I pushed up in the bed, leaning against the pillows. "I just want to feel normal. Like a regular person with a regular life. And I'm not sure I'm ever going to get that." I fiddled with the bedspread as I talked. My voice became a whisper, "But, then I think of the girls that will never even have what I have and feel guilty. So guilty, I can't breathe."

He sighed heavily and the silence stretched between the two of us. He finally said, "I was warned that you'd have these feelings." Looking up sharply at him, he explained, "By the ones who gave you a new identity. They talked to me about what you'd have to face. Counseling would have been offered if you had gone into protective custody, but without that, you're stuck with me. And, Lord knows, I'm not a good counselor."

"Do they do a lot of that? Helping people with new identities?" I asked, suddenly curious about the ones who assisted me.

Nodding slowly, he said, "Yeah. It's what they do...and they're the best at it." After another moment of silence, he said, "I know, right now, you feel like your life doesn't make sense. The past was created by your family, who took away your choices. Until you decided to forge your own path. But, girl, you just started down this road. It's not the end, it's just the beginning of a new you. This new you will have a job, friends, find someone to love and, God willing, you'll get *married and have children...and raise them to be the kind of person you are inside. Strong, willing to take a chance, and willing to right a wrong."*

"But will I find someone who I'll deserve?"

"Oh, darlin' girl, the trick will be for you to find someone who deserves you."

Sighing, I smiled, saying, "At least I have you."

He stood and walked to the door, stopping in the doorway. Looking over his shoulder, he seemed to struggle before adding, "I've never told you the secret of what to do if something happens to me. Just remember, the light will find you." With that, he turned and walked out of the room.

Still sitting on the rug on the floor, she looked back down at the childhood pictures of Nathan and allowed a glimmer of hope to spread throughout her chest. *One day, maybe one day, I'll be able to give him a little dark-haired child that we can raise in love.*

Several hours later, Nathan softly opened the front door and smiled as he viewed the room in front of him. Beau, Red, and Persi were asleep on the living room floor. Scarlett was sound asleep on the sofa with Aggie's body curled around her. Not wanting to wake her, he gave a soft tap on his thigh, and the three dogs on the floor immediately lifted their heads, yawning widely. Looking at Scarlett, he softly ordered, "Stay." Her head flopped back down as the others followed him outside, where he pinned them back into their kennels.

Re-entering the house, he signaled for Scarlett to move from the sofa. As he picked Aggie up in his arms, she woke, but then snuggled into his embrace as he carried her into the bedroom.

She mumbled, "You should put me down. I've got some dinner for you."

"Thanks, babe," he replied, "but you need to be in bed. The food will keep until tomorrow."

Setting her feet gently on the floor, he leaned over and pulled the covers of the bed back. While she pulled her shirt over her head, he grabbed one of his T-shirts. She unsnapped her bra and, taking his shirt, pulled it down over her head. He hated to lose sight of her luscious breasts, but knew now was not the time. Her fingers fumbled on the button of her jeans so he gently pushed her hands away, taking care of them himself. He slipped them down her legs after divesting her of her boots. With a gentle tug, he settled her under the covers, pulling them up to her chin before he headed into the bathroom for a quick shower.

A few minutes later, he slid under the covers with her, after patting Scarlett's head and watching the faithful dog curl onto the rug next to the bed. Wrapping his arms around Aggie, he pulled her back tightly to his front, tucking her next to him. The last thought he had, before going to sleep, was this was how he wanted to spend every night for the rest of his life.

The next day at work, after Agatha had finished all the paperwork that needed to be done, she moved toward the classrooms to check on the women there. Seeing all was well, she walked to the front, greeting the volunteer at the reception desk. Chatting for a few minutes, she stepped outside, grateful for the sunshine beaming warmly. Lifting her chin, she turned her face to the sun, wishing that she were back at Nathan's cabin.

As she turned to go inside, she noticed a pickup truck parked down the street. A man, his face obscured with a ball cap and sunglasses, sat in the passenger side. A strange uneasiness passed over her, reminiscent of the days when she was trying to sneak around her family, keeping them from finding out her plans. The truck was too far away for her to discern the license tag number, so she casually slipped back into the building, immediately dialing Nathan.

His phone went to voicemail, so she called Blaise. He picked up and she blurted, "I tried to call Nathan but he didn't pick up. Maybe I'm just crazy, but I saw an old truck parked down the street. I've never seen it before and it just made me nervous."

"Are you inside?"

"Yes."

"Stay inside, make sure the door is locked, and someone will be right there. We had already been notified and we're on our way."

She smiled at the volunteer and said, "Don't alarm anyone else, but we have to be vigilant about strangers."

The volunteer nodded, but her wide eyes and pale face gave evidence to her nervousness. As Agatha turned back to the window in the door, she saw the truck pull into the parking lot, jerking to a stop just in front of the center's door.

A heavyset man threw open his door and jumped down, landing with both booted feet on the pavement. Slamming his truck door, he stalked to the front of the center, raised his fist and pounded on the door.

"Gail! Let me in! I know you're in there!"

Safely inside, Agatha turned to the volunteer and ordered, "Get to Gail. Tell her to stay in the back, and not to come forward. Make sure she has someone with her. Then call Ann and let her know we have an emergency."

The volunteer hurried off to do her bidding, and Agatha waited, knowing the Saints were on their way.

Within a minute, an SUV pulled in by the front door and three Saints jumped out. Bart, Jude, and Blaise headed straight for the door, as she watched through the window. Bart and Jude quickly subdued the large man, who continued to rant that the center was holding his girlfriend hostage. Still yelling threats, Bart secured his hands behind his back with zip ties, while Blaise moved to the door of the center.

Opening it, she barely jumped out of the way in time as Blaise rushed through. He immediately placed his hands on her shoulders and peered into her eyes.

"Are you okay?"

She nodded, her gaze darting to his side, trying to see what was happening. Before she had a chance to speak, Gail came bursting from the back room, her eyes wild as she said, "Thomas? Thomas is here?"

Agatha broke free from Blaise's hold and turned to Gail. Speaking softly, she said, "Gail...what are you doing here?"

"He came? He came here?"

"Gail, you need to go to the back. Let the police handle this."

Gail's chest heaved as tears filled her eyes, and she said, "Why is he here?"

Outside, with his face still pressed against the brick wall, Thomas yelled, "Gail! I know you're in there!"

Before she could stop her, Gail started around to the door, but her progress was stopped as Blaise placed his arm around her shoulders. She had gotten far enough to be able to see Thomas.

Agatha pleaded, "Don't go back to him. You're strong and getting stronger. Do this for you."

Gail looked at Thomas and asked, in a voice scratchy with emotion, "Why are you here? If you care about me, ever cared about me, you would leave me alone."

"Baby, you belong to me. You should be home with me."

"That's what you never understood," she said, tears sliding down her cheeks. "I don't belong to anybody except me. You never got that. And when I wasn't going your way, you showed me what you thought of me with your fists. That's not love. That's ownership...and I don't belong to anyone but me."

Turning, she fell into Agatha's arms, her chest heaving with exertion. The police arrived, taking Thomas after getting statements from Bart and Jude.

One of the police officers turned to Gail, and said, "Are you going to press charges?"

Ann approached from the back, and said, "The center will press charges."

Agatha looked at Gail and said, "You need to get a restraining order. Ann will go with you and you can do it right now."

Ann nodded. "Gail, what Agatha is telling you, is exactly what you need to do. You've already started the process of standing on your own. We want to help you, and you can help yourself by getting a restraining order."

Gail nodded and wiped the tears from her eyes. The police had Thomas in the squad car, and Ann wrapped her arms around Gail before leading her outside.

Blaise crossed the room, pulling Agatha into a hug. "You okay?"

Nodding, she said, "Yes. I'm sorry to bother—"

"This is no bother, Agatha. This is what you're supposed to do. Nathan's out tracking an elderly man lost from his home, or he'd be here telling you the same himself."

Sucking in a deep breath before blowing it back out slowly, she said, "Thank you."

Blaise kissed the top of her head and warmth spread throughout her body. The idea that Nathan's friends cared so much that they'd drop everything to watch after her, and would go so far as to embrace her, overwhelmed her. She had never experienced that sense of peace with her family.

"Yeah, I saw her," the driver of a black car said in a thick Russian accent as he drove down the road.

"It didn't take her long to call in her protectors," Yurgi growled.

"I circled around, but stayed out of sight and out of range of the cameras. Looks like they got to her within ten minutes."

"We'll keep an eye on the situation. Lucky for us that man tried to get in…now we know she's got protection and we'll have to find another way to get to her."

Scarlett, nose to the ground, trotted at a fast clip along one of the paths in the park, with Nathan right behind. Two police officers were with him, both trained in how to approach a person with dementia.

Confident that Scarlett would find him quickly, he still felt the usual anxiety when someone was missing. His heavy boots thumped sure-footed over the damp ground as his eyes stayed on Scarlett. She left the path, moving through the trees and his anxiety increased as he saw they were nearing the pond. *Fuck, don't let us be too late.*

Scarlett headed out of the trees, causing he and the policeman to increase their speed following her. Nathan looked ahead and saw an elderly man sitting cross-legged at the edge of the pond. Scarlett trotted close before sitting on her haunches, indicating this was the man they had been looking for.

Nathan gave the two police officers a nod and stood back with Scarlett as they approached the man carefully. He watched as the two police officers skillfully engaged the man in a conversation, listening as he described a similar pond from when he was young. Offering him water, they assisted him to his feet and the group began traveling back toward the road.

As the man neared, he looked down at Scarlett, and a wide smile broke across his face. "Had me an old coonhound when I was a boy. Best dog I ever had."

"Yes, sir," he agreed, watching with pride as the older man rubbed Scarlett's head and she patiently allowed the petting. Reaching the street, he observed the police officers carefully settled the man in the back of their cruiser to take him back to the home he had left.

Bending, he scratched Scarlett's ears and under her chin, saying, "You did good again, girl. Let's go home."

His phone vibrated in his pocket and he pulled it out seeing a message from Blaise. Reading it, his heart skipped a beat. *Fuck! Aggie!*

Nathan hurried to the center as fast as he could. Rushing through the front door, his heart pounding, he saw Agatha approaching from the back. Not giving her a chance to speak, he rushed to her, crushing her body against to his.

"I'm fine! I'm fine!" Agatha tried to assure Nathan,

but her voice was muffled, her mouth pressed to his chest. His flannel shirt was soft against her face and she wrapped her arms around his middle.

"Jesus, babe. My heart hasn't stopped racing since Blaise called me."

"It was Gail's ex-boyfriend," she said, her gaze holding his. She smiled and said, "You know what was the best thing to hear? When she said she wasn't property to be owned by anyone. I could have burst with pride."

He peered into her beaming face and kissed her gently, saying, "The work you do here is amazing, babe. You make a difference...you've got to know that."

"Well, you're the one who found her in the first place, so I'd say your work is pretty amazing too."

He looked at the clock on the wall, and said, "It's close enough to the end of day, please babe, tell me that you can go home now."

She nodded, still feeling his heartbeat pounding against her cheek. Turning, she moved to get her purse before walking out the door with him, thinking that she loved hearing the word *home* describing the place they were going together.

2 5

Walking through the woods along the tree-lined path, Agatha thought she was in heaven. Her hand was linked with Nathan's as they walked, the sound of the dogs moving along the trail in front of them mixing with the birds above. She sneaked a peek at him, marveling at his confident stride, his feet covered in his work boots, his legs encased in jeans that strained across his powerful thighs. He had recently trimmed his beard, but she liked it just as well when it was scraggly. Finally, she jerked her gaze back to the sights around her.

The tall trees, thick underbrush, and woodland creatures scurrying through the leaves on the ground captured her attention. The sun cast beams through the limbs above, illuminating the fairy-like woods. "This is beautiful...so peaceful," she said, pulling the fresh air deeply into her lungs.

"What is, babe?"

"This. You. Us. The walk in the woods. The dogs. The sunshine."

He laughed, throwing his head back. "Damn, girl. That just about covers everything."

Scrunching her nose, she lifted her shoulders. "I guess it does, but that's how I feel. I've never had walks in the woods before. I've never been around pets. I've never had a chance to just enjoy the beauty of nature."

Nathan stopped in the middle of the path, wrapping his arms around Agatha and pulling her in tightly. He loved seeing her in one of his flannel shirts, hanging down her thighs, knowing she was safe and warm in his arms. Resting his chin on the top of her head, he closed his eyes as he tried to imagine what life was like before she escaped her family. All the things he took for granted growing up, ran through his mind. "I'd love to take you to my parents' farm sometime. Both to meet them and to let you see where I was raised. It's not fancy, I'll warn you, but it was home."

Agatha looked up at Nathan's face. A sunbeam shot through the trees, illuminating him around the edges with a glow. Her heart squeezed with the knowledge that she loved this man. "I'd be honored to meet your family." She sucked in her lips, before adding, "I never thought anyone would want to take me to meet their family."

"Sweet Aggie, the honor would be mine." Cupping the back of her head with one of his hands, Nathan gently pulled her head back, slightly lifting her lips to his. The kiss was soft and gentle, but with the swipe of her tongue against his, it went deeper and wilder. If not for the bounding dogs that came rushing to them, swirling about their legs, he was sure he would have taken her against a tree.

Lifting his head, he laughed, "As much as I'd like to answer the call of the wild right now, babe, I think the dogs are trying to tell us it's time to go home."

They continued their walk along the path as they headed toward the cabin. The dogs, recognizing they were heading home, trotted ahead, their tails wagging as their noses sniffed the ground. Once there, he went into the kennel to feed them as Agatha headed into the house.

When he joined her inside the cabin, he swooped her into his arms, stalking back to the bedroom.

As he let her body slide down his front, he stopped just before her feet touched the floor, where her lips were at the same level as his. With one hand behind her head, and the other banded around her waist, he gripped her hair gently, angling her head for maximum contact. Tongues tangling, vying for dominance, they bumped noses as their heads moved back and forth.

"I want you naked," she mumbled, her lips not separating from his.

He lowered her to the ground, pulling back as they stared at each other, both panting. With a grin, she whipped her shirt over her head and he did the same. Fingers flew over buttons and zippers as they stripped. Standing naked, their eyes drifted down and back up again, each admiring the view.

Agatha had never had the opportunity to give a blowjob before, but she hoped her racier romance novels would provide the guidance she needed. Before

Nathan could move, she dropped to her knees and took him in her mouth. She swirled her tongue around the tip before moving him in and out. Too large for her to take all of him in, she fisted the bottom of his shaft while sucking.

"Oh, babe," he moaned, his hands tangling in her hair. He gripped her honey blonde tresses tightly before loosening his hold, conscious of hurting her. *My caring man.*

Digging small crescents with her fingernails into his thighs, she held on as she concentrated on pleasuring him and, from the satin tightness of his cock, she could tell she was succeeding. Sparing a glance up to his face, she watched as his head tilted back, the veins in his neck standing out, before he dropped his chin to watch her. Smiling her delight, her lips bobbed up and down over his erection.

Overcome with sensations, Nathan felt his balls tighten and, as much as he wanted to come in her mouth, the desire to come into her tight sex was stronger. With effort, he gently grabbed her hair again and pulled her head back. His cock slid from her mouth and he instantly felt the loss.

Before she could speak, he bent and lifted her up by her underarms, tossing her gently to the bed.

"As much as I love your mouth, babe, I wanna come buried balls deep inside of you."

His words sent a jolt straight to Agatha's sex as she spread her legs, immediately lifting her arms to welcome him.

He reached for a condom, but she halted his arm.

"I'm on birth control. Harlan insisted." At his raised eyebrow, she blushed. "What I mean is, he insisted that I see a gynecologist after I told him that the only doctor I had ever been to was the family doctor." Shrugging, she added, "When I saw the gynecologist and she asked if I was sexually active, I told her no but that I hoped to be. She suggested I go on birth control and, I confess, I liked making that kind of decision and not leaving it up to my mother."

Nathan's breath caught in his throat as he stared down at her beauty. "I'm clean, but I want you to be sure about this."

"Absolutely," she grinned.

"Damn, Aggie," he groaned, "you're perfect." The tip of his straining cock teased her slick opening. As he slowly stretched her tight, accepting walls, he continued to whisper in her ear, "I want to claim every inch of you."

Pulling him tighter to her, Agatha welcomed the feel of his thick cock. Her desire matched her need to be connected to him as he sucked the sensitive spot where her neck met her shoulders. Feeling the nip of his teeth on her pulse sent convulsions through her core.

Losing himself in the sensations, Nathan's movements increased in tempo. Her walls pulled against him with every outward motion and welcomed him with every thrust. Her nipples pebbled against his chest, the soft mounds of her breasts pressed tightly to his pecs.

Kissing a trail down her shoulder to her breasts he latched around a hardened nipple. Pulling it deeply into his mouth, he swirled his tongue around the tight flesh and blew his breath across the bud, watching her shiver in delight.

As Nathan continued to thrust, Agatha felt every movement, her inner walls reveling in the electricity that bolted outward. Her legs ached from clinging to him so tightly, but her desire to join with him as closely as she could, made her lock them in place, even though they trembled with the exertion. She could feel the orgasm nearing as her core pulsed. Crying out his name, she threw her head back against the pillow, her sex convulsing around him.

"I want to watch you come," he said, grinning in satisfaction as she tilted her head forward and her eyes jerked open.

As Agatha's body shuddered in ecstasy, her orgasm washing over her, a blush moved from her chest to her cheeks as she held his gaze. Nathan continued to grind against her clit as he thrust several more times before his neck tightened, the muscles cording as he powered through his own orgasm, emptying deep inside her body. Moving in and out, he continued until drained. Falling forward, he crashed half on her body, half on the mattress.

Agatha welcomed his weight, the feel of his heaviness on top of her, his hips still nestled between her legs. Smoothing her hands over the muscles of his shoulders and down his back, she noted the hard planes melding into the dips and curves.

Neither spoke, both steadying their breathing. As the physical sensations slowly faded, the emotions heightened.

His voice gravel rough, he asked, "Are you okay, baby?"

"Yeah," she breathed, holding his gaze.

Gently moving his mouth down to hers, Nathan captured her lips as well as her breath. Thrusting his tongue between her lips, he plundered her mouth, relishing each curve, ridge, and the taste of her. Agatha matched his ardor, her tongue parrying with his. This kiss was different…this felt like being claimed.

Pulling him to her, she kissed him deeply, hanging on to his shoulders as they allowed their passions to take over. Much later, she curled up in his arms, drifting away into a peaceful sleep.

The dark night had descended, but Charlie was unable to sleep. As she slipped from bed, she looked down at Luke, sleeping soundly. Not wanting to wake him, she padded softly from the room. Once inside their home study, she fired up her secure computer, opening the programs she had perfected over the years, encrypted for maximum security.

Seeing a new email from an address she did not recognize, she opened it, knowing her computer would immediately kill the message if there were any detected viruses. Stunned, she read,

We see you have her protected. We'll assist FBI. She knows the way, if we are needed.

"What the fuck?" She began typing fast and furious, attempting to discern where the message had come from. As brilliant as she was with encryption, she could not believe they used a program that kept her from being able to see who sent the message.

No longer worried about Luke sleeping, she continued to type and grumble loudly. In a few minutes, a sleepy Luke stumbled into the room, bare chested with his boxers slung low over his hips. Rubbing a hand through his hair, causing it to stick straight up, he yawned.

"What the hell are you working on this late?"

She whirled around in her seat, taking in his appearance for the first time. Unable to resist, she stood and placed a kiss on his lips as he wrapped his arms around her. She showed him the message and her attempts to find the sender. "What do you think it means?"

He sat down at the chair and began to work as well, but was unable to break their code. Staring at her, he said, "I have no idea, babe. But we need to meet tomorrow, and I think Agatha's going to have to come in as well."

As they shut the computer down and walked back to bedroom, Luke chuckled. Seeing her lifted eyebrow, he said, "Now you know what it was like for me, when you were helping me by sending cryptic messages. I couldn't figure out who you were and it drove me crazy."

Pinching his naked waist, she darted ahead toward the bedroom, with him fast on her heels.

2 6

Once more, Agatha found herself standing in the standing in the living room of Jack and Bethany's house. This time, Bethany was in the kitchen, bustling about, finishing up with a fresh batch of muffins. After making sure everyone had access to them, she walked over to Jack, standing up on her toes as he gave her a tender kiss. Agatha watched the two embrace before Bethany tossed a wave of her hand at the rest of them.

"I've got another wedding at the cabins to work on, so I'll take the kids with me."

She and the Saints soon settled around the living room, but unlike last time, this time she felt that she was among friends, which soothed her. Jack nodded toward Charlie, giving her the floor.

"I received an email message last night," Charlie began, "and I confess it's so well encrypted I was unable to trace who sent it, where it was sent from, or even when it was sent."

Luke piped up, "As you can imagine, this sent my wife into a tizzy."

"Hmph," she groused. "I'd hardly call it a tizzy. But, the point is, I need for you to look at the message, Agatha, and give us any idea what it means."

All of the Saints looked at the message on their tablets, and she leaned over to peer at the tablet in Nathan's hand. Reading, her eyes widened in bewilderment. Shaking her head slowly, she said, "I don't know what it means."

Jack, his voice gentle asked, "Agatha, can you trust us enough to tell us everything that happened with Harlan?"

She immediately sucked in her lips, doubt flashing through her eyes. Sensing her unease, Nathan twisted around to stare at her.

"What? What is it you haven't told us?"

"Please understand," she begged, "Harlan told me very little. And he always warned me not to talk to anyone about my situation. I know I can trust you, but his lessons were ingrained in me for my own protection."

"It appears that you've had another kind of protection all along," Jack commented.

Continuing to shake her head, she explained, "I had no idea someone was looking after me."

Nathan, a flash of jealousy jolting through him, said, "I'd like to know who the fuck has had their eyes on her."

Agatha cut her eyes to him, seeing the tense set of

his jaw. Sucking in her lips again, a nervous habit, she focused on calming the nerves hitting her stomach. *Oh, Harlan, what would you want me to do?* Sitting up straighter, it struck her that she already had the answer to that question. It was time for her to rely on herself... Harlan was no longer able to look after her and she needed to make her own decisions.

Blowing out a deep breath, she chose to share all she knew, trusting the Saints with her safety and Nathan with her heart. Reaching out to place her hand in his, she began, "The night I was picked up, I was taken to a house, but I don't know where it was. A very nice lady, who I assumed was an FBI agent, stayed with me. She told me that I'd be there until Harlan took charge. He was only in the hospital for two days, and as soon as he was released, he came to see me there. Within two weeks, he knew that I was not going to need to testify against my family, because the FBI had enough evidence to put them away for a long time. Sometime during the third week, he came to pick me up from that house, taking me to his house."

"His house?" Nathan asked, his jaw tight with anger. "Why the hell did he take you to his house?"

Shrugging, she said, "He only said it was for my protection. I was very naïve, and asked very little about what was happening with my family. I knew that they were being charged and, I assumed, with the evidence against them, they were not going to go to trial. Instead, either pleading guilty or making some kind of plea bargain. I was with Harlan for the next year."

She noted the raised eyebrows from most of the men in the room and could feel the ire rolling off of Nathan. "I'm sorry, but I guess I don't see why everyone seems so angry."

"Let's just continue with your story," Jack prodded gently. "The more information we have at our fingertips the better."

"Harlan was very kind to me. He treated me as though I was his daughter, with dignity and respect. Something, I assure you, I had not been given by the men in my family. He told me that I would need to have a new identity. I went along with all of his suggestions, trusting him implicitly. He took me to a salon early one morning, before they opened for business, and told the stylist that I was his daughter and wanted something completely different. My hair was quite long, so she dyed it blonde with highlights and cut it to my shoulders, sleeking it so that the waves were gone, leaving silky, straight hair in their place. He arranged for me to have the colored contacts but did not want me to go from dark brown to blue."

"Why was that?" Charlie asked. "Wouldn't blue have been a more striking difference?"

Nodding, she answered, "That's what I thought, too, but he said blue eyes tend to capture more attention, and he didn't want anyone to have reason to stare at me. So, he said the lighter brown, almost amber, colored contacts would be best. That was also why he went with a darker blonde hair color, instead of a bright yellow."

Nathan recognized that Harlan had a good plan, but still felt an irrational jealousy.

"Continue, please," Jack said, his sharp eyes on Agatha.

"Well, I guess the next thing was my nose. I had a bump along the bridge. He told me that I was going to have surgery on my nose and, once more, trusting him, I just said, 'Okay'. We went out one night, after dark, and drove to an old, brick building. I confess that I was nervous, but went inside and met with the doctor."

Throwing her hand up in front of her, she said, "Before you ask me where I was, or what he looked like, all I can tell you is that I have no idea where we went. The doctor had dark hair and blue eyes, but he wore a hospital mask and a lab coat. He gave me a shot that put me to sleep and, when I woke up, it was the next day and I was back in my bedroom at Harlan's house. I had a bandage on my nose, some bruising and swelling, but was given pain pills for a few days and recuperated just fine."

"This sounds like something from the fucking Twilight Zone," Bart said, shaking his head.

Nathan could feel the tension radiating through Agatha. Lifting his hand, placed it on her shoulder, rubbing gently, to ease the knots he felt in her muscles.

"After a week, the bandages came off my nose, and I noticed that it was a little narrower and the bump was gone. While I had been asleep, they must've made a mold of my teeth as well because, by the time the bandages came off my nose, Harlan had a special retainer, kind of like the Invisalign braces you see advertised on TV, ready for me. Instead of straightening my teeth though, which were already straight, it squished my top teeth together so that now they are slightly crooked."

"All through this, you had no other contact with other people?" Jack asked.

She shook her head, "No. Not during the first months that I was with Harlan. After a while, I started making small trips to the grocery store or to the mall, always with him nearby. He told me my parents and my brothers had been sentenced to prison, but I didn't keep up with the news."

Agatha felt Nathan squeeze her hand and her voice dropped to a whisper as she tried to explain. "I had so much to learn. I began with such fear and had to learn to trust for the first time in my life. I had to learn how to leave Agnes behind and become Agatha. It did not happen overnight, but I was willing to place my entire world in Harlan's hands, knowing eventually I would have a real chance at a new life I could be happy with."

She was silent for a moment, staring into space, her mind swirling.

Nathan gave a silent shake of his head to the others, indicating they needed to let her process whatever she was thinking about.

Finally, looking up, she said, "I still carried a great deal of guilt over the sins of my family and my inaction for so many years. It didn't seem to matter how often Harlan told me that I was not my family. He finally accepted that the guilt was simply part of me. Harlan had met Ann at a fundraiser and felt that being her assistant would be a good job for me. He knew that helping other women, as I had that night, would give me a continued sense of atonement for my family sins. And, he was right."

Jack said, "Harlan knew that Gavrill had gone to prison for tax evasion, but without Agnes' testimony, he would not have been linked to the human trafficking."

"Why did he not push her to testify?" Monty asked.

Nathan, filled with a sense of love for Agatha and wanting to protect her with his life, now understood Harlan's motivation. "Because he loved her." The room was silent and her eyes jumped to his. He rushed to continued. "Not in a sexual way, but Aggie said it herself...he loved her like a daughter. Her bravery managed to put her family behind bars and severely hamper Gavrill's business. He not only ended up in prison, but now had eyes on him, halting the human trafficking business. Because he loved her, Harlan protected her, by keeping her away from Gavrill's eyes."

"Harlan had to have known that Gavrill would not be in prison forever. Wouldn't he have wanted her to know what to do, in case he was no longer around?" Patrick wondered aloud.

"Now that you mention it, he once told me something," she said, her brow scrunched in thought, "but I never understood it. He told me that if anything ever happened to him, the light would find me."

"The light would find you?" several Saints repeated at the same time, their eyebrows lifting in unison.

Nodding, she shrugged. "That's what he said, but I had no idea what he meant."

"And you never asked?" Luke asked, surprised.

Shaking her head as her shoulders slumped, Agatha

replied, "I think I stuck my head in the sand when it came to Harlan. He'd taken over when I needed him most, and I just allowed him to continue to do so." She thought silently for another minute before continuing, "I'm sure it's hard for take-charge people like you to understand what it's like for someone who was never raised to think for themselves. It literally took all my energy to plan how to save those women, so it was easy to let him take control. When you told me that he'd died, I didn't know what to do. And I had no idea what light he was talking about, so I didn't even think about it."

"So, the light..." Charlie repeated, looking first to Luke and, after he shook his head, turning to look at Jack.

Jack remained quiet, but a speculative gleam appeared in his eyes before he quickly shuttered them.

That night, relaxed and snuggled against Nathan's body, as Agatha slept, her mind slid into a memory.

"What are we doing here?"

"You said you wanted a tattoo," Harlan replied. "I don't want to take you just anywhere, so I'm bringing you to a tattoo artist that I know will do a good job."

I looked up and down the street, empty in the early morning hour, and asked, "Are tattoo parlors even open now?"

Harlan chuckled, "Not usually, but this artist wanted you to feel comfortable, so he's opening early just for you."

As I walked inside the building, I was surprised to see it did not look the way I expected. No artist drawings on the walls. No open books of tattoo renderings on the counter. In fact, as I looked around, the room appeared rather blank, other than the screen in the middle of the room. The lights were dim and, as Harlan escorted me around the screen, I was surprised to see the tattoo table with a strong light angled down on it, and a large man rising from his stool.

He greeted me, his manner friendly. "So, Harlan suggested a tattoo of a lighthouse, right?" Seeing me nod, he cut his eyes over to Harlan before they slid back to me, and said, "I hear you're kind of nervous. Got something for you to take, that'll take away the pain and make it easier to relax."

I trusted Harlan explicitly, so took the pill from the man and swallowed it with a glass of water. Soon I felt completely relaxed while still being completely awake. Lying on the table, I pulled my jeans down just low enough to expose my hipbone, but was grateful when the tattoo artist draped a sheet for modesty, as well. Harlan sat with me, holding my hand, and we smiled and talked through the whole thing.

When it was over, the man helped me stand and walk to a floor length mirror.

Before they left, he explained the aftercare to me and gave Harlan a sheet with all of the information, in case I forgot anything. He ushered us to the door and, with a squeeze to my shoulder, wished me well. The loopiness was wearing off, but Harlan wrapped his arm around me and led me back to his car.

Harlan said I had been a guiding light to the women I

saved and to me, he was my light. I loved the look of my tattoo and often, in the early days, held up a mirror so that I could see it clearly. The intricate detail of the lighthouse over-looking the cliffs, with a wave crashing on the rocks below, and the beams of light coming out from the top, seemed perfect.

Nathan hurried through breakfast, barely eating as he explained, "Sorry, babe. I just got a call and Scarlett and I are needed."

Agatha looked up from her plate, her eyes full of concern. "Oh no, who's lost?"

"This time it's a prisoner from the county jail, and he's not lost. He just decided he didn't want to enjoy their accommodations anymore."

Her eyes widened in surprise and she gasped, "Will he be armed and dangerous?"

"Don't think so, but we always go in prepared."

He bent to give her a quick kiss, but she threw her arms around his neck pulling him down, latching onto his lips, pouring all her feelings into their touch. He groaned, saying, "Good God, babe. You make it hard to leave."

Laughing, she settled back on her heels, saying, "Good! I wouldn't want you to forget what you have here at home." Sobering, she added, "Please come home safe."

"You too, sweetheart."

"I'll be fine. Today's just a regular day at the center."

With one last kiss, he was out the door, Scarlett faithfully by his side. She stood in the doorway, watching as they drove down the gravel lane, smiling as she turned back to the house. In a short time, his house, had become her home.

Later that morning, she walked out of her office at the center and down the hall to the computer room. She grinned as she leaned her shoulder against the door-frame, observing the women working inside. Several of them were becoming acclimated to the center, and others had left. She sighed, knowing a few women went back to the man who had abused them, but accepted that each woman had to decide for herself when, and if, the time was right to leave. Her job was to try to give them the strength and the knowledge that they did not have to be abused and there was a place of hope there if they needed it.

Hearing the front buzzer ring, she walked to the lobby. Gail, sitting at the desk, was filling in for the volunteer who had stepped to the back for a few minutes. Tina, chatting with Gail, looked up as she walked through the room, greeting them both with, "Don't get up, I'll get it."

At the door was a statuesque, dark-haired woman whose eyes met hers before dropping to the floor. Knowing how skittish many abused women were, she smiled pleasantly, opening the door wider.

"Hello. My name is Agatha. Welcome to the Safe Harbor Center."

The young woman's eyes filled with tears and her hands shook. "I'm not certain if I'm in the right place."

"Come on in and let's see if we can help you."

"I... I don't know."

"Well, how about if you at least come into the lobby. We can sit right here and chat for a few minutes, if you'd like."

The woman reluctantly followed her in, her eyes darting to the side, seeing Tina and Gail. They both greeted her warmly, introducing themselves, and she motioned for her to sit at one of the chairs.

"We're a safe place for women who are being abused or feel frightened for their personal safety. Women come to us from all walks of life when they need a chance to get their feet on the ground, before deciding what the next step in their life is going to be. We offer a nonjudgmental place for you to feel safe. Does that sound like what you need?"

The woman nodded, her eyes still darting around. "I know this place should make me feel safe," she said, "but I'm not feeling so good. Do you think maybe we could walk around a little bit?"

"Absolutely," she said. "In fact, I was going to take a walk to the little grocery store down the street. Would you like to go with me? Perhaps getting out, and getting some fresh air, would make you feel better."

"I'd like that, ma'am."

The volunteer returned from the ladies' room, smiled at those in the lobby and took her seat behind the desk. Gail and Tina looked over at her, and Tina asked. "Do you mind if we walk with you? We both wanted to go to the grocery store also."

She looked at the young woman, who seemed to carefully consider Tina's request, eyeing the two women with scrutiny. She gave Agatha a little nod of her head, and Agatha turned to the others smiling.

"Come on. We'll make it a group outing."

Together, the four of them stepped out into the sunshine of the late afternoon. She subtly urged Tina and Gail to walk slightly ahead while she hung back with the woman. "I hope you'll feel comfortable enough to let me know your name," she said.

The woman stayed quiet for a moment as they walked down the street, turning the corner near the grocery store. She finally turned and looked toward Agatha, her lips slightly curving. "I thought you might recognize me, but then realized we've never met."

Her brow furrowed, she asked, "Are we supposed to have met?"

"Well, you would think that family would have had a chance to meet before now."

"Sorry?" she asked, turning back to the woman. Gasping, her eyes widened at the smile on the woman's face as she pointed a gun at her.

"Walk," she ordered.

Her feet rooted to the sidewalk, she stared into the cold eyes boring into her.

"Agatha?" Gail called out, turning around, "Tina and I wanted to start lunch early—oh, my God!"

The two women skidded to a stop as the woman

pointed her gun at them, ordering, "Get over with Agnes."

Hearing the name *Agnes*, her blood ran cold, the reality of the situation hitting her. "Leave them alone," she said, with more bravado than she felt.

The woman smiled slowly, her lips curving at the corners. "Oh, how the mighty have fallen. You, dear cousin, are hardly in a position to give orders. At least, not anymore."

"Cousin?"

"Well, something like that. I think I'm more a distant cousin of your mother, but then…we like to keep things all in the family, don't you agree?" She kept the gun trained on all three of them somehow, as she pulled a phone from her pocket. "Got her. Easy, so fuckin' easy. Meet you at the side of the grocery store down the street."

"Who are you?" she asked, racking her brain, attempting to come up with a name to go with the face that, now that she was focused, appeared similar to her mother's.

"Kalina. Kalina Popov." She lifted a perfectly arched eyebrow, tilting her head to the side, waiting, as though for Agatha to recognize her. She remembered her mother referring to a cousin named Kalina, but they had not met.

Narrowing her eyes, Kalina sneered. Staring at them all, each with wide, frightened eyes, she said, "Here's how this is going to go, ladies. We're walking over to that van and if you give me any problems, I've got no problem shooting you."

"Bitch!" Tina breathed, her eyes shooting daggers.

"Temper, temper, ladies. Agnes, maybe you'd better let your friends know that I'm serious…dead serious."

"Gail, Tina, just do what she says." She stepped back a few steps, so that she was standing with the other two women, and reached out to clutch their hands, whispering, "Stay with me. Stay calm."

A white panel van pulled up to the side of the parking lot near where they were standing. The driver kept the van running, while two large men came out and approached them. Both had guns in their hands as well, and one growled, "Which one is she?"

Nodding her head toward Agatha, Kalina said, "This one. This is Agnes."

"What do we do with the other two?"

Her lips curving into a wicked smile, Kalina said, "I think perhaps a few more guests will be fine."

One man approached Tina, grabbing her arm, and as she began to fight him, he hit her in the side of the head with the butt of his gun, knocking her out. Lifting her body easily, he tossed her into the back of the van. Gail, in tears, looked up at the man who had taken her arm.

Agatha turned toward Kalina, her eyes on the gun pointing at her, and said, "Don't do this. Leave the other women here. Don't do this to them."

Shaking her head, Kalina said, "My, my, you do have a big heart for the downtrodden woman, don't you? Too bad you didn't have that same kind of loyalty to your own family. Now shut up, and get in."

ALVAREZ SECURITY OFFICE

Gabe Malloy sat at the computers in Alvarez Security, looking up as the owner, Tony Alvarez, walked into room. "Got something on Agatha Christel," he said, his focus back on the computer screen.

Tony, eyes intent, asked, "What do you see?"

"Not so much what I see, but what I don't." Before Gabe had a chance to explain, his twin, Vinny, walked into the room, followed by the fourth member of their team, Jobe Delaro. Immediately on alert, they listened as Gabe continued, "Saw Agatha and three other women walk out of the center and they haven't come back. That was twenty minutes ago."

"Anything suspicious?" Tony asked.

Shaking his head, he replied, "No…just got a bad feeling."

"Good enough for me," Tony said, moving to a secure phone. "I'll call Jack."

"I'll call Cam," Jobe said, pulling out his phone. Jobe's

sister was Miriam, Cam's wife. He knew he could get hold of his brother-in-law easily.

Tony talked to Jack for a few minutes before turning back to his group. "Jack's on it and checking the tracer they have."

Vinny nodded, saying, "Best idea Jack ever had was giving their women Saint medallions with tracers. Hell, I got Analissa one."

Gabe lifted an eyebrow at his brother. "St. Vincent?"

Grinning, Vinny replied, "Nah. Got her one that says, 'My heart belongs to handsome'."

Tony shook his head before saying to Gabe, "Keep monitoring with the Saints and let me know if there are other developments. Jack said he'd notify us if we were needed."

"Will do," he acknowledged, focusing on his computer screen once again.

Undisclosed Location

"What have you got?"

"Not sure...I got an alert when Agatha was separated over thirty miles distance from her cell phone. Her light tracer says she's moving east."

"Did you patch in to the Saints or the Alvarez Security cameras?"

"Alvarez cameras show her and three women

walking down the street about thirty minutes ago. Never returned. Two of the women were from the center – facial recognition gave me their identities."

"And the fourth?"

"Uncertain. Couldn't get a good angle for recognition. Started a search of the area just as you came in."

They both regarded the screen as the seated man continued to click on the keyboard. Pulling up the security images from the grocery store, they watched as the unidentified woman pulled a gun and forced the three into a van.

"Fuck...send a message to the Saints—encrypted."

"On it."

Another member of their team walked into the cavernous room and the leader turned to him, ordering, "Run facial identification on the woman with the gun."

"On it, boss."

"Message sent to Saints."

"Shit," the third man breathed out.

"What is it?" the leader asked.

"Woman identified as Kalina Popov."

Charlie read the screen, her lips pinched. The person that had sent cryptic messages that she was unable to trace before had just sent some more. Scanning the messages, she called out, "Jack!"

The Saints in the compound looked over as she continued, "Message from unknown source. **Agatha taken at gunpoint from grocery store. Two center**

women with her. She is heading east. Update coming. Second message, **Woman identified as Kalina Popov.**"

As she tried to determine the sender, Luke began tracing Agatha's location from the Saint's medallion around her neck.

Jack's phone rang and he answered, his jaw tight. "Tony." As he listened, it grew even tighter.

Bart, Cam, Nick, and Jude hustled into the weapons room to prepare to head out.

"Who the hell is watching her other than us and the Alvarez group?" Monty asked, staring at Jack.

"Fuck, Nathan's on a tracking case," Blaise said, looking down at his phone.

Jack, off the phone, called out, "That was Alvarez. They lost visual when she left the center's area. I told him we've got someone else we haven't identified with eyes on her and they've just contacted us as well."

Luke called out, "Her tracer has her about ninety miles away, heading east."

"Kalina Popov...they're taking her to Norfolk...my guess is to Yurgi!" Monty surmised.

Marc called out, "Blaise, get hold of Nathan. We can take my plane." He looked at Jack and said, "I'm off to get it ready," before he jogged out the back entrance.

Blaise turned, praying Nathan was near his phone and the fugitive was already captured.

Nathan, having found the fugitive for the deputies to take over, was on his way to the compound. Driving down the road, his mind wandered back to the relation-ship he was building with Agatha. As the lines on the asphalt underneath his tires rolled by, he thought back to the night when he first saw her. In the dark, all alone.

Not knowing much about her story at that time, he had still admired her strength. He smiled, as he always did now, realizing that the woman that shared his life and the woman that had touched him that night two years ago were the same. Glancing at the clock on the dashboard, he wondered if he would have time to swing by and see her quickly before checking in with Jack.

His phone rang and, once connected, he heard Blaise say, "Hold on to your shit, man, and listen carefully. Get to the airfield. Agatha's been taken by Kalina Popov at gunpoint and we're flying to Norfolk."

Heart hammering in his chest as the blood rushed through his veins, he barked, "Who's on them?"

"Charlie and Luke have her pulled up with the tracer. They've got a two-hour lead, but flying we can get there at the same time. Marc's got a private jet to take us in, so get there fast."

Jerking off the highway at the next exit, he looked over at Scarlett. She turned her soulful eyes to him, as though understanding his pain and fear. With his heart in his throat, he reached a shaky hand out to pet the dog's silky coat, gaining comfort from the touch. "Jesus, girl, we've got to find her."

An hour later, he looked out the window at the ground below, Scarlett in the seat next to him. With Marc at the controls and Jude in the co-pilot seat, Jack, Bart, Nick, Chad, Blaise, and he were in seats in the back. Monty was coordinating with the FBI while Cam and Patrick were with Luke and Charlie in the compound.

Looking at his watch, he tried to clear his mind of the fear that threatened to choke him...and was losing the battle to do so.

29

Agatha's body ached from the tension of the last several hours. The driver and Kalina sat in the front, with the two other men in the back seat. The very back of the van was empty of seats, which was where she, Gail, and Tina sat with their wrist taped together in front of them.

For over three hours, she had listened to the conversations of the people in the front, all the while mouthing to Tina and Gail. Tina's face was swollen, but no longer bleeding, and both women's tears had stopped. She had managed to mouth enough words to them, without being noticed by the others, to let them know that she knew who their captors were, that they were after her, and not to worry, someone would come help them. She just hoped she was telling them the truth and that someone would come in time.

As the miles wore on, her mind was filled with thoughts of her family. Her mother, so proud of her Volkov heritage, determined to be an asset to Gavrill...

even if that included selling her soul. Her father, always living in the shadow of a stronger relative, eager to prove that his family was of value. Her brother, Grigory, desiring all the things that money could buy, without the work ethic to earn them honestly. And her other brother, Lazlo, remembering his cruelty to the women that had been brought to him.

As she sat there, stewing over the family she had been born into, determination steeled her spine. *I am not them. I am not my family. They no longer have power over me. I determined my destiny years ago, and will not deviate from it.*

After what seemed like forever, she could tell by the braking and acceleration of the van that they were in a city. Eventually the van came to a stop, and as she looked around, she saw Kalina and the two men in the back seats climb out.

Knowing they only had a few seconds until the back door would open, she rushed to say, "Whatever we do, try to stay together. Don't speak. Don't say anything. Let me handle everything. I know how these people work." Gaining quick nods from Tina and Gail, she faced the back of the van just as the double doors opened wide.

One of the large men leaned in, grabbing her by her arm, and pulled her forward until he could lift her, setting her down outside. Looking over her shoulder she saw Tina and Gail were taken out of the van as well. With a quick look at her surroundings, she knew they were in a warehouse and, while she had never been there, it was not hard to imagine this was part of the Volkov shipping yard.

Working to keep her knees from knocking in fear, she drew in a deep breath, letting it out slowly. She wrapped herself in the cool, unemotional façade she had perfected as a young woman, still as familiar as it ever was. Kalina had disappeared and the driver had moved the van away, leaving the three women with the two enforcers. Lifting an eyebrow toward the nearest one, she watched as he looked dubiously toward the other.

With an imperious voice, having heard it often enough from her mother over the years, she asked, "Are you going to tell me why I'm here? Or are we going to stand around and stare at each other?" She watched the doubt pass through his face and pressed her point, adding a slight Russian accent to her words. "If you know who I am, then you know I am part of the family. I'm fairly sure that my family would not be pleased with how I've been treated."

She knew that he would have only been given the information that he needed, and he confirmed that when he said, "We take our orders from Kalina. If you have a problem, take it up with her."

"Then lead on, by all means."

When it looked as though he was only going to lead her forward and keep the other two women behind, she halted in her steps. "Oh no. They come with me." Not giving him a choice, she hoped that he was used to following directions and would acquiesce.

As the second man nudged Gail and Tina to walk

along with her, she breathed a slight sigh of relief. *Please let them keep us together.* She was sure, with the Saints eyes on her, they would have known she was gone already and where to look for her. What scared her was how long it would take. *Or, if Nathan had finished his job and would be able to come for her.*

The warehouse was cavernous, with a variety of sizes of shipping containers scattered about the room. Groups of men, some workers and some guards with guns, wandered about the place. Their eyes would drift over to the trio of women walking, but when she looked at them, they quickly averted their gaze.

The guards, nudging them along, walked near the back toward a single door. Without talking, one of the men opened the door, stepping through first, while the man behind them grunted for them to follow.

The windowless room was dimly lit. In the corner, was a small desk with a man sitting behind it. Kalina, a slight smile on her face, stood just behind him at his right shoulder. The first man who entered walked forward, turned, and with another grunt indicated for her to stop. Gail and Tina stayed right with her, flanking her shoulders. The last enforcer walked in and closed the door, standing with his back against it.

She had met her mother's cousin, Gavrill, only a couple of times in her life, but even so, she knew the man sitting behind the desk was so similar in looks, he must be related. His black hair and square jaw reminded her of her brother Lazlo.

She refused to lower her eyes, but did not speak,

waiting to hear what he would say first. The silence stretched interminably, but she did not yield.

He finally broke it, and said, "It seems, dear cousin, that you have caused your family a great deal of trouble."

"I don't see how that could be possible," she said. "I'm only a female and hold no power in the family."

"Unlike your parents, Gavrill and I do not underestimate the power of a woman."

She watched Kalina smile, placing her hand on the man's shoulder, giving it a little squeeze.

His hard stare threatened to unnerve her, but she locked her knees into place and kept her eyes on his.

"I am Yurgi, Gavrill's brother. This," he motioned around, "is my domain now." He continued to stare before pondering aloud, "So, what do you propose I should do with you?"

With more bravado than she felt, she replied, "My suggestion would be to treat me well, until you allow me to go back."

Yurgi's eyes widened and Kalina gave an indelicate snort. Pressing her point, she continued, "If you think that my being here is not known, then you are not nearly as smart as you should be. Gavrill may have brought you to run his business, but he will not be pleased when the Feds arrive."

"She's lying," Kalina said, her smile now a sneer. "No one saw us. No one followed us. No one knows you're here."

With a small smile of her own, she replied, "Do not

kid yourself. There are eyes everywhere and, you can be sure, there are many eyes on me."

For the first time since she entered the room, Yurgi's face showed uncertainty. He glanced over his shoulder, up toward Kalina, harshly whispering to her in Russian.

Kalina pressed, "The bitch is lying. I'm telling you no one followed us. No one knows she's here!"

Yurgi growled, "Did you search her?"

"There was no need. She did not have a purse with her. She did not have her cell phone. She's got nothing on her that anyone can trace."

His eyes narrowed, moving back to her, and he said, "Where you are going, you'll be untraceable."

Her stomach lurched and she fought the desire to wipe her sweaty palms on her pants. Maintaining the calm façade, she felt her heartbeat pounding as though it would burst from her chest.

"Take them away," he ordered. Standing, he bypassed Kalina, walking closer to her. "Dealing with you, will go a long way in appeasing my brother."

"And, of course, assuring that he only stays in prison for tax evasion, right? And not the trafficking of humans."

Once more his eyes flashed, a strange combination of doubt and fear, but he said nothing. With a jerk of his head, he turned back toward Kalina, having indicated that the guard should take them out.

As they walked out of the office and back into the warehouse, she heard Kalina call out, "Don't worry, Agnes, you'll have lots of company on your trip."

Understanding the threat, she reached out with each

hand and grasped Tina and Gail, giving each of them a squeeze. She glanced around the warehouse, seeing all the same workers, but a strange sense of being watched filled her, though she could not tell if the eyes were friendly or not.

The two enforcers stopped at the side of a large metal crate, the door partially open, but they moved onward and forced them through another door leading to a small room instead, about the size of the office they had just left. The room was filled with a small gathering of women, huddled together. She stood staring, horror filling her soul, at the frightened eyes of the young women. The realization that they were going to load human cargo into the crate just outside the door, to place on one of the ships, filled her with rage.

The door slammed shut and she whirled around, facing the others. "How long have you been here?"

The blank expressions on their faces told her that the women had been kept somewhere for a while, even if it wasn't here, and were probably hungry...and already defeated.

"We're going to get out of here," she vowed, quickly realizing her words were falling on the ears of women who had already given up hope. Turning toward Gail and Tina, she rushed, "We have to stall...we have to keep them from putting us in the crate."

"What the fuck is happening?" Tina said, her chest heaving.

"These people deal in human cargo. Human trafficking—"

"How do you know about this?" Gail asked, her face registering shock.

"We don't have time to go into that," she said, her eyes darting to the door. "Just accept that this happens and I've worked to shut it down before and will do it again to my dying breath."

"There's no way out…" one of the women said, her eyes haunted.

"Yes, there is," she argued. Looking at each one carefully, willing them to share in her resolve, she said, "They will never take me alive…I'll fight and keep fighting and you can too."

"What…what will happen?" another one asked.

Deciding to not sugar coat the reality, she said, "They'll put you in a shipping container to load onto one of the freighters. You'll probably be let out for necessities and that will include sexually servicing the men on the ship. When the ship docks in a foreign port, you'll be sold."

Ignoring the gasps, she continued, "We are few but we can fight. We can buy a little time until the men who will come to rescue us can get here—"

"Someone's coming?"

"Yes," she promised. Looking to Gail and Tina, she said, "Nathan will come and bring the men he works with."

"But—"

She pulled the St. Francis medallion from around her neck and whispered, "Tracer…they know exactly where we are, so we have to stay together."

Tina's eyes gleamed as she nodded. Turning to the

other women, she said, "I've been used by men all my life. Ain't happenin' no more. I can kick, I can scratch, and I can grab 'em by the balls. They kill me, then I die free. And so can you."

"I been hit by a man for the very last time," Gail vowed, moving to stand right next to Agatha.

"Tell me what to do," one of the women said, her eyes showing a spark of life. "I've been held captive for over a month and I'd rather die than let another man get to me."

"Ladies, we'll get out of here alive, but whatever you do, don't get in that crate outside. Act complacent and it'll give them a false sense of security. It's getting darker outside so they'll probably move us soon. But, my guess is that they'll have the regular workers leave first." A smile curved her lips as she stood tall. "And then, we'll fight like hell."

They did not have long to wait before the door swung open and one of the guards jerked his head to indicate they were to follow him. Walking out quietly, she saw only three guards with guns and all of them were relaxed, their rifles slung casually over their shoulders.

Whirling around, she stared at the nearest guard, and screamed, "Now!"

Catching the man off guard, she rushed him, plowing into his body. As heavy as he was, she barely caused him to step back a foot, but pummeled him with her hands just the same, continuing to scream to the other women, "Fight! Don't give up!"

Gail, spurred into action, her face filled with rage,

rushed the other guard as he was going for his gun. She also began to scream. Getting help from Tina, who managed to bring her knee up in fierce contact with his balls, dropping him to the floor, they continued their assault.

The other women rushed out of the room, a tangle of arms and legs flailing at their kidnappers, screaming just as loudly. The office door opened, Kalina and Yurgi rushing out, their faces registering astonishment at the ensuing melee.

Shoving Kalina out of the way, Yurgi skirted around the women just as the guard Agatha was battling managed to wrap his arms around her, picking her up off the ground. Yurgi nodded his head toward him and ran through the closest door to the outside. Carrying her, the guard ran outside, following him. One of his beefy hands clamped over her mouth, pinching her nose, and she fought to breathe as much as to get away.

3 0

The warehouse suddenly came alive as the Saints burst into the building, along with the FBI agents that had been watching Gavrill's shipping business and were alerted to the kidnapping. As gunfire erupted, Jack and Bart immediately headed toward the women, pushing them down, urging them to get behind one of the crates.

Seeing Kalina dart inside one of the offices, Jude and Chad rushed after her. She was attempting to pull a small revolver from her purse when they got there, but Jude deftly knocked it from her hand. She brought her hand forward to slap his face, but he easily captured her arm, whirling her around and pinning her arm roughly behind her back. Chad had her hands zip tied behind her back within seconds.

She screamed obscenities at them, and they shared a look. With a grin, Jude reached into the pocket of his cargo pants, pulling out a roll of tape. With a snap, he tore off a strip and pressed it over her mouth.

"Hate to say it, bitch, but when that tape comes off,

it's gonna hurt. Maybe that'll teach you to watch your mouth."

She attempted to kick out at him and Chad laughed. Grabbing her around the waist he lifted her up as Jude zip tied her ankles together. Together, they easily carried her to one of the chairs in the room, before heading back out into the warehouse.

Gavrill and Yurgi's men were still returning fire, but between the Saints and the agents, they were soon subdued.

Nathan and Scarlett rushed over to the women, but he did not see Agatha with them. Scarlett immediately began to sniff the area, but stopped suddenly. Following her, he quickly saw why. Agatha's St. Francis medallion was lying on the floor, the chain broken.

Scarlett continued sniffing, at first in circles and then heading toward the office, following the trail of Agatha's scent.

"Fuck!" he cursed, trusting his dog but at the same time, his gaze desperate to catch a glimpse of Agatha. "Did you see her?" he called to the women, now standing, huddled together.

Most shook their heads and he called to Scarlett to come to him. One woman called out, "I saw a man pick her up, but I don't know where they went."

Just then a voice came over the Saints' radios, saying, "Outside. Down the street. Toward the east."

Not recognizing the voice, he hesitated for only a second before running out the nearest door, Blaise and Nick with him.

Jack turned, casting his sharp gaze around, viewing

the occupants in the area. The women were huddled together in one section, their arms around each other. Gavrill's men, and some of the workers, were now subdued, having been rounded up by the FBI agents and placed in another section. His gaze finally landed on a single man, standing in the shadows, focused intently upon him. Recognition flashed through him for a second as he regarded the man's eyes, but there was no way he could be right. No way... The man slid back into the shadows and he took a step forward to follow, but in the blink of an eye, he was gone.

"Jack?" Jude called, handing off Kalina to one of the Feds. "Where did Nathan go?"

Shaking his head to clear it, he motioned for him to follow, catching up with the other Saints as they headed out the door. Running with him, Jude said, "You look like you saw a ghost back there."

Admitting nothing, he continued to run down the street, following after Nathan. *You could say that again...*

Agatha managed to move her mouth just enough to sink her teeth into the fingers of her captor. Crying out, he jerked her head painfully, clamping his arm about her waist tighter. Fearing her ribs would crack, she quieted, thankful that she was now able to breathe easier without his hand over her nose.

Rounding the corner, she viewed the ships anchored in the distance and prayed that was not where they were heading. Struggling once again, she managed to kick his shins with a viciousness she didn't know she was capable of.

"God damn, bitch," he cursed, "I'll break your neck, if you don't stop."

Stopping at the side of a building, Yurgi threw open the door and rushed inside with the two of them following. Looking around, she saw they were in a smaller warehouse with very little cargo inside, giving her no place to hide if she was able to get loose.

Undeterred, she continued to struggle as she was carried toward the back where a row of doors lined the wall. Yurgi chose one, opening the door quickly, and hurried inside, the goon carrying her kicking the door closed behind them. Yurgi flipped the lock as she was tossed to the floor, causing her to stumble and fall backwards.

Ignoring her for a moment, the guard looked at Yurgi and said, "What the fuck do we do with her now?"

As they argued, she hoped enough time would pass that Nathan would be able to find her. Pushing herself to a standing position, she casually reached up to check on the St. Francis medallion around her neck. Her stomach dropped as she realized the necklace was gone. *That's okay... that's okay... I know he'll have Scarlett. Oh shit, I've been carried. Please God let Scarlett be able to find me.*

"I'm not going down for this," the guard said.

"You do what you're told, or you won't live long," Yurgi threatened. "We were told to get her, and that's what we did."

"Yeah, well, if that was the Feds back there, how long you do you think you will still be around?"

Yurgi stayed quiet, beefy hands on his hips, sweat running off his face and dripping down onto his shirt.

Deciding to talk instead of scream, she said, "You can't win this." Noting the heat of anger, mixed with fear, pouring off of them as they both glared daggers toward her, she firmed her resolve. "I know they're looking for you, but more importantly, they're looking for any connection with Gavrill and the transporting of women. What you had back there in the warehouse was the nail in your coffin. And quite frankly, the nail in Gavrill's coffin."

"We dump her, then we got a chance to get out of this. Without her hanging around, no one will know."

Yurgi stared at the man and shook his head. "You are one dumb fuck, if you think you can ever escape the family."

She stared in horror as Yurgi pulled out his gun and shot the other man in the head. As blood splattered on the side of her face and her shirt, she screamed, dropping to the floor, her hands covering her head.

He turned toward her next, his dark eyes bright with rage, and warned, "You want the same? If not, then shut the fuck up."

She had told the women earlier to fight for their lives but, staring at the barrel of his gun, she realized how easy those words had been to say when she was not facing death. Her body shaking with adrenaline, she held his gaze, refusing to look away.

"Go," he ordered, jerking his head toward the door near the back.

She stood on shaky legs and walked to the door, seeing it led to the room right beside the one they were in. Identical—but without a body bleeding on the floor. Grabbing her upper arm in a vice grip, he dragged her through two more doors, each leading to the next office beside it. Coming to the last one at the end of the row, he shoved her through the door leading back into the warehouse, only now they were in the very corner, behind a metal shipping crate on the back wall.

Scarlett appeared confused at first, but Nathan knew if Agatha had been carried, she would need to air track. Thankful she had been trained for that as well, she soon detected the scent and began running down the street, turning at the end of the warehouse toward the wharf.

Trying to both listen and ignore the voices coming over the radio, he focused his attention on his dog.

"Turn south at the next intersection," the unfamiliar man's voice came across the Saints' secure radio.

Charlie's voice broke in. "Who the fuck is this? How the hell are you on my secure frequency?"

"Just do as I say. We've got her on our radar."

"What radar?" Charlie bit back.

From next to him, Jack responded, "Stop the chatter. Whoever's on our line, where now?"

He listened as the man's voice directed them the

same way Scarlett was leading. "Scarlett's got her scent," he said, interrupting them all.

Jack switched his radio to private, and said, "Charlie, let 'em guide us. I'm thinking it's the group that gave Agatha her identity. They must be watching."

"Got it, boss," she replied, the faint sound of keyboard clicks coming through the line.

Not caring about anything other than following his dog at the moment, he halted as she did in front of a door leading into another warehouse. Trying the knob, he breathed easier when it turned in his hand.

Leaning down, he grabbed hold of Scarlett's collar, holding her back and to the side of the outer door. Jack, Bart, and Chad, weapons drawn, opened the door and entered, immediately scoping out the space. The warehouse was not as cavernous as the one they had previously been in, and was almost empty of cargo crates. A few large crates bordered one wall, but the difference appeared to be in a number of doors along the back, all closed.

His hand still tightly holding onto Scarlett's leash, Nathan entered the building, giving a soft command that she stay right by his side. Blaise, Nick, and Jude slipped into the building right behind him, each in military stance with their weapons ready, and began to fan out over the area.

Not willing to wait on their search procedures, he let them know he was giving Scarlett the lead. They halted, calmly waiting, as he gave the command to Scarlett and she immediately began sniffing. She circled around a time or two, giving evidence to the fact that

Agatha may have escaped her captors, darting away only to be grabbed and picked up once again.

Nose to the ground, she crossed the space, leading to one of the doors near the back. Taking her leash, he once more stood them to the side so that Jack and Bart could enter with weapons drawn. Once they were in, he rushed in behind them only to come up short at the site of the bloodied man's body on the floor.

Heart pounding, he jerked his eyes around the room as Scarlett moved past the body, sniffing a spot near the back. "You got her girl?" Scarlett immediately trotted to the door near the back of the room and they continued with the same procedure. He and Scarlett would stand to the side as the other Saints entered and cleared the room, then they would follow. Scarlett continued this process until they got to the last room, where he saw the door leading back to the warehouse open.

He hated to hold Scarlett back, but knew that Jack and Bart needed to make sure they were not walking into a trap. As they moved slowly through the door into the main warehouse he glanced to the main entrance, seeing Blaise, Jude and Nick spreading out. Scarlett immediately began straining at the leash, heading toward the closest crate. He held her back but, making eye contact with the others, they began to move into place for maximum visual on who might be behind the crate.

31

Squished. As scared as Agatha was, that was the only word she could think of to describe how she felt at the moment. Yurgi, with his weapon still in his right hand and his left wrapped around her upper arm tightly, had shoved her behind the crate, crowding in behind her. The space was dark. And even though she tried, the only sounds she could hear was her heart pounding and his heavy breathing on her neck.

Wondering how long they were going to attempt to hide, she tried to shift her body slightly, to be more comfortable. He immediately squeezed her arm tighter, and she knew she was beyond mere bruising, now worried he was going to shut off the blood flow to her hand.

In response to her whispered growl of pain, he gave her arm a jerk. She twisted her head around and up, glaring at him. "You're hurting me."

His tight hold released some and she felt tingles begin to run down her arm. She was still unable to hear anything and was about to ask him how long they were going to hide there, when she felt his body stiffen. Turning her head as much as she could, she noticed he had his head cocked, as though listening.

Trying to listen over the adrenaline rushing through her body, she was able to barely discern the sound of a soft footstep, but had no way of knowing who might be walking on the other side of the crate. Without moving her body, she cast her eyes back up toward Yurgi, noting his attention was riveted to the side in case someone might walk around.

Deciding to take a chance for her freedom, renewing her vow to not go down without a fight, she whirled her body around as fast and as hard as she could in the limited space, lifting her knee to his crotch while simultaneously pushing his right hand to the side, forcing the gun to point away from her. With the scream that ripped from deep inside him, she felt him loosen his hold on her as he fell to his knees.

Stumbling backwards she turned to run to the other side of the crate but he grabbed her foot at the last second. With another scream and kick her shoe came off in his hand and she scrambled forward on her knees, before rising and darting around the corner.

The sight of Agatha rushing around the corner of the crate, blood splattered across her shirt and neck, shot Nathan's heart into overdrive as he gave Scarlett the freedom to run.

Uncertain what she might be facing, the sight of Scarlett running toward her caused Agatha to drop to her knees, tears streaming down her face as she wrapped her arms around the beautiful hound.

Nathan, his heart in his throat, rushed forward, gathering Scarlett and Agatha in his embrace.

Jack and Bart swiftly stepped in, guns trained on Yurgi, still trying to catch his breath while on his knees. He began to lift his gun, but Jack said, "Go for it. Go on, give me an excuse to put a bullet in your brain."

"Easy man," Nick said, stepping in to handcuff Yurgi.

Nathan pulled back away from her, needing to see if she was all right. "Babe, babe, is this your blood?"

"No," Agatha rushed, her gaze searching Nathan's face, seeing fear in his eyes. "It was the other man. He shot him, Nathan. He just shot him."

Wrapping his arms around her he lifted her easily and carried her toward the outer door, with Scarlet trotting happily by his side. The other Saints joined them, each checking to make sure she was all right.

With her arms around his neck, she asked, "Tina? Gail? The other women? What happened—"

"They're fine. They're just fine," he replied. "We got 'em, babe. We got all of them. I promise you, with what the Feds have now, Volkov Shipping will be shut down. Yurgi's caught and Gavrill will find his cushy minimum security prison exchanged for one a lot less to his liking."

Closing her eyes, her words barely a whisper, she said, "We did it. Oh, God…Harlan would be so happy."

"Babe, I'm sure he'd be so fucking proud of you. I know I am." She sunk into his embrace, the adrenaline wearing off, leaving her limp in his arms. "I got you now, babe." The adrenaline slowly began to leave Nathan as well, and he blinked, battling tears, vowing to never let her leave his side again.

Looking down at Scarlett, still trotting along by him, her tongue lolling to the side, he grinned, happy to have both his girls safe with him.

Blaise quickly checked Agatha out, making sure she was uninjured. She kept telling them she was fine and the blood was not hers, but he shushed her gently each time.

"Nathan's eyes are on you, sweetheart, so give this to him. The last hours have been hell for him, imagining not being able to get to you in time. Letting me make sure you're okay will help give him some peace."

Her gaze moved from his face to Nathan's and, seeing the fear etched in his tense jawline, she acquiesced. "You're right," she whispered. As Nathan approached, looking to Blaise and gaining his nod, he let out an audible sigh of relief. She reached out her hand, clutching his and said, "Baby, I always knew you would get here. I never doubted it for a second."

He enveloped her into his embrace, his larger body wrapping itself around her, offering all the comfort and protection he could give.

"In fact," she added, leaning her head back to peer up into his eyes, "I told the other women to fight because I knew you all were coming."

Bart laughed, saying, "Damn, woman. You had those

women so fired up, I've never seen such an impressive sight!"

Nathan's arms tightened and she reached up to pat his face, her fingers sliding along his beard. "What happens now?" He shook his head, having never been involved in a mission like this one.

Nick stepped up to answer that question. "We'll stick around for you to give your statement to the FBI. I know the lead investigator and they'll get to you, Tina, and Gail quickly."

"But, what about the other women? They'll need help—"

"Don't worry," he said, nodding his head in the direction of the gathering outside the warehouse. "They're being well taken care of. The Bureau already has female agents and counselors with them."

She looked over, her heart easing as she saw the women, wrapped in blankets, being well tended with food and water, with a number of women assisting. She grinned as Tina and Gail saw her at the same time and came running over.

Meeting them halfway, the trio hugged tearfully.

"Hot damn, girlfriend," Tina said, finally pulling back. "You look all meek and mild, but you are one, tough, ol' mama!"

Gail said, "Oh, Agatha, I swear, when you told them to never let a man treat them bad again and to fight for their lives, honey, I woulda followed you into any battle right then!"

"I'm just so sorry that because of me, you got caught up in this mess—"

"Girl, you just gotta remember what you always tell us. We can only be responsible for our behavior, not the behavior of others. You're not responsible for the actions of these assholes, they are. You didn't do nothing to us, they did. So, it's all on them, honey," Tina added.

Smiling her appreciation, she hugged the two women tighter, before several agents walked over.

"Agnes? Agnes Gruzinsky—"

"Agatha, if you don't mind. I realize your report will be about Agnes Gruzinsky, but I'd prefer, when talking to me, you call me Agatha."

"Yes, ma'am. So, Ag... Agatha, we need to get a statement from you, as well as these two ladies with you. As soon as we do, we can release you, but will need to have you available."

She looked to the side, seeing Nathan standing nearby, Scarlett sitting patiently at his side, her medallion dangling in his hands, and the other Saints close as well. His eyes bore into hers, a slight hint of fear sliding through them. She smiled, turning to the FBI agent, and said, "Don't worry. Agatha Christel is here to stay. I'll be available, anytime you need me, and especially if this goes to trial."

Nathan's smile lit his face as he and Scarlett walked toward her. His arms wrapped around her and Scarlett leaned her heavy body against both of their legs, a wide smile on her hound face.

"I know you gotta go give your statement, babe. Nick'll be with you, and walk you through it. And I'll be right here waiting on you. When you're all done we'll fly back home together."

Standing with the other Saints, Jack felt the hairs on the back of his neck stand up. Skills honed when he was in the Army Special Forces kicked into high gear and his eyes shifted around looking for the cause. A dark-haired man dressed in a suit, with sunglasses on, appearing to all the world as one of the FBI agents, was standing alone, slightly to the side of the building. Blending into the environment, no one would think anything about his presence. But he knew. He knew that stance. He knew that man.

Disengaging himself from the others, he walked toward the building, casually weaving through the other agents combing the area. Reaching the corner of the warehouse, he stepped just out of sight, stopping in front of the man he never thought to see again. His breath caught in his throat, as he said in a hoarse whisper, "Mace."

The man, like all his former Army SF team, had been like a brother to him for so long, now stared back at him, the barest curve of his lips the only indication of acknowledgment.

"I never thought I'd fuckin' see you again, man," he said, an ache in his chest that he had not felt in years beginning to throb. "Fuck! They told us…you were dead…" Not caring if the man wanted a show of emotion or not, he figured, by showing up like this, he was going to have to take what he got. Stepping forward he grabbed him in a bear hug, holding tightly for a second, blinking as emotion choked in his throat before backslapping twice and moving away.

"Got a lot of fucking questions, but don't figure you're going to give me any answers."

Clearing his own throat, Mason Hanover chuckled a little and replied, "Some secrets are best left buried in Afghanistan."

He held his gaze for a long time, every fiber of his being wanting answers for why his former team member had disappeared in the middle of a mission, was later declared dead, and now was resurrected back in the States, obviously running special ops from here. Totally normal, like nothing had happened. *Fuck.* Finally, recognizing that no answers would be forthcoming, he simply nodded.

Jerking his head behind them, he said, "I figure you're the one who took Agnes and turned her into Agatha." It wasn't a question...he already knew the answer.

"I shouldn't be here, but I couldn't let it pass. Had to say hello to an old comrade...and friend."

"So, this is it. Don't reckon I'll see you again?"

With a small smile, Mace replied, "Been watching the Saints for a while. Alvarez group too. You do good work. Tell your computer gurus, they're good. Don't take it personally that my people are better."

At that, he laughed out loud. "Yeah, I'll be sure to tell them that."

Mace took a step back and, with a nod, began to

turn away. "And, while you're at it, you can give my regards to Tony Alvarez and the others." Almost as an afterthought, he added, "You never know, Jack. This could be the continuation of a beautiful friendship."

Shaking his head as he chuckled, he called out, "Before you go, just gotta ask. How the fuck did you know where Agatha was?"

Eyes twinkling, his smile widened ever so slightly. "You know me…just gotta look for the light."

Then, as silent and as swift as fog, he slid into the shadows and Jack lost sight of him.

Mace continued in the shadows until he reached the street crawling with agents and black SUVs. One of the vehicles pulled close and he climbed into the passenger side.

"You still think this was a good idea?"

He looked at Drew, whose suit and dark glasses also made him appear like any of the other agents in the area. "This needed to be done." As the SUV continued down the road, leaving the Norfolk harbor warehouses behind, he amended, "I needed this to be done."

Continuing in silence for several more miles, he asked, "Josh erasing all traces of our being here?"

Drew looked over, and nodded. "You know him. No one will ever know we were here." After a few seconds, he said, "Except for the man you talked to."

"Don't worry about him. Jack and I go way back." A few more miles passed in silence, as they moved through the Norfolk traffic, finally ending up on the highway, gaining speed. "To everyone else, I'm just a memory. But getting involved in this case, I...well, I just wanted to touch base with him. He deserved that." Leaning back in his seat, his head against the headrest, he added, "Besides, the Saints may be of use in the future."

"Just him huh? And the Alvarez group?"

Chuckling, he admitted, "Figure the same about them, too. Though, I won't make contact with them now. Jack will take that honor...letting Tony Alvarez know I'm still alive."

Drew nodded, no further acknowledgment needed. "Might as well take a nap, boss. We got miles to go to get home."

Mace closed his eyes, but his mind was filled with years before, in the hills of Afghanistan. The Special Forces squad he had served with were some of the best men he had ever known. Being pulled away from them for a black-ops mission, with its long-lasting repercussions, had taken him places he never expected to go. And not having the chance to say goodbye to his brothers, had eaten at him for years.

Sucking in a deep breath, he let it out slowly, knowing he was on the right course for his life. And now Jack, and the others, could feel a bit of peace... without knowing all of the truth.

"Sounds good, man. Take us home."

3 2

Nathan, his eyes pinned on Agatha's tattoo, watched the proceedings carefully. She had carefully pulled up her shirt and slid the waistband of her yoga pants down an inch so that the lighthouse was exposed.

Charlie held the scanner over the image and whistled. "I'll be damned," she breathed. "There's a tracer, smaller than I've ever seen, embedded just under the skin at the top of the lighthouse."

Agatha righted her clothes and turned to Jack. "I suppose the people that Harlan got to change my identity were able to keep up with me with this." Seeing his nod, she said, "Should I leave it in?"

"It's up to you, but you're in no harm."

Shrugging, she turned to Nathan and said, "If it's all right with you, I'd rather not mess with it."

He wrapped his arms around her and looked over the top of her head toward Jack. Trusting his boss, and seeing Jack's nod, he said, "Whatever you want to do is fine with me."

The Saints, plus Agatha and Scarlett, had flown back and all convened at the Saints' compound to debrief. Gail and Tina were being transported by the FBI and Ann was taking charge of their care once they were back at the center.

Nick moved into the room, disconnecting his phone, a smile on his face. "The Bureau got what they needed from Agatha's and the other women's testimonies. Plus, they raided the entire Volkov offices, both personal and professional. It appears that Yurgi wasn't nearly as careful with his correspondence as Gavrill was...and Gavrill wasn't overly careful, so they have records of shipping women. The Coast Guard has boarded one of his ships still in the harbor and the IMO are boarding another of their ships in a German port."

Jack shot Nathan a pointed look and, once Nathan had his arm wrapped around Agatha's shoulders, he added, "They also have captured Harlan's murderer." He paused as she gasped, but seeing her rapt attention, continued. "It was Johan, one of Gavrill's enforcers. His prints matched what was found at Harlan's house and the dumbass still had the weapon used."

Agatha listened, but her mind swirled with the information and she sucked in a ragged breath. Nathan, feeling her body shiver, pulled her tighter against his warmth.

Monty, also in touch with his FBI contacts, added, "Gavrill will soon be having an extended stay in a less congenial environment and will find out his empire has been destroyed."

"But, someone will take his place," she said, her voice

small and tired. The others looked at her and she rushed to say, "What we've done is wonderful, but I was just thinking that there is always evil in the world. Having grown up in it, I know it's there."

"Then we keep fighting," Jack said, his eyes full of determination, "and you keep helping those in need."

Nodding, a small smile slipped over her face before it was replaced with lowered brows. "I don't understand how they found me."

Nick's face fell and his eyes cut over to Nathan. She twisted around and looked up. "What? What aren't you telling me?"

Nathan sighed, not wanting to explain, but he knew the others were waiting to see what he would say. Looking to Jack again, he knew by his nod that his boss was leaving it up to him to decide. Turning Agatha in his arms, so that his body cocooned hers, he held her tightly as he peered into her upturned face.

"Babe, it was your mom. Chessa recognized you from the photograph in the magazine. She messaged Kalina, who visited and took the information to Gavrill and Yurgi. It was her that exposed you and they ordered the kidnapping."

She stared, eyes wide, mouth open, not speaking.

"Breathe, sweet Aggie," he reminded, his heart aching for her, watching astonishment morph into sadness.

"I see..." Agatha said, her voice a hoarse whisper.

"That's not on you—"

"I know," she rushed, her hand pressed flat on

Nathan's chest, gaining strength from his steady heartbeat.

"No, really, Aggie, that's—"

"I know, Nathan. Honestly, I get it. I finally get it. I'm not them. I'm not my family. Whatever poison runs in their veins, it doesn't run in mine. Whatever twisted shit is in their brains, it's not in mine." She sucked in a huge breath before letting it out slowly. "I was born Agnes Gruzinsky, but that's not who I am." She smiled up at him, lifting her hand to smooth the worry lines etching his face, and said, "I'm Aggie. Part Agnes...part Agatha...all your sweet Aggie."

Unheeding the other Saints, he swooped in, his lips taking hers in a deep kiss.

Two days later, Aggie was in the center, glad to get back to her new life. Tina and Gail had returned with tales of her heroics, which she quickly deflected while reminding them of their own heroic actions.

Ann listened carefully to her entire story, from childhood to present, and she braced herself to be fired...or at least to be told it was not appropriate for her to continue working at the center. Instead, Ann hugged her tightly, exclaiming that she knew all along Aggie was the perfect person to manage the center for women.

She had considered asking Nathan to take her to visit her mother, but then realized she had nothing to say to the woman who had done no more for her than give birth to her. Walking down the hall, she felt truly as though the last of her secrets were being let go and life was spreading out before her, ready to be lived.

The receptionist called to say that she had visitors and with a final hug from Ann, she walked to the front. Stepping into the lobby, she was stunned to see the room filled with women...beautiful, smiling women, with Bethany at the lead.

Hands on her hips, Bayley greeted, "I can't believe I'm seeing you again," just before embracing her. Whispering, she added, "I'm so proud of you, Ag—Aggie." Pulling back, she stared at her blonde hair for a second. "This is pretty, but I hope you go back to your natural, dark color."

Grinning, she replied, "I plan on it just as soon as I can get to a salon!"

"I'll book my favorite salon," Angel declared, "and we'll have a full day for all of us!"

Stunned, she stared at Angel's blonde hair with the teal, pink, and purple stripes. Looking around, she wondered what the other women thought, but with smiles on their faces, she assumed it must be a good plan.

Greeting the women she had already met, she was introduced to Dani, Kendall, and Evie. Overwhelmed, she stood, self-consciously, in the room, uncertain what she should say, when Bethany reached over and took her hand.

"Aggie, you're now part of us. We consider ourselves to be a unique sisterhood...think of it like a close-knit support group of friends. No matter how many friends you have, they can never understand what it's like to be with a Saint. So, we will be your new sisters!"

Sucking in her lips, she whispered, "I've never had a sister before. And, to be honest, I've never had any real girlfriends, either."

"Well, then sweetie, congratulations, you just gained eleven of us!" Bayley laughed.

"We know you need to get to work, but we'll have a salon day just as soon as Angel arranges it," Bethany declared, and each woman hugged her as they turned to leave.

As Faith embraced her, she held on tighter for a moment before saying, "I once saw danger in your future." Smiling shyly, she added, "It's gone...I only feel peace with you now."

Aggie was still reeling from that pronouncement when the last to leave, Bayley, embraced her once again. "So...Agatha Christel?"

Laughing, she said, "Your quote that night stayed with me. It seems Agatha Christy knew exactly how to describe my life. So, adapting her name just seemed appropriate."

"I love it," Bayley grinned.

Aggie quoted, " 'I like living. I have sometimes been wildly, despairingly, acutely miserable, racked with sorrow; but through it all I still know quite certainly that just to be alive is a grand thing.' "

Tears filled Bayley's eyes as she offered a final hug before leaving the center.

Nathan walked, hand in hand, with Agatha as they made their way through the cemetery. Coming to a halt at a double gravestone, she knelt, her fingers tracing the words.

Harlan Robert Masten
Devoted husband and friend

"I like the stone," Nathan said, kneeling by her side.

"I wanted something simple…he would have hated anything ornate."

Nodding, he remained silent, allowing her time to just feel.

Bending close to the marble, she whispered, "I found it, Harlan. I found the light. And it's right beside me." With that, she squeezed Nathan's hand and rose from the damp grass. Looking up at his face, she smiled. "I know he can rest in peace now."

Wrapping his strong arm around her shoulders, he escorted her back to his truck.

Nathan, Aggie, and Scarlett walked through the woods, the other dogs trotting along. They had spent the morning playing with Persi's six puppies. She had been entranced with the little bloodhounds, declaring them to be the cutest in the world.

He smiled, listening to her talk about the Saints' women offering more than friendship, but a real sisterhood, knowing she had never experienced that.

"I guess we were both kinda loners," he said, realizing that the Saints were now his brothers as well.

They stopped on the path, the tall trees and thick, green brush creating a wall of privacy, like they were in their own little world. The sun shone down in shafts through the limbs, sending sparks of light all around. He wrapped his arms around her, pulling her body flush with his. Holding her dark-eyed gaze, he remembered the first time he saw her, hidden in the shadows of the nighttime forest. She had captured his imagination then and now had captured his heart.

"I love you, sweet Aggie," he confessed.

Her breath caught in her throat and she blinked back the tears threatening to fall. "I love you, too."

He bent to take her lips, but stopped a whisper away when she spoke again. "Faith said she felt only peace with me now...but it's more than peace. It's love." Smiling, he kissed her, pouring all the love he had into their touch.

Scarlett stopped along the trail and turned her soulful eyes back to her master. A sunbeam rested on her red coat, warming her for a minute. Then, she trotted back to them, leaning her weight against her master's legs, satisfied just to be part of their embrace. If anyone else had been in the woods viewing them, they would have sworn she smiled.

Far away, Mace Hanover climbed the steps of his lighthouse, the caves below housing his security company. As he emerged at the top, the sun was setting behind him, casting a glow over the water, the waves gently slapping the rocks on the shore. Leaning his arms on the rail, he peered out over the horizon, the last few days on his mind. The rescue mission, long in coming. The meeting of an old friend, also long in coming.

Life was not what he had ever expected it to be, but choices had been made and decisions hard earned. He watched the sun as it finished its last decent into the water, shooting brilliant colors across the sky. Standing, he appreciated the view, thankful that it never got old.

His radio, clipped to his belt, called out, "Boss, got a new call."

"Be right down," he responded. With a final glance at the ever-changing sky, he turned and walked back down the stairs.

33

SIX YEARS LATER

Jack opened the front door, watching as Nathan and Aggie pulled to a stop at the side of his and Bethany's home. Walking up the wide front steps, they entered and he bent to kiss her cheek before shaking Nathan's hand.

"Don't run," she called out to Jane, their four-year-old daughter. "Hold your brother's hand." They watched as Jane turned back to grab toddler Evan's hand as he tried to catch up to her.

Nathan moved through the kitchen and, with a kiss to Aggie's head, he headed out the back door to keep an eye on the children, already at play. She joined the few women in the kitchen still putting food onto platters.

Jack followed Nathan, stepping onto his massive, backyard deck that led to a stone patio. Moving to the grill, he unloaded a plate filled with hamburgers ready to be cooked. The large backyard, surrounded with a white-picket fence, covered in thick, lush grass was currently overrun with children playing. He manned the grill, along with Patrick, as some of the other Saints kept an eye on the children.

His children, Peter and Anne, along with Chad's daughter, Amanda, as the oldest ones, herded the younger ones. Cam's daughter, Genevieve, and son, Thomas, played on the swing set with Bart's children, Rick and Shelby. The slide was occupied with Monty's two girls, Ashley and Ariane, and Chad's son, Robert. A small kiddie pool and sprinkler was closely monitored by Blaise and Luke, as they watched Beth and Ben, and Carl and Bill. Nick's children, Bernard, Brooke, and Bryce ran circles around the gathering, chasing Marc's children, Ken and Marianne.

With Jane and Evan in the bunch, the twenty-one children and twenty-four adults made for a huge crowd.

Lowering the hood on the grill, he cast his intense gaze over the gathering of children and adults, and could not believe his life. He expected to have a military career and remembered his Special Forces squad with pride. Their Captain, Tony Alvarez, still ran the Alvarez Security Agency, along with Sergeants Gabe and Vinny Malloy and Jobe Delaro, and the Saints partnered with them when necessary.

After the military, he dedicated himself to the security and investigation business that was his calling. He thought back to some of the many other partnerships throughout the years, especially with Mitch Evans, a former FBI agent who was now the Police Chief of Baytown, a small coastal town where he and the Saints had vacationed many times.

A slight smile crossed his face as he thought of

another former Sergeant, Mace Hanover, whose Lighthouse Security company now occasionally partnered with his as well.

Finally, he thought of the things in his life that were right at his fingertips. A wife and children had never entered his mind, until Bethany came bursting through his property woods many years ago, altering his world for the better. Now, he had love, children, and the honor of watching his men, who were not just employees but also friends, have the same.

The Blue Ridge Mountains cast long shadows in the background and the fresh mountain air filled his lungs. Arms circled him from behind and he reached back to shift Bethany's body around to his side, pulling her in close to him.

"Happy?" she asked, turning her trusting face up to his.

Looking around at the gathering once more, he tilted his head toward hers. "More than life itself, babe." Kissing her gently, they stood together, hearts light.

Hearing a cheer go up from the crowd, they turned and saw the assembly lifting their drinks. "To the Saints!" the others yelled, the children shouting along with the adults.

He nodded, lifting his cup as well. "To the Saints."

To continue this story to the next spin-off series, click here for the first Lighthouse Security Investigation book!
Mace

Cael

Jaxon

Jayden

Asher

Zeke

Cas

Lighthouse Security Investigations

Mace

Rank

Walker

Drew

Blake

Tate

Levi

Clay

Cobb

Hope City (romantic suspense series co-developed

with Kris Michaels

Brock book 1

Sean book 2

Carter book 3

Brody book 4

Kyle book 5

Ryker book 6

Rory book 7

Killian book 8

Torin book 9

Saints Protection & Investigations

(an elite group, assigned to the cases no one else wants…or can solve)

Serial Love

Healing Love

Revealing Love

Seeing Love

Honor Love

Sacrifice Love

Protecting Love

Remember Love

Discover Love

Surviving Love

Celebrating Love

Searching Love

Follow the exciting spin-off series:

Alvarez Security (military romantic suspense)

Gabe

Tony

Vinny

Jobe

SEALs

Thin Ice (Sleeper SEAL)

SEAL Together (Silver SEAL)

Undercover Groom (Hot SEAL)

Also for a Hope City Crossover Novel / Hot SEAL…

A Forever Dad by Maryann Jordan

Letters From Home (military romance)

Class of Love

Freedom of Love

Bond of Love

The Love's Series (detectives)

Love's Taming

Love's Tempting

Love's Trusting

The Fairfield Series (small town detectives)

Emma's Home

Laurie's Time

Carol's Image

Fireworks Over Fairfield

Please take the time to leave a review of this book. Feel free to contact me, especially if you enjoyed my book. I love to hear from readers!

Facebook

Email

Website

ABOUT THE AUTHOR

I am an avid reader of romance novels, often joking that I cut my teeth on the historical romances. I have been reading and reviewing for years. In 2013, I finally gave into the characters in my head, screaming for their story to be told. From these musings, my first novel, Emma's Home, The Fairfield Series was born.

I was a high school counselor having worked in education for thirty years. I live in Virginia, having also lived in four states and two foreign countries. I have been married to a wonderfully patient man for thirty-five years. When writing, my dog or one of my four cats can generally be found in the same room if not on my lap.

Please take the time to leave a review of this book. Feel free to contact me, especially if you enjoyed my book. I love to hear from readers!

Facebook
Email
Website

Made in the USA
Coppell, TX
21 January 2022

72059547R00208